UTTERLY

C000245766

PAULINE MANDERS

To Ann

Best wishes

Pauline Manders

Published in 2020 by Ottobeast Publishing
ottobeastpublishing@gmail.com

Cover design Rebecca Moss Guyver.

ISBN 978-1-912861-06-4

A CIP catalogue record for this title is available from the
British Library.

Also in the Utterly Crime Series by Pauline Manders

Utterly Explosive (first published 2012) - 2nd edition (2019)
Utterly Fuelled (first published 2013) - 2nd edition (2019)
Utterly Rafted (2013)
Utterly Reclaimed (2014)
Utterly Knotted (2015)
Utterly Crushed (2016)
Utterly Dusted (2017)
Utterly Roasted (2018)

To Paul, Fiona, Alastair, Karen, Andrew, Katie and Mathew, and a special dedication to Vigo.

PAULINE MANDERS

Pauline Manders was born in London and trained as a doctor at University College Hospital, London. Having gained her surgical qualifications, she moved with her husband and young family to East Anglia, where she worked in the NHS as an ENT Consultant Surgeon for over 25 years. She used her maiden name throughout her medical career and retired from medicine in 2010.

Retirement has given her time to write crime fiction, become an active member of a local carpentry group, and share her husband's interest in classic cars. She lives deep in the Suffolk countryside.

ACKNOWLEDGMENTS

My thanks to: Beth Wood for her positive advice, support and encouragement; Pat McHugh, my mentor and hardworking editor with a keen sense of humour, mastery of atmosphere and grasp of characters; Rebecca Moss Guyver, for her boundless enthusiasm and brilliant cover artwork and design; David Withnall for his proof reading skills; Andy Deane for his editing help; L Reynolds for ancestry search advice; the Write Now! Bury writers group for their support; Sue Southey for her cheerful reassurances and advice; and my husband and family, on both sides of the Atlantic, for their love and support.

CHAPTER 1

'Awesome,' Nick whispered, and clipped the lid back on his lunchbox.

'Yeah, that Suffolk Gold is right tasty,' Dave said between last mouthfuls of ham and crusty bread. He nodded slowly and glanced at Nick.

'No, I didn't mean the cheese or my lunch. I meant… this.' He swept his hand across the view in a panoramic gesture indicating the neighbouring flat fields, a vibrant green of young shooting wheat and barley. The year was slipping away. Mid-April already.

'You know it's a moated farmhouse, don't you?'

Nick recognised the tone. Dave might be a fellow carpenter and would-be rally driver, but deep down he was a historian, an archivist, someone with a thirst for the past along with his pint of beer. Throw in the fact he'd been Nick's onetime trainer and it was inevitable a homily was about to ensue.

'If we put this lot in the van now, we've still twenty minutes lunch break left before we go back to the roof space. Let's walk; follow the moat and I can tell you all about moated farmhouses.'

'Cool,' Nick said and hid his I-can-read-you-like-a-book grin.

They retraced their steps from the sunny place on the garden bench, skirted a bed of lily of the valley and followed the short gravel path to the Willows & Son van. Beyond it stood the old farmhouse, its plastered exterior imprinted with patterns and hiding the timber frame beneath.

'It'll be this way,' Dave said, barely waiting for Nick to close the van door before heading towards what looked like a shrubby hedge.

It took Nick only a few strides to catch up. He was pleased to be distracted by the promise of a moat tour. So far his day had been spent bending and ducking, claustrophobic in the dusty farmhouse roof space, and sweltering as they figured a way to lay chipboard on uneven joists. It had been slow work running new wooden supports alongside the wormed and bowed oak, and the chipboard slabs were heavy and awkward to manoeuvre. He stretched, enjoying his freedom.

'So the farmhouse is like on a kind of island?' he said.

'Yeah, I suppose so. Of course we drove in where some of the moat will have been filled in.'

They strode along the gravelly track which served as the driveway to the farmhouse.

'It'll be somewhere around here,' Dave said, and slowed as he stepped more carefully onto the roughly mown grass to one side of the track. Nick realised they were heading towards bush-like elm, ash, hawthorn and hazel. Late blossom and April-budding leaves masked their woody branches. It was a common sight; nothing to suggest more than a wild section of hedgerow.

'Was that Defender over there when we arrived? I don't remember seeing it,' he said, pointing at a dark blue 4x4 drawn onto the grass. It was a little way off, but he could see it had a small boat trailer and was backed up close to a gap in the rough hedge.

'I didn't notice; but the boat's gone from the trailer. It must be in the moat.'

Fired by the image of a boat on hidden water, Nick quickened his pace. 'So how wide's this moat going to be?' he asked.

'At least three metres, otherwise it's just a ditch filled with water.' They walked in silence for a few moments. Dave looked thoughtful before adding, 'Not the whole moat of course; over the centuries they tend to silt up if they're not maintained.'

'Centuries?'

'Well yes. This one probably dates from the thirteen hundreds.'

'What? Seven hundred years old? You're kidding me.'

'No. I've read they can be even older; some date back to 1066. There'll have been quite a number round the time this one was dug. As I said – I'm guessing early thirteen hundreds. Apparently the climate was wetter then and the water table was higher.'

'The wetlands of Suffolk. So it was a way to drain a patch of land, right?'

'Yes, along with giving a bit of security. The dugout earth was used to raise the ground in the centre.'

'Cool; make a dry platform for building the farmhouse,' Nick added as he followed Dave. This was turning into more of a moat tutorial than homily.

They walked in single file past the dark blue Defender and empty boat trailer, Nick's thoughts torn between the sheer slog of digging a moat with a medieval spade, and how the water had come to be so hidden. It couldn't have always been concealed like this, surely?

He pushed past a young elm and stood in the gap between the shrubby trees where the ground sloped, at first gently and then more precipitously down to muddy water.

'Wow,' he breathed, taking in the murky surface with no hint to its depth. Three metres seemed a conservative estimate for the width. It was over twice that size, bloating into a rounded shape before extending more narrowly in the line of the moat.

'This has to be where the boat was launched,' Dave said, indicating the breaks and ruts in the turf.

'Well I don't see any boat.' Nick stooped a little to get a better view. His natural height of six foot three set his eyelevel directly through the elm branches stretching across the moat. They touched branches from elm on the far bank, and like lacework they veiled the distance. Sunlight and shade played patterns on the dark water below.

'The boat'll be further on, beyond the next corner I reckon. The moat is likely to be a square or a rectangle shape; come on.' Dave led the way.

They walked on the mown grass. Nick hung back a little to peer at intervals between the trunks and branches, and catch glimpses of the water beyond. Brambles and ivy filled some of the lower gaps. It felt secretive and he couldn't quite shake off the feeling he was walking where he shouldn't. A blackbird took flight and a chaffinch sang loudly. Nick moved quietly. Best not to make their presence too obvious; no need to announce their arrival or break the tranquillity, he decided.

Ahead of him, Dave stopped. 'It seems to widen out here. I expect this'll be where the next section of moat joins.'

'I don't see how you can tell. It's so overgrown. It's like no one's supposed to know it's here.'

'I guess the owners have let it silt up. They probably hope it'll fill in naturally.'

4

'You mean the ones wanting us to make a safe floor up in the roof space?'

'The Coadys? They're new; if owning for a couple of years makes you new. No it'll be the previous owners. This won't have been dredged in thirty years.' Dave stepped carefully around a clump of faded, dying-back daffodils and disappeared between the bushes.

'Hey, wait for me.'

Nick's imagination filled with a vision of liquid darkness merging with layers of decaying twigs and leaves. But maintenance wouldn't be merely about dredging. The foliage extending over the water needed to be tamed as well. He pushed a branch out of his way and followed Dave.

'Why've you stopped?' he muttered, almost bumping into him. Sometimes Dave could be so irritating.

'Does that bloke look all right to you?' Dave asked, tossing the words over his shoulder without looking back.

'What bloke?'

'The one in the boat.'

'Here let me see,' Nick murmured, and pushed Dave lightly to make room to ease past.

'Over there,' Dave said and pointed.

At first Nick couldn't see a boat, let alone a man in a boat. What the hell was Dave on about? It took a moment before his eyes made out the shapes. Objects separated from the water and dappled shade. He struggled to make sense of a neutral fibreglass colour and charcoal patch. Could he be staring at the hunched back of someone kneeling in a dirty water-coloured flat boat?

Something about the shape chilled; it was eerily still. An unnatural stance. If it was a person there should be a head. So where was the head? *I need to see a head*, Nick's inner voice faltered.

'What's he looking at?' Dave asked.

'How'd you mean?'

Dave didn't answer.

Now Nick made sense of it. The figure was hunched all right. It was bent over the bow of the boat. And the head? He made out the back of a head; the face was submerged in the water. The arms were outstretched, the hands and forearms immersed and out of view.

'It looks like....' Nick was going to say *like he's reaching into the water for something*. Instead he yelled, 'Hey, are you OK out there?'

He waited, tense and anxious. Dave stood next to him, for once silent. There was no answer. No movement. Nothing.

'Do you think...,' Nick steeled himself to say the unspeakable, 'he's dead?'

'Are you OK?' Dave bellowed at the figure.

God, what if he wasn't dead? They were wasting time. Life or death – it could hang on a few seconds. He needed to wade in, swim over, get the man's face out of the water, push him back into the boat and drag the boat to the bank. Nick strode forwards.

'Hey what are you doing, Nick? Stop! You can't go in, you'll drown.'

Nick wasn't listening. He'd keep his clothes and trainers on. And his watch. It was showerproof. 'Look after my phone, will you?' he said, dragging it from his jeans.

'No Nick. He hasn't moved the whole time we've been here. He... I think he's... I think we're too late.' Dave grabbed his arm.

'How do you know? We can't be sure.'

'If you go in and get into trouble, then I have to go in after you. I'm sure about that. And we'll both drown. For God's sake Nick, look at the man. He could have been here like that for hours.'

Something made Nick drag his eyes from the figure and fix on Dave. Perhaps it was the vice-like grip biting into his arm or the urgency in Dave's voice. Realism cut in. Nick might be athletic and close on twenty-four, but Dave was portly and middle-aged. Could he even swim? He'd never asked. And the bottom of the moat – imagine sinking into all that silt or getting tangled in weed?

'A rope. There's rope in the van. I'll get it, I can run faster,' he rasped.

'I'll phone for help.'

Nick hesitated. It was a last chance moment; hurl himself into the water or run for rope?

'Go!' Dave boomed.

The command was the decider. It propelled him into one leaping stride, then another. A rope. The van. It filled his mind; a single objective. It carried him over nettles, brambles, rough grass and the gravel driveway. He tore open the van door and reached for the coil of rope hanging on the side frame. 'I need a grapple,' he panted, 'something to catch on the boat. This'll do.' He grabbed a heavy sash cramp, slammed the door, turned on his heel and ran back.

Dave was still talking into a mobile phone and standing mid-calf deep in rough grass close to the bank. Nick pushed past. He cast an anxious glance; the figure in the boat didn't look as if it had moved. Nothing had changed. He hoped for his conscience's sake they'd always been too late to save him.

'Stand clear, Dave. Give me some space. I'll need a backswing on this,' he shouted as he tied one end of the rope to the metal cramp. It was old, but strong. Its metal sliders and clamping plates stood proud of the short metal shaft. There'd be something to catch on the side of the boat.

He stood facing the boat, his legs planted, and swung the cramp on the rope. He reckoned twenty feet. 'Watch out!' he yelled and with final accelerating power let go. It arched forwards across the moat, trailing rope behind, the end still secure in his left hand. Splosh! It landed short. Water heaved and rippled, rocking the flat-bottomed boat.

'Shit!' he muttered and tugged on the rope, reining it back.

It took several throws; the first too short, the next too far right, and finally *smack* onto the stern of the boat.

'Got it!' he yelled.

Dave ended his call and hurried to help. Together they pulled on the rope, easing it towards them. Nick felt a sudden resistance. The cramp had caught against something.

'Steady. Keep the tension,' Dave muttered.

Slowly the flat boat turned and its stern lined up with the pull of the rope. It felt as if it was taking forever, but the boat inched towards them.

'Keep holding the rope, while I secure it,' Nick said and hurried down the bank. His foot plunged into icy water. Down it went, well beyond his knee before his trainer touched the bottom. Clouds of silt mushroomed up through the murky water. Oh God, his foot kept travelling deeper. Mud engulfed his trainer… then his ankle. Instinctively he grabbed the side of the boat and hauled himself in.

'Careful, Nick,' Dave shouted. 'Tie the rope to the rowlock or something.'

'Give me some slack on it.' He worked quickly, and the weight of the cramp still attached, held the twists of the rope.

But the figure didn't move. It knelt beyond the front plank seat, hunched forwards over the side of the bow. 'Right,' Nick muttered and grasped a handful of the bloke's tee-shirt.

He tugged and the boat rocked but nothing happened. The body was too heavy; his purchase on it too flimsy. He strained to lift the man's head and get the face out of the water but the weight of the dangling arms pinned him over the side. God, he'd have to bear hug the man's body to yank him back into the boat.

'Careful,' Dave shouted again.

The boat pitched as Nick heaved and lifted and pulled. 'Argh,' he groaned with the effort as he worked the man's shoulders, head and arms back into the boat.

'Is he dead?' Dave asked.

Nick didn't need to look. He'd felt the chill of the man's arms, seen the ashen blue of the skin and face, and there'd been no heartbeat to sense in his bear hug.

'Yeah.'

Something glinted in the bottom of the boat as sunshine seeped between the branches.

'What the hell's that?'

•••

Nick sat on the roughly mown grass. He was close enough to the bank to keep an eye on the boat, but not too close. He'd seen enough. And so, while Nick tried to distance himself, Dave stood talking to Mr Coady, or rather Victor, as he'd insisted they call him. He'd come running from the farmhouse, hotfoot after the phone call from Dave.

'He was measuring the depth of silt – you know, down to the level of the clay. We're going to have the moat…. Oh God, I need to ring the dredging firm.' Victor's soft voice drifted across on the edge of panic. 'I guess that pole sticking out of the water was his measuring gauge.'

What pole, Nick wondered, and scanned the water. Oh that. He'd thought it was just a tall bit of cane caught in the moat and hadn't paid it much attention. An image formed in his mind. A body hunched over the side of a boat. *Block it out*. He shivered and forced it away. What to do? *Fill your head with other stuff. It's risky leaving space for intrusive thoughts*.

He hummed, first a tuneless note and then a melody. Had he always been like this? It had taken him years to toughen up. The banter of colleagues at Willows & Son didn't allow for much expression of emotion, unless it was about joinery or football. Dave was different, but then he'd been his trainer and Nick the raw carpentry apprentice. And his mates from the band? The ones he'd known since his school days? He guessed they expressed their emotion through music, lyrics and melodies. None of them actually spoke about their feelings.

For an instant a body hunched over the side of a boat. *Block it out*.

Dave had once told him he could be impulsive. *Me? Impulsive?* Of course Nick had argued at the time but deep down he'd known it was true. Was it such a bad thing? Impulse might have been described as bravery if they'd taken an earlier stroll around the moat and a life had been saved. To Nick's way of thinking, it was an expression of his passion and ideas. Part of his core.

Take his application to Exeter University for an Environmental Sciences degree course. Had it been a whim? At eighteen, had he been too young? And now, almost six years on, did he reckon it had been impulse or passion that threw him into the destructive path of Melanie in that ill-fated Freshers' Week? His first year had been a disaster. He'd dropped out and come home to Suffolk. But now at twenty-four? Had his decision to follow his passion and work with his hands been an impulse? To create things from wood, train to be a craftsman and enjoy the freedom of outdoors and the Suffolk countryside – had it all simply been on a whim? No. The line between passion and impulse was blurred. Chrissie seemed to understand, and so did Matt... sometimes.

CHAPTER 2

Chrissie looked across the old barn workshop. She had shared the space with Ron Clegg for almost four years, the first two as his apprentice and since then as his business partner. The wooden door stood open and spring sunshine streamed in, casting shadows beyond the workbenches and highlighting the woodturning lathe where it stood against the far wall. The scent of wood dust, beeswax and white spirit filled the air. She had spent the day working on the broken leg stretcher of a gateleg table. A country piece dating to around 1660, Ron reckoned.

Her thoughts drifted to the long weekend ahead. The Easter weekend complete with two bank holidays tacked on, Good Friday and Easter Monday. It would have been nice to go on a short trip with Clive, but once again, his work had put paid to that. As it was, she expected she'd barely get to see him.

Brrring brrring! The ringtone burst from her mobile. She had forgotten she'd slipped it into her pocket, and for a moment it took her by surprise. The time and caller ID were clear on the screen as she pulled it from her linen work trousers. 14:55.

'Clive?' she said, pleasure mixed with surprise.

'Hi, Chrissie. I'm glad I caught you. Are you busy? I mean… something's come up and… would it be OK if you left work now? I need your help.'

'What? Has something happened? Are you all right?'

'Yes of course I am, but I'm not sure about Nick.'

'Nick? What's happened to him?'

'I don't think anything's happened to him exactly, but I've just had a call from Stickley. A man's been found dead out towards Eye. A possible drowning.'

'Oh God. You mean,' she struggled to find the words, 'are you saying–'

'No, no. But Stickley said a Nick Cowley helped pull the body out of the water.'

'Nick pulled a body out of the water? God that must've been awful. And Stickley's there with Nick, you said?'

'Yes. Stickley called because... well he wanted to ask if he should call the SOC team in. I said to stop the ambulance carting the body off and to get the police surgeon. If the doc thinks it's a sudden, unexplained or suspicious death then he'll call the SOC team in. It all sounds a bit odd. I'm driving over.'

'Poor Nick, of course I'll come,' Chrissie breathed. She'd only met Clive's detective sergeant a couple of times, but his voice had the qualities of a cheese grater and she doubted Nick would cope with his abrasive style. Clive must have known it as well.

'I'm not far from the workshop. I'll pick you up in... ten minutes, all right?'

'Yes, but–'

The call cut dead.

'Is everything all right, Mrs Jax?' Ron asked from his workbench. He was standing, half bent over a plank of elm held firm in the bench vice, a metal plane in his hands. His arthritic knuckles were obvious even from a distance.

'I don't know, Mr Clegg. I'm trying to get my head round it.'

The lines on Ron's aging face didn't give anything away, but she guessed he'd heard enough from her half of the phone call to draw his own conclusions.

'It's Clive,' she blurted. 'He wants me to go with him to the scene of a drowning somewhere near Eye.'

'I thought I heard Nick's name mentioned. Is he all right, Mrs Jax?'

'It was Nick who pulled the body out of the water, and Clive reckons....'

'Nick may need a friend with him.'

'Yes.'

'Hmm, well Clive's probably right. Now don't get any ideas while you're there. You know what you're like.' He ran a hand along the edge of the plank and turned his attention back to planing it.

You know what you're like. What was that supposed to mean? Couldn't everyone see the curious puzzle solver and lateral thinker buried deep inside her? Words like meddling and nosey were unfair. She'd expected more from Ron; he was usually so insightful. But then he hadn't actually used those words. A dog with a bone is how he'd described her once and, to her way of thinking, tenacity was a good thing.

By contrast, Clive, when he was being DI Clive Merry, could be singularly blunt. He usually thought she was interfering with his investigations. But when was the last time he'd asked for her help near a crime scene? 'I reckon this is a first. And he'll be here in about ten minutes,' she murmured, rounding off her train of thought.

'Then you'd best start packing up. I imagine he'll be in a hurry when he arrives,' Ron said between planing strokes.

She hadn't meant the *he will be here in ten minutes* for Ron's ears, didn't want him thinking she was bunking off work early, but then his response was so Ron; practical, straight to the heart of the matter and sparing the questions. Perhaps she should take a leaf out of his book; the *sparing the questions* bit. Her mind raced on as she swept up her wood shavings scattered around the woodturning lathe.

Nick must be in a bad way. How was he coping? And his flashbacks? She pictured him humming soulful tunes; a bad sign. Agitation ate at her composure. Best wait outside in the sunshine.

'I'm going now,' she said abruptly and checked the wood shaving bin so that Ron couldn't read the angst in her face. She kept her voice even as she continued; 'Have a lovely Easter, Mr Clegg. I'll call you on the workshop number as soon as I know how Nick is. You'll be here for a while, won't you?'

'Yes, I want to get this elm glued and clamped before I pack up. And thanks; if you give me a call it'll help put my mind at ease.'

'Bye, Mr Clegg.' She hurried outside. The old wooden barn stood close to a brick outbuilding. Feral hedges spread along its neighbouring field boundaries. A light breeze ruffled her short blonde hair. The rhythmic sound of an engine with rotor blades rumbled overhead. She shielded her eyes from the sun and squinted at a helicopter flying towards the nearby Wattisham Airbase. She tracked it as it flew, forcing herself to keep her mind as well as her eyes on its angular silhouette. 'Apache,' she whispered and momentarily forgot her worries about Nick.

Toot! A car horn startled her. She spun round to see Clive's black Ford Mondeo slowing to a halt in the roughly concreted courtyard in front of the barn workshop. He wound down his window. 'Hi, Chrissie.'

'You made me jump! The Apache was so loud I didn't hear you,' she said, breathless.

'But you must've been expecting me. Are you ready? Bag? Keys? And don't forget to lock your car. I may not have time to drive you back here for it tonight.'

Good; so she'd be going in his car. At least that way there wouldn't be any risk of her getting separated and lost on the way. And more to the point, she'd have plenty of opportunity to ask Clive…. Oh no, what had happened to her resolve to take a leaf out of Ron's book?

A few moments later she was sitting in Clive's front passenger seat as the Mondeo rocked its way along the rutted and potholed track from the workshop. Within half a dozen seconds they were onto the Wattisham Airfield perimeter lane, with its grassy verges and tall untamed hedge.

'How long ago was this person found?' she asked as Clive drove through gently rolling Suffolk countryside to join the main roads. They headed east of the A14 towards the so-called old Roman road, the modern A140 which eventually leads to Norwich.

'I guess a couple of hours ago.'

'How far is it?'

'This side of Eye. We turn off at Thornham Magna.'

'Thornham Magna sounds kind of Roman,' she said mildly.

'Well the Thornham bit is Old English. Thorn for thorny – I suppose there must have been lots of hawthorn trees. And ham means a hamlet, a village, a homestead – that type of thing.' He sounded relaxed and easy with her questions. They were on safe ground. She waited. Experience had taught her that if she stayed quiet, he'd fill the silence with some further snippet, and hopefully, this time he'd volunteer some scene-of-drowning information rather than more of the Old English.

'After Thornham Magna it's Thorndon and then towards Eye,' he said after a long pause.

'Thorndon? More farmsteads and dwellings among hawthorn trees?'

'Yes, I suppose so,' he laughed. 'But we're looking for a moated farmhouse in the middle of nowhere. Literally nothing nearby.'

She watched the satnav on his dashboard console. 'Was Nick doing some work at the moated farmhouse?'

'Stickley didn't say. You know I still find it hard to believe you've been friends for so long. You seem such an unlikely trio, what with Matt as well.'

'But people get thrown together on those types of courses and Utterly Academy was no exception. I suppose I must have been the carpentry misfit.'

'You probably still are. But Nick? He seems–'

'What d'you mean, *I probably still am*? Being female and old enough to start on a second career doesn't make me an oddball for ever. If anyone is, it's got to be Matt.'

'And you and Matt are also friends, and I kind of get that. But Nick?'

'I guess we seemed safe, Matt and I. Nick makes friends easily enough but he's wary of letting them close. And Matt and I, we were across from him on the same workbench. He helped us out a lot at the beginning. He's a good bloke. He's OK, you know.'

'Hmm.' Clive's expression was impossible to read. His face told his age; mid-forties, much the same age as her but with many more smile lines around his eyes.

'I'm guessing Nick will have to wait around until the police surgeon's seen the body, right?'

Clive didn't answer. His silence confirmed her fears for Nick.

'Why do you think it isn't just an accident?' She checked his face. He appeared to be concentrating on the road ahead, deaf to her question. Her thoughts raced on. What if the only strange thing about it was Nick's involvement? Was Clive driving to the scene simply because Nick's account didn't add up? She wrestled with the implications.

While the sleek Ford Mondeo ate the miles, Chrissie watched acres of rapeseed fly past, the intense yellow already brilliant in stretches of early flowering fields. It should have lifted her mood and soothed her anxiety, but the yellow only served to heighten her sense of danger. She focused on the more restful green patchwork of young wheat and barley fields.

'We turn off here,' Clive said. He hadn't spoken for at least ten minutes.

The vista of flat and gently rolling farmland was temporarily screened by a thick wild hedgerow. A moment later, it was easily visible again beyond roadside ditches. Chrissie lost her bearings as they passed isolated farmworkers' cottages and took turnings leading onto ever narrower lanes.

'It's somewhere down this one,' Clive announced.

Death's proximity felt palpable. They followed a winding gravel driveway off the lane. Until that moment she'd been detached from the drowning, her focus on the living and Nick, curiosity and anxiety mixed in equal measure. Wild overgrown hawthorn, elm and ash formed an inner perimeter ahead. A sense of mortality coloured her view. It was oppressive.

Clive eased onto roughly mown grass to the side of the track to let an oncoming ambulance pass. He wound down his window and caught the driver's attention.

'Hello, I'm Detective Inspector Merry. Has the police surgeon released the body?' Clive held up his police ID as he spoke.

'The doc wants the hands and feet bagged by the SOC team for forensics. They're getting the body ready to take to the coroner's pathologist. You can ask the doc yourself, he's still back there. Sorry we can't stop - got another call.' The ambulance squeezed past.

Chrissie bit her lip and glanced at Clive. She sensed his shift into detective inspector mode. The tension in his jaw and his frown said it all. Even his short auburn hair looked darker and more severe as they drove further along the gravel and parked next to Stickley's car. Chrissie didn't allow her eyes to dwell on the white panel van with *FORENSIC SERVICES* printed in large letters along its sides. Her stomach twisted. Where was Nick?

'I'll go and find Nick,' she murmured and left Clive to talk to his DS. She walked past the cars and vehicles assembled like guests at a country event and headed for the farmhouse which was dominated by its roof, with wooden beams projecting along the eaves. The pale Suffolk-pink walls didn't speak of death and the moat wasn't immediately obvious. She followed her nose past a bed of lily of the valley.

It was Nick who spotted her first. 'Chrissie! What the hell are you doing here?'

'Nick? Hey, and Dave. I-I finished early today so I dropped by to see Clive. I was with him when the call came through,' she lied. 'As it was you, he reckoned it'd be OK if I came along. But I had to promise to stay out of the way. I heard you pulled someone out of the moat. Are you all right?'

It was Dave who answered. 'Yeah, my stupid idea to walk round the moat. We should have cut our lunch break short and gone back to work. It would have been a damned sight easier. We're working in the farmhouse attic,' he finished by way of an explanation.

'So did someone take a swim in the moat and get into trouble?' She had to know.

'It wasn't like that,' Nick muttered.

Dave glanced at Nick before adding, 'There was a bloke in a boat measuring the depth of silt for the dredging team. He'd kind of flopped across the side of the boat with his head in the water.'

'He was well dead by the time we saw him,' Nick said, the strain sounding in his voice.

'But that's awful. And his head was in the water? How come?'

'We don't know.'

She let the sense of it sink in. 'How strange.'

'I'll tell you what's strange; since we've been hanging around, I've had a chance to talk to Shaun. He's Tuscan's boss from the dredging firm,' Dave's tone was conspiratorial.

'Tuscan?' Chrissie echoed.

'Yes, Tuscan Grabb - he's the dead bloke. Shaun drove over as soon as he heard what had happened. But the odd thing about it is there were loads of little gas canisters like silver bulbs in the boat. Apparently they don't use anything like that for dredging or depth gauges. Shaun can't think why they were there.'

'How strange. Little silver gas cylinders, you say?'

'Shaun reckons they're cream chargers.'

'What's a cream charger?'

'Something you use to make cream frothy.'

'Really? In the boat? But it doesn't make any sense.'

She was about to ask where the moat was and if she could have a look, but something in Nick's face stopped her. What was wrong with her? She was there for Nick, but already her mind was darting off on questions and tangents. 'You didn't have to do any mouth-to-mouth, or chest compressions to get water out of his lungs, did you?'

'No, nothing like that. But it was weird manhandling him back into the boat.' Nick pulled a face.

'Nick's got a theory, haven't you Nick?' Dave said before Chrissie could make a comment.

'What? Oh yeah – I've seen those cream chargers at one of the gigs we did in Ipswich. They're filled with nitrous oxide.'

'Isn't that laughing gas?'

'Yeah. People fill balloons with the stuff and then take puffs from it like you would a smoke - or some even breathe it straight from the dispensers. Apparently it gives an awesomely fast high. It's trending in the London clubs.'

'My God, now I've heard everything! But you don't actually know what's in the canisters in the boat, do you?'

'No.'

21

'It's only a theory. Something to think about while we try not to dwell on… Tuscan,' Dave said.

'Right,' Chrissie breathed. Poor Nick. Thank God he'd had Dave with him. Now Clive had arrived, maybe everything would get moving.

CHAPTER 3

Matt tipped liquid polish onto the rag and made small circular movements as he rubbed the blackberry bubblegum-coloured bodywork. It was a first for him. He'd never polished anything before, but if he was going to exert himself, then what better reason than to make his retro-styled 125cc Vespa the envy of everyone on the Easter Sunday scooter ride-out to Dunwich? He'd always thought Good Friday was a bit of a dead day as far as bank holidays went and this one was no exception.

He wondered how his mates were spending their Friday, but his imagination didn't run to complete guesses. He supposed he should call Chrissie and ask. It would be an opportunity to get her to explain her message about cream dispensers and chargers. *What do you know about them?* was how she'd ended her text the evening before. It had struck him as odd at the time. He'd never thought of her as a whipped cream type of person; he couldn't even recall seeing her eat cream.

He straightened his back and wiped his forehead with a plump hand. This polishing malarkey wasn't all it was cracked up to be. All he could see were swirls and circles of smeary white covering the vibrantly-coloured legshield. Not the look he'd hoped for.

He pulled his mobile from his cargo shorts and pressed Chrissie's automatic dial.

'Hi,' he said when she finally answered.

'Oh hi, Matt.'

He waited for her to say more, maybe launch into cream speak but when she didn't he searched for suitable words.

'Er... them chargers are small metal cartridges you slip into them cream dispensers.'

'Hmm, I know that, Matt. Tell me something I don't know.'

'They're made of steel and they fill 'em with nitrous oxide coz it's kinda soluble in fat.'

'Soluble in what?'

'Well cream's got fat in it aint it?'

'So?'

'When you discharge the cartridge into the cream in the dispenser, the nitrous oxide dissolves in the cream coz of the fat an' all that pressure. Then you pull the trigger–'

'Trigger?'

'Yeah, open the valve. The pressure shoots the cream out the nozzle. Once it's outside in the air the nitrous oxide comes out of the fat and forms into bubbles. It's kinda neat since it's them bubbles expandin' that froths the cream.'

'Right, but I thought you were checking out the nitrous oxide scene.'

'You didn't say. It weren't clear, Chrissie.'

'I kind of assumed, with all your people-searching you'd know all about the trends coming from London.'

He hadn't connected her text last night with the drug scene. He might work for an online people tracing agency, but a simple question about cream chargers and dispensers had seemed just that. He felt stupid and the Suffolk in his voice thickened. 'Are you wantin' to try some laughin' gas then?'

'Don't be a duzzy woop! God, you've got me talking like you now. Hey, where are you calling from?'

He glanced around, as if he needed to check. 'Home. I'm out the front.'

'Well if you're not doing anything, why not ride over? Clive's working. I was thinking of catching the Viking exhibition up in London. You know, the one at the British Museum? But it's closed today. Any other Friday would have been OK but not Good Friday. Trust my luck.'

'Will you be cookin'?'

'Later.'

'Yeah OK, cool. I'll ride over.'

Matt slipped his mobile back in his pocket and surveyed the Vespa. Its side panels, central cover and rear mudguard could wait. He had the rest of Friday and all of Saturday when he could polish, and besides he didn't feel comfortable hanging round for too long outside the front door; didn't want to attract more raucous calls of *you'll have to rub harder, mate if you want to make that pink turn red*. It might be a Special Edition and say pink on the registration document but to his eyes it was blackberry bubblegum, retro and awesome.

Dismissing the imagined colour-shade card, he stowed a sweatshirt, donned his helmet, started up and rode out of Tumble Weed Drive and away from his mum's semidetached bungalow. Time had dulled his eyes to the flaking paintwork. It had even acclimatised him to its oppressive atmosphere. He'd never thought to judge it. Critical appraisal was a term he'd read about, not dished out.

It didn't take him long to leave Stowmarket behind and his mood rose with every mile as his thoughts focused ahead on Woolpit and Chrissie's kitchen.

Rat-at-at-at-at-at! Chrissie's faulty doorbell stuttered its metallic notes while Matt stood, the journey completed and his Vespa parked in the lane. He hugged his helmet, gazed at her end of terrace cottage and waited for her to answer.

'Bleedin' malware - same bricks as Utterly,' he muttered. At least time and soot had dulled this yellow Suffolk clay to a stonier grey. 'Eighteen seventy-nine? Killer app!' The words slipped out as he read the date on the plaque high on the central cottage.

Footsteps approached and the door opened with a swish. 'Hi, Matt.'

'They're the same bricks.'

'How'd you mean the same bricks? Are you all right?'

'Course I am. I aint the one askin' 'bout laughin' gas.'

She held his gaze for a moment, made a kind of shrug and inclined her head in a backward gesture.

He lingered hoping she'd say something. Making sense of body language didn't seem to get any easier.

'Well don't just stand there; come in.' She disappeared into the gloom of a narrow hallway with barely room for more than a staircase. 'And leave your helmet on the table out here,' she tossed over her shoulder.

'Cool. I aint brought me laptop but I can look up stuff on yours if you like.' He blinked in the sudden half-light and shoved his helmet onto a narrow table tucked against the wall. It sent something clattering.

'Careful with Bill's photo.'

'Yeah, sure.'

Bill's photo; he couldn't remember it ever not being there. Chrissie rarely mentioned him. She'd told them he was dead. Matt reckoned if that was the case then Bill couldn't mind when he didn't make any attempt to pick up the photo.

He followed her through to a tiny kitchen offset from the corridor hallway. Light flooded in through an old sash window. The butler sink was empty and a couple of plates, cups and glasses stood on the rack to drain.

'Did you mean it? You know, about looking some things up on mine? Would you show me some of your tricks, like… how you do a people search at work?' She'd turned to face him, one hand brushing the small kitchen table before coming to rest against her laptop.

'I don't get it, Chrissie. I thought you were into cream dispensers an' nitrous oxide? Laughin' gas? The London scene?'

'Yes I am, but something happened yesterday and now I want to find out about a man as well. Goes by the name of Tuscan Grabb.'

'So you're sayin'…?' The pieces of puzzle came together, 'Clive? You aint had a bust-up with Clive?'

'No, but I will if he ever finds out I've been looking up Tuscan Grabb.'

Matt paused, torn between asking more and heading for her laptop. The straightforwardness of the laptop won.

'No wait. Not in here – there's not enough space for you at this table and I won't be able to see how you're doing it. Let's take my laptop into the other room. I'll make us some coffee. Is that OK for you?'

He would have preferred a can of lager but settled instead for a mug of milky coffee with a heap of sugar. The other room, the cosy living room, spanned the remainder of the back of the cottage. He carried Chrissie's laptop balanced on her portable printer as they headed back into the hall and through the end doorway.

'Put the printer on the coffee table before you drop it,' Chrissie said, business-like all of a sudden.

'Scammin' hell,' he muttered, feeling a bit pressured. The two-seater sofa beckoned and Matt sank into it. He settled the laptop on his knee. A geometrically patterned rug of burgundies, midnight blue and beige added a splash of colour on the stripped floorboards, momentarily distracting him from the laptop.

'Shove up a bit and make some room for me, will you?' She settled next to him on the sofa, leaned across, and blocking his view with her shoulder, keyed in her password.

'Why all the cover-up? I reckon I can guess your password, anyway. It'll be somethin' like an old car reg number, right Chrissie?'

He watched her frown lines appear; they had to mean something. Was this one of those times when a frown meant yes and a smile meant no? He changed tack; 'Is Grabb spelled with one or two Bs?'

'I don't know. I haven't seen it written.'

'Cool.' He rubbed his chin and caught at the sandy hair growing there. He hoped playing with his beard made him look focused and professional. 'Right, let's try typin' the name in inverted commas in Google People Search. I reckon Tuscan sounds like a moniker.'

'A nickname?

'Yeah, but let's see what we get with Tuscan and all them different spellin's of Grabb first.'

'That'll be Grabb with one and two Bs, and with or without an E. That's four variables.'

'You sure you aint seen it written?' he groaned and worked his way through the sequence. 'Phishin' hell – we aint got any hits for individuals but we're gettin' websites for leather goods.' He clicked on each site in turn. 'Hey, this *Tuscan Grabb* site with a double B and no E looks more your kinda bloke. He's sellin' old glass bottles. D'you think he's the one?'

'And why would selling glass bottles make him my kind of bloke?'

Matt didn't answer. He was on a roll. 'OK, let's try just a plain T as the first initial and drop the Tuscan moniker. It'll widen the search.' He signed into Facebook and keyed T Grabb in the people finder. A dropdown appeared with a selection of Facebook members, each with a T initial and a spelling variation of the Grabb surname. He narrowed the field to males and read them out as he scrolled the cursor down the list. 'A handful of Ts, an' now we've a Terry-Tim, Tomas, Tuathal, Toussaint and Trojan!'

'But Trojan is Trojan Greeb.'

'Yeah, it's a pain in the codec the way they give you names nothin' like the one you've entered. An' there aint no Tuscan. Do you recognise any of them thumbnail faces with a T initial an' Grabb-like surnames?'

She didn't answer.

'How about this Toussaint bloke? He's got a link to that bottle-sellin' website on his public access page.'

'Hmm, let's save that and come back to him later. What else have you got?'

'Twitter, Instagram, LinkedIn, and if I wuz in the office I'd go through the newspaper sites next. What kinda age is 'e? An' you still aint said what he looks like.'

29

'The thing is I would have had to ask Nick and I didn't like to. At least not yesterday when it was all a bit raw still.'

'What? What you on about, Chrissie? Were you off on laughin' gas or somethin'? And what's Nick got to do with this Tuscan bloke?'

'I can't say. I promised Clive I wouldn't tell anyone.'

Matt blinked as he struggled to follow the thread of it all. He'd already gathered Clive didn't like it when Chrissie asked too many questions about his cases. Matt knew because Chrissie had told him years ago, and it followed she'd have been sworn to secrecy. He supposed it was down to her being so spammin' nosey. Well he could do nosey as well.

He thrust his hand into his cargo shorts and retrieved his mobile. With a couple of deft thumb moves he pressed automatic dial for Nick's number.

'What are you doing? Who are you calling?' Chrissie hissed.

'Hey?' he said when the ringtone finally cut short.

'Wotcha mate,' a sleepy voice croaked.

'Who's the Tuscan Grabb bloke Chrissie wants me to do a people search for? She won't say.'

'Hey stop! You can't, Matt. Leave Nick alone!'

Silence answered his question.

Matt ploughed on. 'No one's sayin' what happened yesterday. Chrissie reckoned if I want to know I'd have to ask you.'

'No I didn't say that,' she moaned.

'He's… I fished him out of a moat. Not literally, but you get the idea.' Nick's voice sounded flat.

'What? Tuscan Grabb? Is he OK?'

'No.'

'So what you sayin'?'

'He's… h-he was dead.'

'Blog almighty! You pulled a stiff out the drink?' He became aware of Chrissie shaking her head next to him. 'But why all the secrecy? It'll be headlinin' on all the local news sites. You shoulda said, Chrissie.'

'Are you at Chrissie's?'

'Yeah.'

Chrissie mimed frantic drinking movements and tapped her chest.

'Fancy a pint in the White Hart?' Matt said in a rare flash of interpretation.

'OK. See you in the bar in twenty-five, but I may not be good company.'

'Right, mate.' The line went dead.

Matt turned his attention back to the laptop and keyed Eastern Anglia Daily Tribune in search.

'I would've done this right at the start if I'd known what it was about, Chrissie.'

'But I don't have a membership.'

'Yeah, but the Utterly Academy Library do an' I got their code in me head.'

Within seconds they were looking at the day's head-lines. Friday April 18th 2014.

Mystery Man Found Dead in Moat. - A man thought to be in his early thirties was found dead in a small boat yes-terday on an isolated moat near Eye. Emergency services were called but he was pronounced dead at the scene. It is unknown how he died or how long he had been in the boat. It is understood that the moat was scheduled for dredging but work had not yet begun. A police spokesperson said the case had been referred to the coroner. The name of the dead man will be released after formal identification has taken place and the relatives have been informed.

'An' we still don't know how to spell his fraggin' name,' Matt groaned.

CHAPTER 4

Nick let his mobile slip from his fingers onto the duvet. *So Matt wants to meet up for a lunchtime drink, does he?* At least it was a reason to get up. *Meeting in twenty-five minutes?* Sleep had come late and heaviness weighed behind his eyes, not from drinking but from a disturbed night. If he lingered in bed he knew he'd doze off again, and the half-sleep would let in the demons. He couldn't risk it.

He threw off the duvet and staggered bleary-eyed to the tiny shower squeezed between the eaves in his garret lodging. There was barely enough height for him to stand, as tepid water drizzled over his short brown hair and formed rivulets down his back and chest. The scent of cedar wood filled his nose as he lathered shampoo.

There really was no need for him to wash again. He'd stood under the shower for what had seemed like forever the evening before, but already he craved water to purge the overnight memories. He still sensed the coldness of Tuscan Grabb's chest pressed against him. Brackish droplets had splashed and chilled from the man's head. A sodden arm had swung heavy against his bear hug embrace. Nick shivered.

What had Chrissie said? *Did you have time to feel all that while you were pulling and heaving or are you just registering it now*? *Do you think it's a kind of retrospective experience*? She was right of course. If he hadn't clocked it at the time, why dwell on it now?

He soaped his head more aggressively and thought about Dave's approach in both coping and in helping him. Dave had adopted a policy of distraction by the simple means of keeping up a torrent of chatter. Once Chrissie had arrived, he'd backed off a little and left the talking to her. But Dave was a work colleague, and Nick wondered if he ever let his guard down. Could either of them be sure that nothing would filter back to Willows about how they'd handled it?

His thoughts raced on as the water trickled from the showerhead. Matt already had questions for him; he'd made it clear in his call. Would he also want a minute by minute account of what had happened yesterday? Well he wasn't going to get one. Clive had said to keep the details to himself. The steel canisters, tubes and balloon found in the boat were all evidence. The look on the DI's face had left no doubt about that.

Nick hadn't let on to Clive, of course but he'd seen that type of paraphernalia before at some of the gigs with the band. Fronting the vocals meant he faced the audience, and while he sang he spotted the stunners, sexy dancers and come-ons. He'd always noticed the balloons, the silvery helium-filled ones with *congrats* and *happy birthday* written across them. More recently he'd started seeing the old-fashioned rubber ones in primary colours so common at children's birthday parties. But why bring them to a gig in a pub? And why keep taking puffs from them and passing them around for your mates to breathe in and out of while you bopped and drank?

Jake, the lead guitarist had explained what it was about. That had been over six months ago.

'Bloody laughing gas. Bloody nitrous oxide,' Nick muttered and turned off the shower. He towelled himself roughly and threw on clean underwear, tee-shirt and jeans.

Outside stairs led down from his single room above his landlady's double garage. He took the steps two at a time and kept the speed going at a fast pace. It was almost half a mile to the White Hart pub in the centre of Woolpit but while he ran he couldn't think – and he'd already done too much thinking in the short time he'd been fully awake. He weaved into a lane and headed past beamed cottages and historic Suffolk-brick houses. A half-barrel planted with daffodils jutted onto the narrow pavement fifty yards ahead. It was his goal, the floral marker outside the door to the saloon bar. He took a sharp left without shortening his stride and jogged into the pub.

'Hiya!'

He recognised Matt's voice. He was lounging against the scrubbed pine counter while Chrissie sat perched on a bar stool close by. A handful of drinkers stood at the bar. It struck him as busy for Friday lunchtime, until he remembered it was Good Friday.

'The menu looks pretty good,' Chrissie said by way of a hello and how are you.

He knew her style. She was fishing. How he answered would tell her if he was still eating or had lost his appetite and was in danger of heading into what his mother would call a decline. It was her way of checking on his state of mind.

'I'm OK, Chrissie. You can stop worrying. Matt's call woke me up so I haven't had a chance to eat yet. I reckon I'll be ready for something after I've had a pint.'

'Well it looks like the specials for today are *Herb-Battered Haddock and chips* or there's *locally reared Red Poll Beef in a quarter pound burger*,' Chrissie said, craning her neck to read the specials board on the chimneybreast above the old brick fireplace.

'Why'd anyone put herbs in the batter?'

'Beats me Matt. Have you tried the Easter Special Edition Pale Ale?' Nick pointed at the *Guest Beers* list. He knew it was a stupid question; Matt was a lager drinker, but while he was asking the questions he felt in some kind of control. He turned his attention to the barman and ordered a half pint taster, all the while conscious that beside him, Chrissie and Matt would be building up to ask about Tuscan Grabb.

Pale-coloured ale slopped into the glass as the barman pulled the tap, and while Nick watched the liquid swirl and bubbles form, he became certain of something. He needed a break from the nightmare of yesterday. If he didn't have to revisit the memory of Tuscan Grabb then he wasn't going there voluntarily, and anyway, he didn't actually know anything about the bloke other than he'd been a dead weight to pull back into the boat. The rest, as DI Clive Merry had said, was evidence.

He sipped the pale ale and thrashed around in his mind for an escape from his torment.

'Are you OK, mate?'

Oh God, his face was giving him away. What to do? And then he saw the answer; it had been staring him in the face all along. Dave's technique – the method of distracting talk. In fact he might even make it easier for himself by repeating some of Dave's chatter.

'Dave told me something yesterday that might interest you, Chrissie.' He smiled. He had a strategy.

'Really?' She sounded interested.

'Yeah, it seems Willows have had an odd request from Utterly Academy.'

'How'd you mean, odd?' Matt chipped in.

'Well it seems they're looking for one of the local joinery firms to take on a carpentry apprentice who needs relocating.'

'Why does he or she need relocating?'

'I don't know, Chrissie. It's a bloke and he isn't from this area. Dave said old Mr Willows wasn't at all keen on the idea and turned it down. But my point is they'll be looking for some other firm to take him on and Dave reckons they may ask you.'

'But Clegg & Jax isn't a joinery firm. We're cabinet makers and furniture restorers.'

'That was Dave's point. He reckons, despite what the Academy have said, you would be a better fit for this bloke.'

'But why?'

'Something about him wanting to spend most of his time in a workshop.'

'What?'

'Dave reckons you may get a call from the Academy after the Easter weekend. I'm not saying you will, but give it some thought in case you do.'

Nick sipped his beer. One look at Chrissie's face told him he'd played his cards perfectly. Right now Tuscan Grabb was the last thing on her mind. He figured she'd be working out the logistics of taking on an apprentice; the disruption versus financial incentives and kudos. As for Matt – well he was frowning.

'A relocatin' apprentice? I can do some snoopin', find his name if you like, Chrissie. The Academy's closed over

Easter but I got me IT pass. I reckon they'll have to register him on the release day teachin'. What you say?'

Perfect, Nick thought and silently made a toast to Dave. Without his shining example he'd never have shifted the spotlight so smoothly from Tuscan Grabb, at least not without causing some kind of offence for being secretive.

'I wonder why he wants to relocate,' Nick said, stoking the distraction topic.

CHAPTER 5

The prospect of being asked to take on a relocated apprentice had been a surprise to Chrissie. She was still having trouble digesting Nick's effortlessly planted rumour. Her immediate inclination had been to ring Clive and Ron and tell them. But what would she have said? There were no specifics to share and most of what she said would have been little more than repeated gossip. She could almost hear their voices; an exasperated *oh for God's sake* from Clive and a more measured *I think we should wait and see if we hear anything from the Academy first* from Ron. Worse still, she knew they were reasonable responses but knowing it didn't quell the nervous excitement threatening to take her over. The one certainty was that there was no mileage in running it past them, at least not yet. It would have to wait until after the long Easter weekend. By then she'd have had a chance to contact the Academy's carpentry course director, Mr Blumfield and find out what was going on. It was a pity her rapport with him had never been anything other than strained.

Chrissie stood in her kitchen and gazed though the narrow sash window, her thoughts centred on her worries. Did she want an apprentice? Would the workshop have sufficient space? Was she good enough to train someone? Was the kudos of having an apprentice worth the hassle?

It was still Saturday and the prospect of waiting several more days to find out if there was any truth behind the rumour was proving hard. The Easter weekend stretched ahead and inactivity made it more difficult to bear. Friday had passed easily enough; Nick being surprisingly chirpy in the White Hart had helped. In fact if he hadn't seemed so relaxed, she wouldn't have felt she could transfer her anxiety about him onto the supposed apprentice, who might be on the horizon. But Saturday was dragging. Clive was working again. And there was Easter Sunday and Monday to fill as well.

Of course there was still the Viking exhibition at the British Museum. She'd decided to combine it with meeting up with her cousin Angela in London. But would Clive want to watch a re-enactment of a siege at Framlingham Castle on his day off? If his enthusiastic following of the London Marathon only a week ago on the TV, was a clue to go on, he might well prefer to start training for the Ipswich Half Marathon instead. If that was the case then she'd ask her bubbly friend Sarah to go with her. A local radio presenter had said there'd be *gruesome tales from the medieval surgeon* along with *rallying cries from the generals*. She wondered if the sights a medieval surgeon encountered on a battlefield were so very different from a modern-day police surgeon's call-out experience. God, now her thoughts were back on Clive's case, the dead Tuscan Grabb.

She gave herself a metaphorical shake and focused on the view outside her kitchen window. A clump of cow parsley had spread between her garden fence and flowerbed. The white flower heads swayed in a breeze while a pink peony stood tall and bowed gently from the border. If the afternoon sun had been stronger it might have cast a shadow. *Use the time to live in the moment,* her inner voice whispered as she dragged herself back to the here and now.

'The hot cross buns!' She'd forgotten her dough. It needed to be knocked back and divided into bun-size portions before a final proving and the oven.

While she worked the fruity bun dough her thoughts drifted. Matt's search record would be on her laptop. Why not visit the Tuscan Grabb site and take a closer look at the bottles? Matt had assumed she'd be interested in them and Clive could hardly complain if he found out. After all, antique furniture and old curios were her thing. What could be more natural than to check out a site selling antique bottles?

Soon the hot cross buns were safely in the oven and her kitchen began to fill with warm cooking aromas. She settled with her laptop at the pine kitchen table and keyed in her password. Oh hell, should she change it? If Matt had guessed it so easily, then so would…. Her programmes opened. She clicked on the Tuscan Grabb site listed in her recent searches and forgot about her password issue. Within seconds she was on the site and reading an *Introduction to Antique Bottles and Bottle Collecting*.

She was fascinated. It seemed many collectors started as children grubbing around in ponds and rivers, picking up old bottles, or finding them in rubbish tips. And of course the adult Tuscan would have been well placed to find bottles in the course of his dredging work. There must have been barrel loads of bottles tossed into ponds, rivers and moats over the centuries. Dave had told her a little about moated farmhouses while she'd kept Nick company on the fateful Thursday. If what he'd told her was accurate, most of the moats in Suffolk dated from the thirteen hundreds. It followed there would have been more than old bottles for Tuscan to dredge up.

A hint of burning raisin and candied peel tickled her nose. 'Oh no!' she squealed. Hot air billowed into her face as she flung the oven door open. She threw the tray of buns onto the counter and fanned them with a tea towel. Once she'd picked and flicked the carbonised fruity lumps away with a pointed knife, she reckoned the buns would be edible. They weren't perfect but it would have to do. 'Just in time,' she breathed, inpatient to get back to the bottle site.

She didn't hear Clive arrive an hour or so later. She was too engrossed in reading about old bottles as she moved from site to site. Terms like *pontil marks*, and the names for the various types of bottle lips and bases were a revelation; they reflected an evolution through the different production techniques developed over time. And the colours – she was amazed by what could be achieved simply by adding traces of cobalt, copper, selenium, carbon, nickel or iron to the glass.

'It's like carpentry,' she murmured.

'What's like carpentry?'

'Clive!' She caught her breath. He stood in the kitchen doorway, a trim figure in classic fit lightweight trousers and shirt. 'Hey, I didn't hear you come in.' She blinked her surprise, and dragged her mind back from the intricacies of push-up bottle bases.

'Sorry, I didn't mean to startle you but you were completely absorbed in your laptop. So, what's like carpentry? Hey, are these okay to eat?' The frown in his question was obvious as he lingered near the counter and surveyed the hot cross buns.

'They should be all right with plenty of butter. I just managed to save them. So how was your day?'

'It's been interesting. But you're doing that thing again, answering a question with a question. Tell me, what's so like carpentry? You were about to say when I came in.' He crossed the small kitchen and kissed her lightly.

The faintest hint of sweat wafted from his blue striped shirt. She guessed it meant he'd had a stressful day and wrinkled her nose. *You're not the only one who can play detective*, she thought.

'I reckon dating old bottles is like carpentry. You have to know about the way they were made and when the different styles and production techniques came in. The manufacturing methods reflect the age and value of the bottles.'

'And that makes it like carpentry?'

'Yes, because with carpentry the styles also reflect the tools in use and production techniques, plus the availability of different woods and the manufacture of things like nails. Of course changes in fashion and demand will throw a spanner in the works, but what I'm saying is you can only date and value the piece if you know the background stuff.'

'So why this sudden interest in old bottles?'

'I've been asked to give a quote for repairing a... George III oval mahogany and brass wine cooler. It got me thinking about the bottles being cooled.' She smiled and held his gaze, secretly a little appalled by the ease with which she'd just lied.

He doesn't know about the Tuscan Grabb antique bottle site she realised as she read his face. If he had she was sure she'd have seen his jaw set for a moment while he decided how to "play" her sudden interest in old bottles. Instead, all she saw were tired smile lines around his eyes.

'Come on; let's try the hot cross buns,' she said, changing the subject and flipping down her laptop screen. 'Tea, coffee or beer? Oh, and while I remember, how do you fancy watching a re-enactment of a siege at Framlingham Castle?'

'What, now?'

'No. It's on tomorrow and Monday. I meant to print out the details, but I left the printer in the other room. I can't think why,' she added, remembering Matt.

She hadn't told him about Matt dropping by yesterday. She'd said about having lunch with Nick and Matt in the White Hart, but not the rest. Not the bit about the Tuscan Grabb site or the relocated apprentice rumour. Her face flamed. Now she looked guilty of something. Damn.

'Just tell me you haven't been meddling in my case, Chrissie.'

'Of course I haven't, but... well I wasn't going to say until I'd had a chance to check it out with old Blumfield. Nick told me Clegg & Jax might be asked to take on an apprentice who's moving into the area.'

'And why would Nick know about it?'

'I don't know. That's why I hadn't said anything to you yet.'

He seemed to think for a moment, as if he was taking it on board. She knew it didn't explain her guilty blush, but assumed he'd put it down to excited scheming around the prospect of an apprentice.

'So what's the Framlingham Castle thing about?'

'I'm not entirely sure but apparently there'll be *gruesome tales from the medieval surgeon*.'

'God, as if I don't hear enough gruesome tales.'

'But most people watching aren't going to be like you.' She stood up and gave him a hug. 'So how's your day been? No gruesome tales, I hope! I suppose it's too soon to expect anything back from the post mortem or forensics.'

'You mean for Thursday's sudden death? You must be joking. You're talking about a weekend with two public holidays tacked on. Four days of emergency services.'

'You always get landed with the long weekends. Are you sure you don't want a beer?' She filled the kettle and eyed the hot cross buns.

'I'll have a mug of tea with the burnt offerings, please. I'm still on emergency duty.'

They carried their tea and hot cross buns through to the living room. The printer sat accusingly on the low coffee table. It wasn't even plugged in and looked abandoned and inert; as dead as the small Victorian fire grate set in the narrow chimneybreast. She ignored it, inwardly daring it to make her feel duplicitous.

'Come on, tell me about your day,' she said and settled beside him on the two-seater sofa. She sensed his tension from the way he sat with his long legs tidy. She knew whenever he slumped into the seat, stretched out his legs and threw his head back on the cushions it meant he was exhausted but relaxed. Neatness reflected stress control. She'd already caught the smell of his faintly sweaty shirt. Poor Clive. 'So how was your day,' she coaxed.

'I had a long chat with the police surgeon.'

'And?'

'Did you know the concentration of oxygen in the air is about twenty per cent?'

'Yes, I think so. Why?'

'It's also how much oxygen you need to stay alive when you're breathing nitrous oxide for any length of time.'

'So?'

'Those nitrous oxide canisters for the whipped cream dispensers only contain nitrous oxide; one hundred per cent nitrous oxide under pressure. So if you breathe it for recreational purposes–'

'To get a high?'

'Yes. You'll still need oxygen to stay alive. Nitrous oxide abusers have a tendency to forget that.'

'So how much do you need to give you a high?' she asked.

'The police surgeon said a few breaths of at least fifty per cent. He was talking percentages of the volume you breathe in. But for your average abuser it'll be one breath of neat nitrous oxide followed by some breaths of air. Apparently the high comes almost immediately.'

'And what's the high like?'

'He said there's euphoria, disinhibition, body numbness, a feeling of floating, maybe dizziness, uncontrollable laughter and then sedation.'

'So people get happy and impulsive. But the numbness? Is that why dentists use it?'

'I was told it's used to help with pain control, but in medical and dental situations they use pure oxygen mixed with the nitrous oxide, not air. Using air wouldn't give enough oxygen to be safe.'

Clive frowned, closed his eyes in concentration and continued, 'But there's something inherent in the properties of nitrous oxide – something to do with it having a very low blood-gas partition coefficient.'

He held up his hand. 'Don't ask; I don't understand exactly what it means. But the doctor said it helps to explain why there's an increased risk of death with nitrous oxide due to oxygen starvation. It's to do with the ease the nitrous oxide comes out of the blood and fills the air spaces in the body, like the lungs and in the bowels. Now the relevance in the lungs is that if an abuser has taken a breath of nitrous oxide and then starts to take a breath of air, the nitrous oxide is already coming out of the blood and filling the lung alveoli when the breath of air is taken. It means the air can't reach the alveolar membranes because of the nitrous oxide and therefore the oxygen in it doesn't get absorbed.'

'And what are alveoli when they're at home?'

'The doctor assumed I knew so I didn't like to ask. But I read later they're the tiny balloon-like sacs in your lungs at the end of your breathing tubes. It's where gases are absorbed and expelled from the blood.'

'But what's the relevance?'

'It's a reason why nitrous oxide abusers can die or come to harm though lack of oxygen, despite thinking they're safe breathing air. It's particularly dangerous in an enclosed space like a car or rebreathing it into a balloon. They asphyxiate when the oxygen is depleted.'

'God, you must have felt like you were back at school having to listen to all that.'

'Not really. The doc made it sound interesting and of course it all made perfect sense when he was explaining it. We'll have to wait for the post mortem to distinguish between asphyxiation from drowning or from nitrous oxide.'

'Poor man,' Chrissie murmured.

'It seems he was addicted to the stuff. At least that's what our enquiries suggest. Poor bastard must have been desperate for it.'

'But how d'you know he was desperate for it?'

'He had frostbite on his lips and tongue.'

'Frostbite? But it was sunny on Thursday.'

'It wasn't anything to do with the weather. If you breathe nitrous oxide directly from the pressurised canister then it's very cold - freezing cold - but the numbing effect stops you being aware of that. The post mortem will tell us more, but from the photos at the scene I think he put the canister to his mouth and opened the valve.'

'That's really sad.' There wasn't anything else she could think to say. Her head was swimming with Clive's tutorial on nitrous oxide.

'Right, time to try a hot cross bun,' he said and reached for the plate.

She watched him bite into it and chew. 'What do you think?'

He didn't answer for a moment; a faint frown creased his forehead.

'Come on, it can't be that bad.'

'No, you're right, Chrissie. It's not quite hard enough to load into one of those huge catapults at the siege re-enactment.'

CHAPTER 6

Tuesday 22^(nd) April 2014.

Man Found Dead in Boat Near Eye Named by Police.
Matt read the headline on the news site a second time and
let the air escape between his lips in a low whistle before
skimming on.

*A 33-year-old man found dead near Eye on Thursday
has been named by police as Toussaint (known as Tuscan)
Grabb. He was thought to have been assessing the build-up
of silt prior to dredging a moat and was discovered dead in
the small boat he was using. It is unclear how he died, although canisters of nitrous oxide (laughing gas) were found
at the scene. A police spokesman said the case was being
investigated as an unexpected sudden death and there
would be more information following the coroner's post
mortem.*

'Fraggin' malware,' Matt breathed. 'So he aint Tuscan, he's really Toussaint. What kinda name is that?'

But he remembered seeing it on Friday's search with
Chrissie. He closed his eyes and pictured her laptop screen.
It took a moment before he visualised the Facebook page
like a screenshot, complete with the people finder
dropdown box. There'd been a *Toussaint Grabb* listed
above a *Trojan Greeb*. He focused on the name *Toussaint*.
There wasn't a thumbnail photo of his face, just a plain blue
disc with the letter T on it. Matt replayed Friday's mouse
moves in his mind. Public access had been allowed for the
Toussaint Grabb home page but there'd been minimal information apart from the link to the bottle-selling site.

'Looks like we found Tuscan Grabb after all, 'cept we dint know it at the time,' he muttered.

He knew the change from Toussaint to Tuscan ought to make him suspicious. In his line of business people frequently changed their first names when they wanted to become less visible. Yeah, but with a name like Toussaint? Blog Almighty! Who wouldn't want to change it? Under the circumstances Tuscan seemed a pretty cool choice.

He shot off a text to Chrissie. *Have u seen news 2day? Tuscan is really Toussaint Grabb*. He left it at that; he was already running late.

With a sudden burst of energy, he laid his laptop carefully on the floor by his bed and tossed the duvet to one side. Familiarity blinded him to his faded grubby bedroom; his focus simply pinpointed the clothes discarded on the floor where he'd shed them the night before. They'd do again for today – the baggy jeans along with his favourite tee-shirt from the weekend. With no further decision to make about what to wear, he dressed quickly, raked his fingers through his dark sandy hair and smoothed his beard. Any combing could wait. Without looking back, he hurried heavy-footed along the bungalow's narrow hallway, past the greasy kitchen and out into April sunshine.

The ride from Tumbleweed Drive to Bury St Edmunds, via the back roads at eight thirty in the morning, took him a customary twenty-eight minutes. He scootered past fields of sprouting winter wheat and barley, wind beating into his chest and rippling his denim jacket. Exhilaration lifted his spirits as he leaned into the bends and then accelerated out, moving his body to balance the scooter with more poise and speed than he could ever achieve on his own. It made him feel how his paunchy slow body could never make him feel. If he could have fused with the Vespa to become a part-man part-machine superhero of his childhood comics, then he would have, and without a second thought.

The roads became busier as he approached Bury, finally clogging into near stationary lines of traffic. He threaded past the cars and nipped across a roundabout into Southgate Street. From there he wove into the Buttermarket area of the old town. He was heading for the offices of Balcon & Mora, a people and debt tracing agency housed on the first floor of a stucco-clad building leaning into an alley.

He parked the Vespa, stowed his helmet and plodded up a narrow old staircase to the unmanned reception and waiting area. 'Frag!' he yelped. His shin smarted as he knocked into the low coffee table and flipped a pile of fly-ers onto the floor.

'Hi, Matt. Sounds like you had a good Easter.' A voice travelled through a partially open door with *DAMON MORA* in bold letters across it.

'Yeah, it were OK,' Matt grunted and pushed the door wide open. He nodded a morning greeting to a man in his late twenties. 'Hi, Damon,' he added for good measure.

The office was a cramped, informal first-names-only kind of a place befitting the techie vibe of an internet-based service. Damon, mousy-haired and of slim build, lounged back in a faux leather office chair surrounded by computer paraphernalia. He was the boss - he'd set up the business, he lay down the rules and he paid Matt's wages. He fixed Matt with his tawny eyes.

It was unsettling and Matt's cheeks flamed. 'Damon, you know that stuff 'bout not gettin' us mixed up in police investigations?' he mumbled.

'You mean your tendency to poke around murder victims?'

'Yeah, well this one aint a murder victim. Least I don't reckon so, yet.'

'But it's a death?'

'Yeah, he's blue-screened it all right.'

'Are we getting paid? Otherwise it's in your own time and you're not using my system.'

Matt had to think for a moment. 'I dunno. It were over the Easter break.'

'Hmm, well tell me the name and I'll decide.' Damon sat forward, his hands ready at the keyboard on his trestle table desk.

'He's called Tuscan Grabb, 'cept it turns out his real name's Toussaint Grabb.' Matt squeezed behind the desk to look over Damon's shoulder at the screen.

'Is that Grabb with a double B? And how do you spell Toussaint?'

Matt told him the letters as Damon opened a news site and keyed the names in its search box.

Almost at once the headline *Man Found Dead in Boat Near Eye Named by Police* came up on the screen. Matt didn't bother to read the piece; he'd already seen it on his laptop at home. He waited while Damon digested the salient points.

'So, it's an unexpected sudden death, there was nitrous oxide at the scene, and Toussaint sounds French,' Damon said. He made a couple of mouse moves and the screen divided to make space for a second tab – *Names: Their Origins and Prevalence*.

'Awesome,' Matt murmured as he scanned the blurb about the name *Toussaint*. 'It says it's French for all saints,

52

and can be a surname or a given name. Hey, d'you s'pose his birthday is November 1st? It's All Saints' Day, accordin' to this. That's a bloggin' awful name to dump on you coz you got born on November 1st.'

'Not if you're French and Roman Catholic.'

'Yeah but 'e changed his name to Tuscan. D'you s'pose it means he aint either of them things?'

'Maybe he didn't want people to think so. The person who named him thirty-three years ago must have thought he was.'

'Right.'

Damon might call it profiling, but to Matt's way of thinking they were combing for background information; snippets to put together to build data. Simply go back thirty-three years from April 2014 but allow for a November birthday and it was a safe bet that Toussaint Grabb was born on November 1st 1980 to a French mother or into a family with French ancestry. Matt was about to say this but Damon cut across his thoughts.

'So who's asking for info on this Toussaint character?'

'Er, one of me mates found him. I reckon I were just nosin' for 'em.'

'So no one's paying?'

'I wouldn't a thought it.'

'Well you know the rules, Matt. This is a business and we've a long list of names just come through from the credit card company. It's time to earn your bread and find the up-to-date contact details.'

Matt knew the score. It was a set routine and he was comfortable with it. 'I'll have a cola, thanks - if you're offerin',' he said and eased his way around Damon's chair and back into the body of the room, its carpet dulled by

wear. He shed his denim jacket and settled into his customary seat at a table set against the wall. There was barely
space for the keyboard and screen, but he'd come to like it
that way. It felt safe. In the early days he'd found sitting
with his back to the boss unnerving but now, like most
things, he'd got used to it.

He logged on and waited for the first batch of names
from Damon to open, while in the background the newly
acquired coffeemaker clinked and hissed and released warm
aromas into the stale air.

'Thanks,' he said, swivelling round to take the proffered cola.

'D12? Wasn't that thought to be code for Dirty Dozen,
or Detroit Twelve? The group had Eminem in it,' Damon
muttered, eyeing Matt's tee-shirt.

'Yeah, kinda cool and edgy, don't you think?' Matt
smoothed the distorted cotton stretched across his chest and
ample belly. Large splodges of purple morphed into a vista
of hills and writing coiled like a road between them.

Damon squinted at the writing. 'PURPLE HILLS,' he
read out slowly. 'But D12 had a massive hit with Purple
Pills. I reckon you're wearing their censored version for
American radio. The original was about drugs – ampheta-
mines, speed, that kind of thing.'

'Yeah well Maisie got it for me coz of the colour. See
it matches me Vespa paintwork. I got loads of comments
when I wore it on me scooter ride-out to Dunwich on Sunday.'

'I bet you did.' Damon's voice sharpened, 'This Toussaint Grabb you're searching – it isn't about the laughing
gas, is it? I've told you before; nothing linking us with
drugs, and that's procuring as well as dealing.'

'Yeah, I got it. But I aint into laughin' gas. An' anyhow, it's legal aint it.'

Matt couldn't tell if Damon was convinced by his denial.

CHAPTER 7

Chrissie slowed to 5mph and steered around a pothole on the rough track leading to the Clegg & Jax workshops. It was Tuesday, the first day back at work after the Easter break and she'd determined to turn over a new leaf. For once she felt unruffled and in control of her inquisitive mind, rather than controlled by it. The day spent in London wandering around the British Museum with her cousin had restored her sense of proportion and wellbeing.

Ping! A message alert sounded from somewhere deep in her handbag on the passenger seat. She quelled the urge to reach across and rummage for her phone. The calm, no-longer-nosey Chrissie of Tuesday morning should be able to resist looking at her mobile - at least for five minutes while she parked and made a mug of tea, she reasoned.

'Good morning Mr Clegg,' she said brightly as she opened the door to the barn workshop.

'Good morning, Mrs Jax, and thanks for letting me know Nick was all right on Thursday.'

'No problem. Another tea?' She plucked the empty mug from his workbench, pulled her phone from her bag and breezed towards the kettle.

She couldn't stop herself from snatching a glance at the alert still lighting her screen. A preview of Matt's message *Have u seen news 2day? Tuscan...* leapt off the screen.

Her stomach lurched. What news? Clive hadn't said anything about a press release that morning. Before she could resist, she'd opened the full message. It read - *Have u seen news 2day? Tuscan is really Toussaint Grabb.*

In itself the alias wasn't a complete surprise. The link to the bottle website had been a clue, but it begged the question - what had happened to all her resolve? The new no-longer-nosey Chrissie hadn't even managed to curb her curiosity for five minutes before opening the message.

Mortified, she switched on the kettle.

'I'm going to ring Utterly Academy this morning, Mr Clegg. I should be able to catch someone if I wait until after ten o'clock. Nick said something about an apprentice being relocated to the area. He'd heard a rumour we might be asked to take him. I thought I'd speak to Blumfield and find out what's going on?'

There – she'd salvaged her newly turned-over leaf. She'd proved to herself that she could treat a sensitive subject calmly. Damn it, she'd even built in a planned one-and-a-half-hour delay before phoning.

'Well Mrs Jax, my experience of taking on apprentices has been very positive.'

'But you've only taken on one apprentice, and that was me.'

He nodded in a stiff arthritic way. She knew the subject was closed until after her call to the Academy. For the moment it was time to drink her tea and get back to repairing one of the broken oak bars joining the legs on the antique gateleg table, a so-called leg stretcher. She didn't want to dismantle the whole table simply to free up the broken stretcher; it would be difficult, time-consuming and she was bound to cause further damage to the old wood in the process. The line between restoration and conservation was a tightrope she walked daily.

She'd already drilled out the wooden pegs holding the stretcher tenons in their mortise joints. If she could free one

57

end of the damaged stretcher, then it should be possible to draw out the other end with its tenon. It all depended on how much give there was in the table's other joints. It was going to be a make or break moment and the point at which she'd know if she'd have to dismantle the table.

'It's circa 1660 so it pre-dates using glue to hold the joints,' she murmured.

'That's assuming no one's tried to mend it in the last 300 years since glue of one sort or another has been around,' Ron added.

'Thanks for instilling the cold note of doubt.'

'Well you wouldn't be the first to get caught out, Mrs Jax.'

She'd known that of course, but there were no signs of a previous repair so she was hopeful. She was also amused by Ron. It was so like him; forever the teacher. Perhaps a new apprentice was just what the workshop needed.

For the next hour or so, she lost herself to the damaged stretcher as she tried to free one end from the leg. But it wouldn't move however hard she wobbled, rocked and pulled. It was time for some lateral thinking. The damage to the stretcher took the form of a bad split in the oak, along with heavy wear and missing wood. She reckoned if she cut along the line of the split with a fret saw, she could divide the stretcher in two. If she still couldn't free the tenon from its mortise joint, then she would simply saw it off and pull, pick or drill out the retained tenon.

She drew lines along the stretcher for her saw cuts so that she could repair it later with a scarf joint between original and replacement old wood.

'Oh no! Is that the time?' It was just after ten o'clock and the sudden flutter in her stomach signalled a rush of angst. 'I almost forgot I was going to ring the Academy, Mr Clegg.' She hoped the surge of hyped-up anticipation wasn't obvious in her voice.

'Use the workshop phone, Mrs Jax.' He put down his tools and waited.

Her call to the Academy was put through to Mr Blumfield's office but there was no answer. She swallowed her frustration and tried again. When this time she was put through to the main Admin and HR office a young female voice answered. 'Hello, did you say you were Mrs Jax from Clegg & Jax?'

'Yes, Chrissie Jax. I was trying to contact Oliver Blumfield but he isn't answering his extension number at the moment.'

'I probably shouldn't ask, but is this anything to do with the new carpentry apprentice? I was going to contact you but it's been really busy in the office this morning.'

Chrissie steadied her voice. 'Yes, it is about the new apprentice.'

'Oh good. Mr Blumfield said he thinks your firm would be the ideal fit for her.'

'For her? Did you just say her?'

'Yes. Why? Is that a problem for you?'

'No, not at all. I just wasn't sure I'd heard you correctly,' Chrissie soothed, covering her surprise while she collected her thoughts.

But why shouldn't the new apprentice be a girl? She was a girl, if you considered her age of forty-five years as still being a girl. Was being a girl the reason why Willow's hadn't taken on this new apprentice? Nick had said something about wanting to be largely workshop-based. But that was just an excuse. She sensed it. No, she knew it. The chauvinistic bastards! Well, if the boys could look after the boys, the girls could look after the girls.

'What's her name? Remind me,' she said as a red mist threatened to descend.

'Gayle Corby. You sounded surprised she's a girl. I thought Mr Blumfield–'

'Corby… yes, well I'd caught the name Corby and assumed it was a boy's first name. My mistake,' she fibbed, not wanting to appear completely in the dark to the HR department. 'Look, can you ask Mr Blumfield to phone us here. You said you were about to call us when I rang you, so I assume you've got our number.'

'Yes of course, I'll get right onto it. Do you want me to put the paperwork in the post, or would you prefer I emailed you?'

'No, post it please. But we do need to talk to Mr Blumfield before we finalise anything. Make sure he understands that.' Chrissie ended the call.

She let her breath escape in a silent whistle and raised her eyebrows at Ron.

'Well, Mrs Jax, from what I heard you say, the new apprentice is a girl called Corby, not a bloke going by the first name of Corby! Did they tell you anything else?'

'Not really. I asked her name and it's Gayle Corby. I figured we'd find out the rest from Mr Blumfield. You heard me say we had to talk to him before we–'

'Finalised anything was what I heard you say. So you reckon that's enough?'

'Well yes, Mr Clegg. She's a girl. According to Nick, Willows didn't want her. And she's having to relocate from somewhere else, probably because she's a girl. Of course we have to take her. You took me.'

'But you came with recommendations from the Academy. It was nothing to do with whether you were a girl or boy; you came because of what you're like. We should be told why Gayle is leaving her current apprenticeship. We don't want personality clashes in the workshop. It wouldn't work.'

Ron's words stayed with Chrissie as she went back to the gateleg table. He was right of course; she was being blinded by her reaction to supposed male chauvinistic and sexist behaviour. But something Ron had said was news to her. She had come with recommendations from the Academy. Good God, old Blumfield must have said something nice about her! And then another thought struck; he might have lied to get rid of her.

•••

Chrissie was surprised later that day to find Clive had got home before her. He was wearing his running shoes and shorts, and for a moment she wondered if he'd had one of his rare half days and she'd forgotten.

'Hi,' she said, as she walked into the kitchen and headed for the fridge. 'You're back earlier than usual. I had to hang on for a call from Blumfield. I'm afraid it rather delayed me, otherwise I'd have been home sooner. God, I need a drink. Would you like a lager?'

'I think I'll wait until after my run, thanks. It sounds like you've had a difficult day.'

She opened the fridge and took a bottle. 'I suppose it has been a bit difficult but it's all sorted now. So how come you managed to escape work early?'

'It seems early, but I just got away on time, for once.'

'That's nice,' she said and gave him a hug. 'So tell me about your day.'

61

'A few surprises. And now the DCI is talking to the Regional Organised Crime Unit about the Tuscan Grabb case. Forensics found something odd. But I've told you before, the Organised Crime lot aren't the easiest. I guess someone will eventually think to tell me if they're taking the case over or if I'm still on it. But in the meantime–'

'It was time to come home. But what do you mean, Forensics found something odd about the Tuscan Grabb case?'

'This is between you and me, Chrissie, and we don't know yet if it was a malicious prank or if Tuscan was targeted, but....' Clive paused as if he was trying to find the right words.

'Go on,' she prompted.

'The forensic team are examining the balloons, tubing, release valve and nitrous oxide canisters found with Tuscan in his boat. I suppose they're checking fingerprints, that kind of thing. Anyway they noticed the balloons didn't look as if they'd been inflated. That's when they discovered there was a reason. All the balloons had their necks sealed up with glue. It would have been impossible to inflate them with anything, let alone with nitrous oxide.'

'But why glue up the balloons?'

'Well that's the question. Could whoever glued them up have known Tuscan didn't have any other balloons in the boat to fill and therefore couldn't inhale the so-called laughing gas directly from a balloon? If so it was a safe bet he'd have to breathe the nitrous oxide directly from the canister, or rather the release valve. In other words, not only at a high pressure, but also at a freezing cold temperature as it shot out of the canister.'

'My God!'

'And we assume that's exactly what Tuscan did. The pathologist found damage consistent with him breathing freezing cold gas. There was frostbite of Tuscan's lips and tongue. His soft palate was swollen. And his vocal cords and the lining of his larynx... yes, I'm sure the pathologist said larynx, were also swollen.'

'You mean his voice box?'

'Yes. The cold injury as good as closed off Tuscan's airway so he couldn't get air into his lungs. He suffocated. It was... murder, or aggravated manslaughter.'

'What?'

'Of course the blood and tissue toxicology and analysis of any fluid in his lungs aren't back yet, but the pathologist doesn't reckon he had any moat water in his lungs.'

'So he was dead before his head went in the water. But surely he realised the laughing gas was freezing cold and stopped before....' She let her words drift.

'You're forgetting the nitrous oxide is a painkiller. The pathologist said it would have numbed him and deadened the discomfort. Hey, but I've been going on for ever about my case. You haven't said why you were hanging around for a call from Blumfield?'

Chrissie steeled herself to appear cool about her news. 'Oh that. Yes, it seems we may be taking on a Gayle Corby from the Midlands. She's partway through her first year of a carpentry apprenticeship but it didn't work out and so she asked to be relocated.'

'Relocated to Wattisham? It's a long way from the Midlands, isn't it?'

'I know, but apparently she wants to move to Suffolk. A childhood dream of hers and now there's an opportunity to fulfil it. The Midlands programme director thinks she'll be better suited to having a female trainer in a workshop, rather than being assigned to a male-dominated firm. Also, the apprenticeship has to be a recognised one. You know; affiliated with a college or academy and with proper training release days etc. I guess there aren't many apprenticeships around that fit the bill.'

She smiled at him. It had made perfect sense when Mr Blumfield had spoken with her less than an hour ago. In fact he'd spoken with both Ron Clegg and her. She might be nominated as the official trainer, but they'd all agreed Ron would be sharing the training with her.

'So how will it work?'

'For me it'll be a job-share trainer's post with Ron, except the forms are so archaic they assume only one named trainer. And amazingly the financial deal means it's good for our business. So it's a win-win situation. It makes it difficult to justify not taking her. Why are you frowning?'

'I don't know. I suppose the Midlands end sounds… unusual.'

'Oh come on, stop thinking like a policeman for once! Go and do your run and then we can have something to eat at the White Hart to celebrate.'

'Right then, I'll be about forty minutes.'

She watched him as he filled his water bottle from the swan-necked tap at the sink.

She might have schooled her face to appear calm, but inside she was a whirlwind of emotion. She had assumed the *not working out* for Gayle in the Midlands to be code for unsympathetic male trainers. But Clive had just sown the seed of doubt. What if there were other reasons and Gayle had issues with motivation and ability? And now there was this business with Tuscan. Was it about to spiral into a full-blown murder investigation? Poor Nick.

'I better warn him,' she murmured.

'Sorry, I didn't catch that,' Clive said as water splashed onto the drainer.

'What? Oh, have a nice run and don't be too long.'

'No, forty minutes max. Bye,' and he was gone.

CHAPTER 8

Nick answered his mobile. 'Hey Chrissie.'

'Nick, hi. Is it OK to talk?'

'Yeah sure.' He checked the time. 18:12. His garret room over the double garage felt warm and airless. 'I was just about to head out for a jamming session with Jake. But that's not till seven. What's up?'

'Nothing really. It's just I thought you ought to know the latest about this Tuscan Grabb bloke.'

'Except his name's apparently Toussaint Grabb.'

'Yes, Toussaint a.k.a. Tuscan. But what I wanted to say was… according to Clive his death is starting to look like there may be more to it than a simple accidental over-dose. It's something to do with the drug scene, except I'm not sure why Clive said that.'

Nick took a moment to focus on Toussaint a.k.a. Tuscan, then drove the image away. 'So why'd I want to know?'

'It's just in case the police come round asking more questions. I didn't want it to put the wind up you. I can't believe there'll be anything in it as far as you're concerned.'

'Right.'

'Sorry, I probably shouldn't have said anything.'

'No, that's OK, Chrissie. Thanks.'

'Have a good jamming session. See you Friday. Bye.'

He collected his thoughts before slipping his phone back into his jeans. What the hell was all that about? He'd known Chrissie for a number of years, but even by her standards her call had come across as odd.

'Something's rattled her,' he murmured, barely registering he was staring at his naked feet as he stood on the threadbare carpet.

He didn't normally meet up with his band mates on a Tuesday evening, but after the trauma of pulling Tuscan's head out of the water, he'd fallen back on his music and was determined to keep busy. It was his way of coping; there was no point in collapsing on his bed with a six-pack of beers at the end of a working day.

Melodies and one-liners born of the incident milled around his head and needed an outlet. Suggestive phrases such as *laughing water* and *laughing lies* swirled in his mind. Moody associations in *glassy water* and *crying skies* beat a rhythm and lent themselves to a song. Jake, a friend from his school days and the lead guitarist, had been happy to meet for a jamming session. The rest of the band, namely Jason, Adam and Denton, couldn't make it. But that didn't matter. He was pretty sure Jake and he would quickly fit the words and phrases to the repeating riff floating somewhere in his thoughts.

'What the hell,' he muttered and mentally shelved Chrissie's call. It was time to slip on his new trainers, reach for his battered acoustic guitar case, grab his car keys and head out to meet up with Jake.

•••

The next day was dull and overcast. Nick didn't mind, in fact he preferred it to the bright sunshine of the previous week. Working in the roof space in the old moated farmhouse near Eye had been sweaty and dusty. Heat had only added another layer of discomfort but at least today he'd be spared the high temperatures.

67

The Willows van was loaded with more chipboard. Dave drove while Nick sat on the passenger seat, swaying with the movement as they headed along the A140 before turning east towards Thorndon and then north towards Eye. They'd be there soon. The riff, tweaked and polished with Jake the evening before, ran around his mind in a loop with the motion: *laughing water, laughing lies, glassy water, crying skies*.

'We'd be finished by now at the Coadys' farmhouse if it wasn't for this business with the dredgers,' Dave said, looking ahead and directing his words at the windscreen.

'I don't know why you say dredgers. There was only one of them. If there'd been more than one, maybe the accident wouldn't have happened in the first place,' Nick muttered, his words interrupting the riff looping in his head.

'Yes, well Shaun, the man in charge, seemed pretty agitated. You can imagine the red tape he'll have to go through with an accident like that.'

'Yeah, right. Tuscan wasn't wearing a life jacket. I'd have had something to pull him by if he'd had one on.' A memory of the bear hug streaked through his brain.

'Shaun said there was one in the 4x4. Bloody fool must have forgotten to put it on.' Dave's tone had a final ring. It was obvious he didn't want to talk further on the subject.

They travelled in silence for the rest of the journey, each deep in their own thoughts. Nick spent his time banishing the memory of the cold wet bear hug and concentrating on the day ahead. It hadn't proved easy to lay a flat floor where nothing ran dead straight, no two pieces of wood abutted evenly, and there were no true 90° angles. Added to that was the challenge of working with old wood.

It was either wormed to a state of powdery weakness, or aged and dried to something as hard as iron.

He'd spent most of his time attaching new straight edged timber to the side of the old roughly hewn joists where they'd bent, or beetle and worm had partially destroyed them. They had only ever been meant to serve as ceiling joists, not weight bearing floor joists for the restricted roof space above. They certainly hadn't been chosen with a flat upper surface in mind to lay boards on.

The van's tyres crunched on gravel and brought Nick's focus sharply back to his surroundings. Overgrown hawthorn, ash and elm marked the line of the moat, and an apron of roughly mown grass stretched from it towards the entrance track. Dave slowed to walking pace and Nick's eyes ran along the Police Keep Out tape cordoning off part of the bank.

The ground where Tuscan and the flat-bottomed boat had been dragged out of the water looked chewed and rutted by the rescue and recovery vehicles. The dark blue 4x4 had gone. Flattened grass and tyre treads left the only signs it had ever been there. It felt raw; bleaker than the sight of Tuscan out on the moat with his body flopped over the side of the boat and his head in the water. The scarred ground was Tuscan's epitaph. Nick shivered.

'Are you OK with it now?' Dave asked as they drove on past.

'What? Yeah, yeah,' he lied.

'Well I try not to think about it. Mind you, when I see the police tape and the tyre marks it gives me a jolt. But it's getting easier each time.'

Nick wasn't sure it got any easier, but rutted ground, footprints and crushed grass might make a good second verse to go with the riff looping in his head.

'The sooner we get this job finished, the sooner we won't have to drive past this,' Dave muttered and accelerated across the moat and parked to one side of the farmhouse.

'It can't be too good for the Coadys,' Nick said.

They unloaded the chipboard. It came ready tongue and grooved and they'd already cut it into half-width strips using the table saw back at the workshop. 'Ease of handling,' Dave had said and winked. At the time it had taken Nick a moment to work out he'd meant ease of access through the relatively narrow hatchway into the roof space.

The next couple of hours were backbreaking. They ran lines of adhesive to help fix the chipboard to the upper surface of the new wood re-enforcing the joists. 'Did you put glue on that tongue,' Dave asked as he used a heavy rubber hammer on the edge of a board to drive the tongue into the groove of the adjacent board.

'Yeah, yeah; you've told me a million times they squeak if you don't glue'em.'

Nick followed Dave outside when they stopped to take a break. The staircase between the first and the ground floor ran in the width of the wall and turned sharply on the top and bottom steps. 'This'll have been built in the wall alongside the chimneybreast when they added an extension a century ago,' Dave tossed back at him.

'As long as they're not the only stairs in the place,' Nick said and ducked to miss a beam at ceiling height across the second to last step.

They headed to the van to collect their thermoses and made their way to the garden bench where they could admire the view across the fields of green-shooting wheat and barley, sown the previous autumn.

'I like your tip of drawing the line of the joist on the surface of the chipboard. Makes it a damn sight easier nailing or screwing them down,' Nick said and poured himself some milky tea.

'Hey, that's Shaun isn't it?'

'Where?' Nick saw the movement before his brain had made sense of it. A stocky man with a shock of dark hair emerged from between the elm trees and nettles bordering the moat.

'Those waders'll be bloody hot and sweaty,' Dave muttered.

'Better than standing in freezing muddy water up to your thighs.' Nick shuddered with the memory.

Shaun waved and walked over to them in a laboured way.

'How's it going?' Dave asked.

'I've been checking the bank. Working out how close to it we can start dredging without causing the bank to fall in. They said I'll have the boat back in a few days, so until then it's waders for me.'

'Do you have many people working for you?' Nick asked.

'You mean can I replace Tuscan?'

'Well not exactly. I was just wondering how big your operation was.'

'It takes three of us on a job this size. We can't drain the moat and we don't want to damage the banks. So we put one man on a floating pontoon on the moat with a small digger. But in order to protect the bank, we need a small skip on the pontoon as well. Then we have someone on the bank to winch the pontoon back and empty the skip at intervals onto our conveyor belt.'

'A conveyor belt?'

'Yes, it helps to separate out the worst of the rubbish from the sludge as it delivers the dredging into a larger skip.'

'What do you do with it?'

'We can empty the skip somewhere on the clients land or fill specially designed bags and lay them on their land instead. You know, to build up the ground height. The water and moisture leaches out and the bags eventually rot. Of course we can, if the client prefers, simply miss out the conveyor belt and take the un-separated dredged material straight for disposal as landfill – but that works out more expensive.'

'And the rubbish; do you ever find anything interesting or valuable, and who gets to keep it?'

'Ah – we're bound by the same code of conduct as metal detectorists. Everything belongs to the landowner, unless it's deemed to be treasure. So we draw up an agreement with the landowner before we start dredging. Most landowners are interested to see what's in their silt and mud but might not want to keep every last fragment of a glass beer bottle or bits of 19th century pottery. They get first pickings. But, if it's treasure it belongs to the state and no one automatically owns it. So all treasure has to be handed in or reported to the coroner. You only get to keep it if no museums want it.'

'Treasure? That sounds awesome.'

'You must be joking. You can't believe all the stories you hear. The odds are stacked against us. We aren't archaeologists. We're working in sludge and muddy water with heavy diggers. I'd have more chance of winning the lottery than finding any treasure. Believe me.' He looked at each of them in turn, his tanned face almost line-free. It made him look young, but Nick reckoned he was likely to be the wrong side of his mid-forties.

'It's treasure if it's 300 years old, right?' Dave said, butting into the conversation for the first time.

Shaun frowned. 'It's anything defined as treasure by the 1996 Treasure Act, which means anything over 300 years old and having its weight made up of 10% precious metal. Needless to say, it isn't quite as simple as that. Take coins - if they're 300 years old and 10% gold or silver then if you find two together it's treasure, but if there's less percentage gold or silver in them you only call it treasure if you find 10 together.' Shaun shrugged and looked heavenwards.

'So find 9 coins and you get to keep them. Find 10 and you hand them in?' Nick said.

'I suppose it has to work on honesty,' Dave added.

'Trust is everything. At least running behind schedule on our job out Walberswick way means it hasn't been a complete disaster getting delayed here before we can start work. I haven't had to lay anyone off work.'

'Yeah,' Nick murmured, mildly shocked Tuscan's boss could refer to his death as a delay. 'Had Tuscan worked for you long?'

'A few years. He was a bit younger than the rest of us. I suppose that's maybe why I never got to know him well.' Shaun raised his hand in a weary goodbye salute and headed off along the gravel path around the old farmhouse.

'I hope you never refer to me as a *delay* if I'm ever found dead and slumped over the side of a boat with my head in the water.'

'Course not, Nick. *Bloody idiot* tends to spring to mind.'

'Thanks. But seriously, Shaun didn't seem too cut up just now about Tuscan's death.'

'Well if Tuscan was into using laughing gas, maybe he was using other stuff as well. I guess Shaun must have been pretty hacked off if he was working alongside someone with a drug habit. And if he wasn't, he'll certainly be hacked off now with all the red tape over a death at work.'

Chrissie's words came back to him. *It's starting to look like there may be more to it than a simple accidental overdose* she'd said. Oh God!

Ping! He opened his text message. It was from Chrissie. *New apprentice, Gayle joining Clegg & Jax this wk. I'll bring her to meet everyone Friday. See U Nags Head.*

CHAPTER 9

The atmosphere on Friday night in the Nags Head was electric; at least it felt electric to Matt. He edged a little closer to Maisie and slipped an arm around her slim waist.

'So where's Gayle from?' Maisie squealed, her voice strident above the jukebox as Ed Sheeran's *I See Fire* rose in a crescendo.

'How'd I know, Mais? I aint seen her yet. I told you Chrissie were bringin' her along to meet the crowd.' He tried to lip sync his words with Ed Sheeran's vocal. It didn't quite work.

'What you just say, Matt?' The pink highlights in her blonde hair looked like flames in the pub's strip lighting.

He waited while guitar and strings underpinned the chorus riff before Ed's voice soared in. 'I aint seen her,' Matt said, nodding his head to the rhythm. He reckoned he looked like Ed; same beard, similar hair shade. But tubbier. Much tubbier.

'You aint doin' that Ed Sheeran thing again are you?'

'What? I'm the very spit of 'im. It's open mic later.'

'Yeah, but it aint karaoke an' you're wearin' the wrong tee. How come you aint looked Gayle up yet?'

He smoothed the *Purple Hills* tee-shirt as she pulled away from him. He'd put it on to please her. The American hip hop reference might have been cool scootering out to Dunwich on his Vespa, but was it the sort of tee Ed would wear? And to an open mic evening? He had no idea.

'Nick an' Jake are singin' later,' he said, his thoughts on the evening ahead.

'Yeah? So why you not answerin' 'bout Gayle? You fancy her or somethin'?'

'What?' To be honest he hadn't given her much thought. But now when he stopped to consider he supposed it was because Chrissie hadn't asked him to. He'd also been busier than usual working with Damon to find contact addresses for the card companies' lists of names.

'Don't be a duzzy woop, Mais.'

She seemed happy with his response and sipped her rum & cola. They made their way across the stained floorboards to a bench seat against the wall in the main bar area. It was on one side of the old fireplace and faced a scrubbed pine table marked with beer stains and seared by past cigarettes. A couple of microphones had been set up on stands in front of the dartboard. An amplifier was balanced on one of a pair of speakers.

'Cool,' Matt said as he eyed the set. Oak beams darkened the low ceiling and made a den of the corner.

It wasn't long before the bar had filled with a sea of drinkers. Voices ebbed and flowed on the stale beery air. Nick was easy to spot when he arrived. He stood taller than most and carried a battered guitar case. Jake emerged from the throng near the counter with a beer and a flat oblong case. His electric guitar, Matt reckoned. By the time Chrissie arrived trailing a solid-looking girl with medium length hair tied back into a messy bun, Seth and Andy had also joined them.

'She must be Gayle,' Maisie whispered leaning close. 'Them highlights weren't cheap.'

Matt focused on the girl's hair. It looked a kind of nondescript mid-brown, possibly fairer. He wasn't sure he could make out any streaks. He was about to ask, 'What highlights?' but a glass smashed behind the counter and the moment had passed.

'Seth and Andy were on the carpentry course a couple of years ago, and Nick and Matt, a year or so before that,' Chrissie said by way of introductions.

'Hi, I'm Jake. Don't ask me to saw anything up.'

'And I'm Maisie. Where you from, Gayle?'

'Leicester.' Her voice sounded too small for her body.

'Oh yeah, where in Leicester?' Jake asked.

'I wasn't there long. Just a flat on an estate. Something to forget. Nothing special.'

'Are you singing the new song you've written?' Chrissie butted in.

'*A Last Laugh* – yeah we thought we'd try it out,' Jake said.

'Hey, is it about that Tuscan bloke?' Matt asked.

Gayle frowned and Chrissie explained, 'It was in the news last week. A death from laughing gas. The man was in a boat and Nick found him.'

'I'll see if I can pull up the news item on my iPad. Nick keeps adding new verses so I've brought it with my guitar for the words.' Jake reached for his guitar case.

Matt watched. He'd got used to slipping his laptop in his backpack, but an iPad might be a cool substitute for it in his out-on-location people tracing kit. He glanced at Maisie. She seemed to be more interested in Gayle, so he stood up and moved closer to Jake.

'Blog Almighty!' he breathed as he read the breaking news headline: *More Deaths from Laughing Gas. Suffolk Follows London Trend. A man has been found dead in Dunwich, surrounded by canisters of nitrous oxide. This is the second death in Suffolk thought to be related to so-called laughing gas in just over a week.*

'What? What's happened? Let me see.' Chrissie put out her hand for the iPad. 'My God. This is horrible. I must ask Clive about it when I get home.'

'Who's Clive?' Her voice was tiny.

'He's a policeman. But he's okay coz he's Chrissie's fella. Can I 'ave another rum 'n cola, Matt?'

'Sure, Mais.' He was already standing so he couldn't really say no, but secretly he'd hoped to have a go on Jake's iPad.

'Hey, Ed Sheeran,' Maisie squeaked as she handed him her empty glass, 'get one for Gayle as well, while you're about it. OK, Gayle?'

'I-I'm not sure I–'

'Nah, he don't mind gettin' them, Gayle,' Maisie insisted.

CHAPTER 10

It was late by the time Chrissie dropped Gayle back at her lodging on Restitution Road. It was to be a starting place for Gayle – close to the centre of Stowmarket, the Leisure Centre, the main bus routes and train station. It wouldn't have suited Chrissie, but then Chrissie was independent and a rebel at heart. She would never have been happy to be a lodger with one of the staff from the Academy, even if they were non-teaching and from the catering department.

'Bye, Gayle,' she called after her through the car window, 'It's the apprentice release day on Monday, so see you on Tuesday at the workshop. OK?'

Had introducing her to the Nags Head and the ex-student crowd been a mistake, Chrissie wondered as she drove home to Woolpit. As far as Chrissie could see, Gayle was quiet and withdrawn and didn't seem to know anyone in Stowmarket. So surely it was better to be included and made to feel welcome, than to be ignored. She hoped they hadn't overwhelmed her.

It was dark in the lane outside her home in Woolpit; no lights on in numbers 1 or 2 Albert Cottages, just a dim light showing through one of her upstairs windows. She reckoned Clive must be still awake, unless of course he'd fallen asleep while waiting up for her.

She opened the front door. 'Hey, are you awake?' she called softly.

A snore from the living room answered her question. She tiptoed into the kitchen and made herself a large mug of tea.

Clive barely stirred when she carried her tea into the living room. She stood on the rug of burgundies, midnight blue and beige and watched him for a moment. He was still wearing his jacket and had sprawled awkwardly on the two-seater sofa, his head propped on the arm and his feet on the floor as if he'd fallen asleep sideways from a sitting position. A full mug of coffee looked untouched on the low table. He must have sensed she was there because his breathing grew quieter and lighter.

'Chrissie? Hi,' he said, opening his eyes, his voice full of sleep.

'Hey. You were out for the count.' She almost slopped tea on him as she leant over his head and kissed him. 'Did you get in late as well?'

'Hmm,' he sighed wearily.

'Move over a bit and make some room for me.'

'God, what a day,' he yawned. 'I expect you've heard about this latest laughing gas death. It'll have been all over this evening's news by now. It's only turned out to be Tuscan's boyfriend.'

'What?'

'We'd kept Tuscan's sexuality out of the news. Mind you, it took us a few days to discover because he'd kept it under wraps. But now with this second death, well there'll be panic in the gay community. You know the kind of thing – are they being targeted?'

'Well are they?' Chrissie blinked, instantly wide awake.

'No, not as such. At least I don't think so. It looks as if Tuscan's boyfriend took his own life, either by accident or on purpose. Or rather I guess that's what we're supposed to think.'

'But you're not convinced?'

'Well, there was no suicide note. He was found with his head in the tumble dryer, along with canisters of laughing gas and the dispenser.'

'What? Sounds like a risky way to use laughing gas, although it could still be an impulsive, broken-hearted way of following Tuscan, right?'

'I don't know. You see we never got a proper opportunity to speak to him. It was only when he didn't show at the station to be interviewed that someone went to check on him. That's how his body was discovered.'

'Do you think the police wanting to question him could have tipped him into killing himself?'

'Again, I don't know. We're waiting for the full post mortem results, but the pathologist phoned to tell me he's found some superficial bruising to the chest. He wondered if it could be from the rim of the drum in the tumble dryer. We'll have to wait for the SOC officers to take a drum rim imprint before we can be sure, but if it is it could mean he was held down.'

'God, how horrible. Was the dryer a condenser or an air vented one?'

'Christ, Chrissie, you do ask some anoraky questions.'

'No – it's just he wouldn't have stood a hell's chance if it wasn't the vented type.'

'I don't think he stood a chance anyway. I should have mentioned he was only wearing one shoe – no I'll rephrase that. One of his thong sandals was in the living room and the other was only half on one foot.'

'So,' Chrissie sipped her tea, 'you think… he was dragged or forced from the living room?'

'Possibly. There was some fresh blood in his nose, but it doesn't look as if he'd been hit.'

She took a moment to digest the implications. 'And Tuscan's death? What did our Regional Organised Crime Unit think about his death?'

'First tranche of enquiries indicates Tuscan, or should I say Toussaint's death was most likely a targeted premeditated murder. There doesn't appear to be any evidence of balloon tampering elsewhere across the laughing gas drug scene.'

'But if it was murder, what's the motive?'

'Well, the most likely motive is the gay angle – a lover's tiff. Tuscan wasn't a known dealer, just a user. He collected old glass bottles, but nothing of great value. His bank accounts might hopefully shed more light when we're granted access. At the moment we're waiting for the gas chromatography on his brain and various other tissues to come back. It should confirm the nitrous oxide. And of course his hair analysis for other drugs will come back eventually.'

'And that's it? Tuscan's gay lover murders him with laughing gas, and then filled with remorse, kills himself with the same agent?'

'That's what I think we're supposed to think.'

'And our Regional Organised Crime Unit? What's their view on this second death?'

'They've only just been informed about it. I'm sure they'll get back to me eventually – but in the meantime I'm investigating both deaths and keeping the ROC Unit in the loop.'

'D'you think that's why Toussaint called himself Tuscan? To keep his double life secret? I'm starting to feel rather sorry for him.'

'If you're going to feel sorry for anyone, spare some for me. I've got to go in tomorrow on my Saturday off to make an announcement to the press about this latest death. There's bound to be a bucketload of questions to field. At least we'll be able to release the name by then. But you haven't told me how your evening went? Did Gayle enjoy the Nags Head open mic thing?'

'I don't know. She doesn't say much. I can't really read her yet. Mind you, it's not surprising; I only met her for the first time yesterday when she came to the workshop. She's definitely reluctant to talk about her time in Leicester.'

'Is she any good, though? Has she got the makings to be a carpenter?'

'It's early days. With Ron and me teaching her, she's bound to be a star.'

Clive laughed. 'I doubt she'd dare to be anything but. Come on, time to go to bed.'

•••

Chrissie had trouble sleeping. She lay awake, her mind alive with the news of this latest death. Clive hadn't told her the man's name, but he'd said enough to fire her imagination. Sleep, when it finally came, plunged her into fitful dreams. By morning she felt exhausted and mostly slept through Clive getting up, showering, dressing and leaving to face the local press. For another hour or so she dozed until at last she felt ready to emerge from under her duvet and pad downstairs to make a mug of strong tea.

She felt as if she was jetlagged as she settled at her narrow kitchen table and sipped her tea. Was there any point in checking the news sites online yet? It was still only 10:00 am. Clive's announcement wouldn't have filtered through to the internet yet.

'What? 10:00 am?' she squealed as a memory surfaced from the nightmare of her restless dreams. 'The project for Gayle - I was going to find something for her to work on. That antique apothecary medicine box!'

She'd noticed it earlier in the week amid the list of sale items at Bury St Edmunds auction rooms; or rather the old glass medicine bottles had caught her eye. What was its lot number? Hell, was she too late to get to the auction this morning in Bury?

She flipped up her laptop screen and logged in. Within moments she was on the auction room site and scrolling through the catalogue. *19th Century Antique Apothecary Medicine Box*, she read. Its lot number was 149, which placed it early amongst the five hundred or so lots. There was no reserve price on it, and the auction was about to start. God, she wasn't going to make it to Bury in time.

What had Ron always told her? *Don't buy without viewing first.*

In a flash of time-pressured ambivalence, she logged in to the online bidding option and registered her details.

When lot number 149 came up, the bidding was slow. Chrissie felt like a stalker, hanging in the shadows, waiting for her moment. Was interest in lot 149 poor because of the mediocre condition of the teak box, brass handles and glass bottles? Was it a warning? Should she back away? On a sudden impulse she keyed in a late bid. No one bid above her. She held her breath. The auctioneer's gavel slammed on its sounding block. What had she done? The medicine box was hers.

Brrring brrring! She grabbed her mobile and checked the time and caller ID. It was 11:00 am. 'Hi, Clive. How did your news release go?'

'It went as uneventfully as I could have hoped it would go. I kept information to a minimum and basically said the man's name was Jon Dareham. His death was unexpected and he was found with canisters of laughing gas, but the cause of death was unknown and we would know more following a post-mortem examination. There weren't any awkward questions and none of the reporters have had time to link Jon Dareham and Tuscan.'

'Oh good,' she said, her mind still fizzing with the excitement of the auction.

'It'll break soon enough.'

'But you'll know more by then and be better prepared. Hey, I don't suppose you'd want to meet me up in Bury for lunch? I've got something to collect from the auction rooms.'

CHAPTER 11

Nick flicked on his car radio. It was Saturday morning and he was driving home from band practice.

This is the twelve o'clock news… the newscaster's voice merged with the sound of the Ford Fiesta's engine… *Saturday 26th April.* Nick reached to change the channel but stopped as he caught… *a forty-year-old man was found dead yesterday. He had died unexpectedly in his home near Dunwich, Suffolk.* Nick slowed to listen. *The man has been named as Jon Dareham. His body was found with canisters of nitrous oxide, commonly called laughing gas. It isn't yet known if his death was related to the laughing gas. He had lived in the area for over ten years and was thought to have dealt in fine objects. The police are waiting for the results of a post mortem examination.*

'Laughing gas canisters?' Nick breathed. What the hell was going on? This was the second person found dead with canisters of nitrous oxide in just over a week. Hadn't Chrissie phoned to warn him about the nitrous oxide found with Tuscan, or rather to say it was unlikely to be a simple accidental overdose? Her call had been only four days ago. The Regional Organised Crime Unit, or drug squad as he preferred to think of them, were likely to be sniffing around - except no one had returned to ask him more questions. Well, he reckoned they would now.

He followed the road out of Stowmarket towards Rattlesden, his mind running the *Last Laugh* melody. What the hell were fine objects? At this rate he'd have to pen another verse, he thought as he took the turning for Woolpit. He needed to get back to his garret lodging and catch up on sleep before it was time to leave for the band's evening gig in Southwold.

At least the Saturday morning band practice had gone well, which was a miracle, considering both Jake and he were feeling decidedly the worse for wear after the Nags Head open mic evening. The band had really got behind the new song. Adam, the bass guitarist, added an urgent rhythm and Denton on keyboards brought in a funky harpsichord effect. Their drummer Jason picked up and embellished Adam's underpinning rhythm. All in all, it was shaping up well.

CHAPTER 12

'We should've gone to Nick's gig in Southwold yesterday,' Maisie said, pausing to face Matt.

'Dunwich on me scooter ride-out were far enough. How in scammin' hell were we s'posed to get to Southwold and fit Gayle on the back as well? It aint legal, Mais.'

'Yeah but....' She shrugged and fell silent.

They sauntered through the small grassy square in front of Stowmarket's old Corn Exchange, extended with Suffolk bricks way back in the 1860s. Except it wasn't the Corn Exchange anymore, it had been reborn as the prestigious John Peel Centre. Neither had the grassy square always been a grassy square. It was hidden behind the old marketplace. A handful of stone tablets, memorials and sarcophagi hinted at its past graveyard status. The church of St Peter and St Mary shielded it from the busy Station Road. To Matt's way of thinking nothing was what it appeared to be.

'So why'd you want to take Gayle with us, Mais?'

'I were tryin' to be friendly. She aint got her own crowd.'

'But she aint been here long.'

'Yeah, s'pose so. But she's kinda my age, so I thought it'd be nice. See I reckon she's a bit of a dancer. You know, like she might've wanted a bit of a bop at Nick's gig?'

'But she weren't dancin' at the Nags Head on Friday night.'

'No, but she were tellin' me she done dance classes as a kid. An' she were wearin' them orange sneakers.'

'Yeah, you told me they were trendin', and her hair were done in a *windswept updo*. That's what you called it

88

and then you said a white blouse and denims were cool with orange sneakers.'

'Well they are. I thought she were goin' to be right into her fashion but then she said she aint got no pastel winter coat. Everyone's got a pastel coat.'

'But you aint, Mais.'

'Yeah I 'ave. Me 60s PVC raincoat. It's pale orange, right? Lucky I work in the vintage shop. I'd never've found one otherwise.'

'Right.'

'S'pose her voice aint too wicked awesome, either.'

'So is she cool or aint she cool, Mais?' Matt was confused.

'I dunno. That's the whole point – I dunno. I'm surprised you aint looked up stuff about her. I mean, why's she moved away from Leicester? She wouldn't tell me. She don't add up for me.'

'I thought she seemed quite nice. Hey, what's that for?' He fended off a playful shoulder slap. 'But serious, she were nice. What's wrong with sayin' that, Mais?'

Maisie squealed by way of an answer and he gave up trying to understand. 'D'you fancy a cola an' sub?' he asked instead.

'Yeah, I fancy a ham an' cheese one.'

They ambled along Church Walk and through the paved cutting into the old marketplace. 'Bacon an' sausage with ketchup, I reckon.' His words conjured flavours to die for between two halves of a soft bread baton.

•••

It was Monday morning and the ride from Stowmarket to Bury St Edmunds cleared Matt's mind. The cool buffeting breeze on the Vespa transformed his muzzy, barely awake thoughts to something sharper and more focused. For once he felt ready for the Balcon & Mora office as he trudged up the narrow stairs to the unmanned reception and waiting area. The pile of flyers on the low table had been cleared and replaced with Balcon & Mora leaflets spread out like a fan. Was it an omen or something to discourage casual flyer dropping? He frowned. Maybe Damon was in on a marketing drive. The door to his office was closed. Matt knocked and waited.

'Hi, Matt,' Damon said opening the door with a flourish.

'Mornin'. You been tidyin' out here?'

'Yes, I hate it when people leave flyers like it's a free advertising space.'

'Yeah, but at least someone's trudged them stairs an' knows we've a table for stuff.'

Damon opened his mouth to say something, seemed to think better of it and headed back to his office chair. He looked mildly faded as he sat at his pale trestle desk, his taupe tee-shirt casting him as an extension of the wooden worktop. His tawny eyes fixed on Matt.

'Any tailin' or location watchin' today?' Matt asked, his morning Vespa ride still fresh in his mind.

'No, but I've had an interesting search request. Are you going to stand at that door all day or are you coming in?'

Of course he was coming in. Why did Damon need to ask? He lumbered into the stale air, slung his backpack onto the plastic chair and unzipped his denim jacket.

'Yeah, so what's so interestin' 'bout this search request?'

'It can wait. I'll tell you once you've worked through the latest list of names.'

Matt didn't like secrets, and certainly not the ones he was excluded from. He felt a stab of disappointment and hurt. Being left out might only be temporary but his instinct was to side-step the hurt and lose himself and his feelings surfing the internet. And besides, searching and detecting were exciting. They came close to the exhilaration of a scooter ride or the quests of his childhood comic-strip heroes. He grabbed a can of cola from the economy pack near the coffeemaker and settled at his computer.

The list of names Damon sent to his computer was the usual motley collection of first and second names and initials. They were the names printed on credit cards, and along with last known contact addresses and phone numbers, it was the only information their client (the card company) gave to Balcon & Mora. Matt's job was to find a current address and phone number for each name. His searches were generally clear-cut and for the most part he found the name had moved and forgotten to set up a forwarding address service, or their mobile phone had been lost or stolen. Of course it was never so straightforward if the name had intended to disappear.

He pulled the tab on the cola can and started working his way in alphabetical order through the list. A couple of hours into his searches he found himself looking at the Google Earth view of a J-J Jones' last known address. The card company had provided J-J's mobile number but when Matt made a call from the office phone he quickly discovered J-J wasn't answering. Was that all calls, or only those not on his phone's contact list? It was starting to look as if J-J was goin' to be difficult to *cop a houd* of, as Matt might say when alcohol loosened his Suffolk tongue. 'Slippery codec,' he breathed instead, before adding, 'the sneaky weasel,' when he discovered photos posted by J-J at the weekend on his Facebook page. They clearly caught the frontage of a house which looked identical to J-J's last known address, as shown on the Google Earth view.

'This bloke aint moved. He's pretendin' he aint livin' there, when really he is.'

Behind him, Damon stirred. The familiar sound of him pushing his office chair away from the desk; the pause when Matt knew he'd be stretching his arms; another pause and....

'Time for a coffee or another cola?' Damon asked.

'Yeah, a cola, thanks. D'you reckon I should stake out the address? I could check it this evenin' on me way home. Maybe take a few time an' date stamped photos – you know, of him arrivin', an' the like?' Matt didn't bother to clarify who he was talking about. He knew Damon would have been monitoring his screen.

'For a moment there, Matt, I thought you were asking me about the interesting search I was about to let you in on. But yes sure, if this is about the J-J Jones you're search-ing... if it's on your way home, why not?'

'Cool. And the interestin' search?'

'Ah yes; it's a Nick Cowley. My preliminary search tells me you know him.'

'What? Nick? He's me mate. Why'd anyone want to search anythin' on him?'

'I don't know, I thought you might be able to tell me. It's a bit of a departure from our usual bread-and-butter card names.'

'So who's askin' and anyway, what they want to know? If it's his address an' mobile number – well they aint a secret. I've got 'em.'

Matt watched as Damon fussed over the coffeemaker. He could hardly be described as sporty, but his movements were fast.

'The client called from a BT phone box – so I can only trace the call box ID, not the caller.'

'A call box? I thought they were history.'

'This one's in Elmsett. The signal's so poor out there it's the most used phone box in Suffolk.'

'Fraggin' hell. D'you reckon it were one of them fans. You know Nick sings in a band?'

'Yes, I've looked at the band's Facebook page. It was a bloke's voice.'

'Right... but how'll you get the info back to 'im? He must've given you a name or email.'

'He said he'd call again.'

'OK, an' how's he goin' to pay? You can trace somethin' about 'im then.'

'Not if he uses a prepaid card that doesn't have his name on it.'

'Right.' Matt lapsed into silence while the coffeemaker hissed and gurgled.

'The thing is, the client only wanted a phone number and address. It's not particularly sensitive information; the address is already out there on the electoral register. The client could have looked it up for himself if he knew how or wanted to.'

'I reckon you'll have got Nick's parents' address in Barking Tye, not where 'e's a lodger.'

'True.'

'So what you gonna do, Damon?'

'I wanted to talk to you first. The client said he'll call again tomorrow, 8:30 in the morning. I thought, as Nick's a mate of yours, you could ride here tomorrow via Elmsett. If you're there for the call, you can be here by 9:30.'

'Yeah, I can get a time shot of him in the phone box. An' if he's drivin' I'll get his car and reg number.'

'Of course, I don't know anything about Nick being a lodger anywhere, and for the record, I haven't had this conversation with you.'

Matt felt a surge of confusion, but then Damon winked. It took him a moment to process the signal. He reckoned he must be doubly in on the secret. 'You'll record the time the bloke calls, though?'

'You know all our office calls are automatically logged by date and time. Now for God's sake don't talk to Nick about this. Have you got that?' This time Damon didn't wink. Did it mean that being doubly in on the secret was a secret?

A sense of unease and confusion descended on Matt as he pulled the tab on his second can of cola. He reckoned there was nothing else for it but to immerse himself in searching the current contact details for the next name on his list.

When Damon next pushed his tired faux leather office chair back from his desk and stretched his arms, it was lunchtime.

'I've got to go out for about half an hour, Matt.'

'Yeah OK, see ya,' Matt called over his shoulder as the office door closed behind Damon.

He waited, listening for the soft creaks from the old floor and stair boards as Damon hurried down to the ground floor. At last he had the office to himself. It wasn't that he minded Damon being there, he liked it, but sometimes he wanted to look something up without Damon's prying eyes fixed on his back. Yes, Damon could still check on his search history, but Matt had discovered if he hid a search within the search thread for one of the names on his morning's work list, it tended to slip under Damon's radar.

Gayle Corby fitted that bill. If he was going to keep Maisie happy then he had to do a quick online search for the new apprentice at the Jax & Clegg workshop.

He typed her name between inverted commas in Google search. There was nothing; at least nothing which seemed to match the Gayle Corby he'd met at the open mic night. He tried Facebook, Instagram and LinkedIn, and then the news sites. He even looked through death announcements, although without a date of birth or death there wasn't a lot to feed his search. He had just started sifting through carpentry courses and joinery apprenticeships in the Leicester area, when he caught the familiar creak on the stairs and floorboards. He clicked out of his search and onto the news feeds.

'Hi,' he said as Damon hurried back into the office.

'Hey, any interesting news breaking?' Damon asked and headed for the coffeemaker.

'The police 'ave just detained a fifteen-year-old boy for stabbin' a female teacher to death in front of fellow students at a school in Leeds,' Matt said as he paraphrased a news feed.

'What?'

'Stabbed her multiple times, accordin' to this.'

'That's…sick.' Damon strode over to look at Matt's screen.

Matt nodded. It was sick all right but his mind was torn between the horror of the stabbing and relief he'd cleared his search. At least he wasn't having to explain Gayle Corby to Damon, and to be honest, how could he explain an internet ghost, if indeed that was what Gayle was. The whole point about an internet ghost was that you couldn't find it. Except, in the same vein as quantum physics and maths, she did exist. She was a reality. How was he going to explain it to Maisie? He hadn't really processed it himself.

'Are you OK?'

'What? Yeah, just thinkin'.'

'Right, well you better get back to your list of names. You need to get them finished; there's J-J Jones to stake out on your way home, remember.'

CHAPTER 13

Matt shut the front door quietly behind him. He didn't *do* quiet very well, but this Tuesday morning he had an added incentive. He really didn't want his mum on his back for waking her before her morning alarm.

He had dressed as he deemed an undercover stakeout operative would dress. His jeans were unremarkable and underneath his denim zipped jacket he wore a black tee-shirt. His laptop was in a soft backpack slung over one shoulder. He looked around and breathed the cool air as he sharpened his focus. Early morning light cast a leaden wash over Tumble Weed Drive. Even the blackberry bubblegum paintwork on his 125cc Vespa looked muted where it stood close to the side wall of his mum's bungalow. Its front wheel was angled in its locked position like a broken limb.

He pulled on his full face helmet, slipped his key in the ignition lock, pressed the starter button and rode slowly out of the Flower Estate. He had worked out the route he would take; southwest from Stowmarket on the B1115. He'd leave the B road before reaching Hadleigh and weave a path along narrow lanes to Elmsett. The traffic was light and he made good time. The Google map street view had already told him the phone box would be standing across the road from a pub and post office stores. All he needed to do was park his scooter and wait.

He rode past the village green and into Elmsett. On one side of the road there was a hedge and playing fields that could have passed for a meadow. It felt like a barrier holding back the houses and cottages across the way. A long parking bay ran alongside and a few yards on from it he saw the phone box. 'Killer app,' he breathed. He was on target.

He slowed as he passed and turned into the forecourt of the pub. The building's pink wash gave warmth to the early morning. Hanging baskets added a touch of green, but the season was still a little early for the plants to be showing many flowers. It felt friendly, welcoming and relaxed. He had a plan; all he had to do was follow it through. As long as the client showed up to phone Damon, nothing could go wrong. He parked and checked the time. 08:16.

He watched as cars drew into the long parking bay and drivers or school kids got out and hurried over to the post office stores. As far as he could make out they were commuters or on the school run. No car stayed for long, and as the minutes passed and 08:30 approached, he shed his helmet and sauntered down the road. A placard hung above a doorway into a cream painted brick house. *Elmsett Post Office, General Stores & Newsagents*, he read and paused to look at the newspapers on the rack. He took out his mobile and then remembered there wouldn't be any signal.

'Frag,' he muttered. It was why people used the phone box. A flash of panic twisted his guts. Would his phone camera work? *Duzzy woop*, it worked independent of signal.

In that millisecond of distraction, he'd missed a black Toyota Land Cruiser as it drew off the road. One moment it hadn't been there, the next it was parked behind a silver Audi saloon. He watched a stocky man step down from the driver's side. No one else appeared to be in the Toyota. The man looked to right and left and then strode along the road towards the phone box and pub.

'Fraggin' hell,' Matt breathed as he thumbed his phone camera on and selected the time and date stamped photo option. He swallowed his surge of excitement and took shots of the black Toyota and its number plate. All the while the man seemed unaware of everyone around him as he neared the phone box. Was he the client? Matt willed him to step into the phone box. Yes... he was opening the glass door, now rummaging in a trouser pocket. Was he looking for a phone number? Coins?

Matt moved from his vantage point near the newspaper racks and crossed the road in what he hoped was a relaxed manner, towards the phone box. He slowed as he got closer almost pausing as the man lifted the receiver, half turned to face the box's keypad and hunched in concentration.

Click! He zoomed the focus and clicked again. He'd caught the man's dark hair, a profile and then... yes, a full face shot as the man began his call.

'Are you waiting to make a call?'

'What?' Matt spun on his foot.

'Are you in the queue? For the phone?'

'W-what?' Blog Almighty, a man in a loose khaki nylon jacket stood close to him. He must have been followed.

'I said, are you in the queue? Eight thirty's always busy here.'

'No! N-no. I were checkin' to see if I got the number - but I aint saved it on me phone. I'll 'ave to wait till I get to Ipswich; I'll call from there. You go ahead, mate.' Matt backed away.

'Thanks.'

It was Matt's moment. He made as if to put his phone away while firing off some shots of the man beside him.

'Cheers mate,' he said and walked back across the road to the pub and his scooter.

He took his time fussing with his parking stand, top box and helmet and when the moment was right, stole timed shots of the man with black hair leaving the phone box and then the khaki jacket man making his call.

The Vespa's four-stroke engine chortled gently as Matt rode for a few seconds along the road in the direction for Ipswich. Just out of sight of the phone box, he stopped and doubled back, taking care to remain concealed. He was curious to see if the khaki jacket man had come in a car, and if so, he wanted the registration number.

He took a photo as the man left the phone box and crossed the road. Matt edged the Vespa forwards, but the man disappeared from view down a narrow lane between the houses. Matt accelerated, but by the time he reached the lane, the man had vanished.

When Matt trudged up the stairs to the Balcon & Mora office in Bury St Edmunds at around ten o'clock, Damon's first words were, 'You're late.'

'Yeah, well there were a complication, weren't there.'

'So what exactly was the complication?'

'Lots of people use the phone box at 08:30. How'd I know which one it were? I had to stay and clock 'em all.'

'You could have phoned me and asked if the call had come through?'

'Yeah, but you're forgettin' there aint no signal out there. How'd I check with you on me mobile? It's why the phone box is busy, right?'

'OK, so how many were there?'

'Two.'

'Two? Come on, get yourself a cola and tell me about it.'

CHAPTER 14

Chrissie waited in her car for Gayle. She'd pulled up at the side of the road skirting the Recreation Ground to the west of central Stowmarket. It was Tuesday morning, the day after Gayle's first apprentice release day and the start of her first week at Clegg & Jax. Chrissie figured it was easier to give her a lift from the corner outside the Recreation Ground than fight a way through the morning traffic to Gayle's digs. If the Clegg & Jax workshops had been on a bus route, then she could have left her to find her own way.

Her mind drifted back to Matt's phone call the evening before. He hadn't found anything on the internet about Gayle. She didn't know why he was telling her; she hadn't been the one to ask him to look. 'Maisie were curious,' Matt had explained.

He'd wanted some nugget; any piece of information Chrissie could tell him to aid his search. 'I'll think about it,' she'd said and here she was still thinking about it.

Did it matter if he hadn't found Gayle on the internet? Chrissie doubted he'd find much about Chrissie Jax either, although she'd never thought to search about herself. She supposed there'd be something about her working as an accountant in Ipswich in the noughties, and Clegg & Jax would come up somewhere. A sharp stab reminded her there'd be newspaper articles about Bill's death. The *Anaphylactic Shock as Local Man Chokes to Death in Czech Republic*, and the *Rubber Recycling Death of Local Man Abroad*.

She switched on her car radio to distract herself while she waited.

A knock sounded on the passenger window.

'Hi, Gayle,' she said and leaned across to open the passenger door.

Gayle slipped into the TR7. She looked ready for work in faded jeans and mint sweatshirt, an edge of white tee-shirt showing at her neckline. She'd changed Friday's orange sneakers for a charcoal grey pair with white trim.

Chrissie was about to ask if Blumfield had made a comment about her footwear. He'd certainly taken Chrissie to task over her preference for wearing pumps rather than steel toe safety boots. She bit her tongue. It might not sound like camaraderie to Gayle and she didn't want the girl taking it the wrong way.

'Cool car,' Gayle said by way of a greeting, 'the yellow's awesome.'

Again, Chrissie bit her tongue. Gayle hadn't remarked on her 1981 TR7 convertible on Friday. Perhaps it was just that this morning she felt more confident. 'Mr Clegg shields his eyes when he looks at it,' Chrissie said and smiled.

She started the engine and turned up the volume on the radio. The newsreader's voice ran in the background as she concentrated on turning into the flow of traffic. *Yesterday's fatal stabbing of a 61-year-old teacher by a 15-year-old student continues to shock Leeds and indeed the country. The frenzied knife attack took place in front of a classroom of students.*

The newsreader's words passed over Chrissie's head as her thoughts followed their own thread. She must be relaxed with Gayle and not bombard her with questions about the apprentice release day. It might come across as threatening rather than as genuine interest. She'd take a leaf out of Ron's book and wait to be told. It was all right to drive and not talk. She'd let the radio fill the space.

Today's weather will be windy with increasing cloud and a high chance of rain by mid-afternoon. Temperatures will reach a maximum of 13° C.

'Can I turn the radio down?' Gayle's tiny voice was barely audible.

'Yes, of course. The weather doesn't sound too good. Turn it off if you like.' Chrissie glanced across at Gayle. Her face looked pale, her square jaw set. 'Do you get car sick?'

'No. Hey, I like this song,' she said as OneRepublic's catchy pop rock hit *Counting Stars* began to play. Her body language didn't invite further questions and the rest of the journey passed without either of them saying more. The background tones of the car's radio and 2 litre engine bathed their silence. It felt surprisingly companionable to Chrissie.

'We're here now,' she murmured as she turned off the Wattisham Airfield perimeter lane and onto the rough track leading to the Clegg & Jax barn workshop.

'Good morning, Miss Corby, Mrs Jax,' Ron said moments later as Chrissie followed Gayle into the old barn.

Having an apprentice join them didn't seem a good enough reason to change her routine, and Chrissie automatically slung her soft leather hobo-style bag onto a bench stool and headed for the kettle.

'Tea? Coffee?' she asked in an all-inclusive way.

'I haven't seen the mahogany apothecary box yet,' Ron said, limping over with his empty mug from where he'd been fiddling with the settings on the thickness planer.

'Then I must show you. Hey Gayle, can you take over with the kettle here for a moment? Strong tea for Mr Clegg and me, and there's instant coffee if you don't want tea.'

She left Gayle with the kettle and mugs and fetched the antique box she'd bid for online at the weekend. It was still wrapped in the calico dustsheet she'd protected it with when she'd collected it from the auction rooms. She knew Ron had already seen it because she'd shown it to him. She also knew how his mind worked. This was his way of engaging Gayle in its restoration. By the time they'd drunk their mugs of tea, she reckoned Gayle would have volunteered to work on it and genuinely believe she'd chosen the project herself.

'What do you think?' she said, setting it down on the workbench close to Ron and pulling back the dustsheet.

She was pleased to see Gayle walk over to look at it of her own accord.

'Is it solid mahogany?' Gayle asked.

Ron seemed to consider her question before answering, 'You have to look at the patterns of the wood grain and the way the pieces are joined together. If you can't see the joins, or they don't look like the type of joints you'd expect, then it could be because you're looking at where the sheets of veneer meet each other, not the wood underneath. Sometimes you can see or feel where the veneer is lifting away from the carcass wood. Here let's open the box and have a look on the inside as well. Yes, you can open it - go ahead.'

'Do I use this?' Gayle grasped the brass swan neck handle on the top of the lid.

'You can, but it was meant as a carrying handle. You might prefer to use your hands on the sides of the lid; you'll get a better feel of the wood and the lid's weight.'

Gayle hesitated, as if unsure what to do.

'Go on then, Miss Corby, open it. There's no key in the keyhole, so I guess it won't be locked.'

'W-what are all those?' Gayle gasped.

'Ah, the antique apothecary bottles,' Ron said softly and proceeded to lift each one out in turn.

Chrissie had kept quiet while she watched Ron teach and engage Gayle, but the sight of the antique bottles grabbed her attention. She found them too interesting to notice Gayle's reaction. Her eyes focused on the glass stoppers and yellowed labels: *Calcined Magnesia...* Calcined? *Powder of Bark*, *Spirit of Lavender*, something–*uble Epsom Salt*. The words were difficult to read with unfamiliar abbreviations and shortened forms. Some of the bottles still contained powder remnants or liquid. A couple of compartments had been empty and the bottles missing.

'What's apothecary mean?' Gayle asked, cutting into Chrissie's absorption with a hollow voice.

'What, Gayle? Oh I suppose it means pharmacist, an old-fashioned name for someone who prepared and sold medicines and drugs. Look,' Chrissie pointed, 'there, on the back edge of the inside of the lid. See the old label? *G Marshall & Co, Chemists & Druggists. Brewer Street, Golden Square*. It's in London; I've looked up the address.'

'Good,' Ron said, 'now all the bottles are out we can have a proper look at the inside. Ah, as I suspected, the dividers for the compartments need attention. Why don't you take out the drawer at the bottom next?' Ron removed the brass retaining pin and turned the box around for Gayle.

The brass drawer handle was inset and hinged so as to sit flush with the drawer front. Gayle slipped a slender finger under it and eased the drawer out. She didn't say anything, just stared at the contents with her jaw clenched.

'Hey isn't this neat,' Chrissie said, hoping her excitement was infectious, 'a glass measuring cup, and a glass pestle and mortar.' She lifted out lightweight beam scales and held them up. 'Look, there are even some brass leaf weights. Do you think this is original to the box?'

No one said anything. Had she overplayed her excitement? She glanced at Ron. He was looking at Gayle, so she followed the direction of his gaze. Oh God, the girl's face had turned ashen.

'Gayle! Are you all right?' she asked.

Gayle's eyes rolled upwards and then her knees gave way. Down she went. A bench stool crashed over. Chrissie lunged at her, grabbed her arm and broke her fall.

'Oh God, do you think she's fainted?' Chrissie panted. She knelt beside Gayle, panic threatening to take control. The girl lay, eyes closed and unmoving on the concrete.

'She seemed to be OK until she opened the box,' Ron murmured.

'Hey, Gayle! Come on, open your eyes! I don't think she's having a fit.' Chrissie touched Gayle's forehead. It felt cold and clammy. She knew she was supposed to check for specific things; but which things? The girl was breathing – that was good. Pulse? Which pulse? Her wrist? Chrissie fumbled. She couldn't feel anything. Try somewhere else on her wrist? Maybe her neck?

'Her colour's coming back. I think she's coming round,' Ron said.

'What? Oh thank God. Gayle! Gayle! Are you all right?'

A breathy moan escaped Gayle's lips. She opened her eyes and frowned. 'I-I'm sorry… I-I came over light-headed.'

'There's nothing to be sorry about. You seem to have just fainted, that's all. No - don't try and get up. Stay where you are for a moment otherwise you might faint again.' Chrissie hoped she sounded confident and in control, but inside she felt like jelly. 'Do you tend to faint easily?' she asked.

'Yeah, it's a right pain. Sorry.'

The next hour was somewhat disrupted. Gayle insisted she was fine and Chrissie suggested she sat at one of the workbenches and practise her French polishing skills on a wooden board. That way she'd be sitting down and they could keep an eye on her. Secretly Chrissie was kicking herself for not having noticed sooner when Gayle turned pale. God! Looking back, hadn't she gone a bit pasty in the car as well?

•••

'You know the worst thing about it?' Chrissie said that evening as she relaxed with Clive in the White Hart.

'You mean about Gayle fainting today?'

Chrissie sipped her Pinot Grigio. 'Yes. The worst thing was not being able to talk it over with Ron. I mean, how could I with Gayle still there with us? I didn't even like to put my car radio on when I drove her home. I didn't want to risk… I mean in case I missed noticing if she went pasty on me again.'

'What do you mean, went pasty on you again? Has she gone pasty before?' Clive leaned back on his pine chair and seemed to appraise her.

It was a difficult one to answer and Chrissie closed her eyes as she relived the memory of Gayle lying on the workshop floor, her square face chalky-pale. All trace of smiles and frowns had been erased by unconsciousness and when Chrissie had looked more closely she'd seen a fine angular scar faintly marking Gayle's temple. A star-shaped scar? Chrissie didn't remember having noticed it before. The drama of the faint had driven it from her mind until now.

'She must have hit her head fainting in the past,' Chrissie murmured.

'You're not making any sense.' Clive took a mouthful of beer, stretched his legs under the pub table and waited as if he had all the time in the world.

'Gayle has a tendency to faint. I thought when she went pale in my car she was getting travel sick. That was about half an hour before she actually fainted in the workshop. The Academy didn't give us any health records, and our workshop health & fitness questionnaire didn't flag any issues. The point is she didn't tell us about her tendency to faint until it happened. What if she'd been diabetic or epileptic and hadn't told us?'

'Then I think the Academy would have had to have told you. Look, as long as you've advised her to see her GP and you allow her time off for her appointment, what else is there to do? How old is she?'

'Nineteen.'

'There you are then. She's an adult.'

'I know, but I feel responsible for her. I can't help it. What if she comes over all faint while she's using the band saw or something?'

They lapsed into silence. Clive looked untroubled by Chrissie's revelations about Gayle, and his casual common sense responses were becoming close to irritating. It was all right for him, he didn't have to take responsibility for workshop safety.

Chrissie switched her thoughts to studying the neat chalk writing on the specials board. It was attached high on the old chimneybreast, and for once they were sitting at a table close enough to be able to read it without having to get up and walk nearer. The *mushroom & lentil ragu on linguine with shavings of Parmesan cheese* sounded nice. The temperature had dropped and the evening air felt cool. The ragu and linguine would do nicely.

'Have you decided what you'd like?' she asked.

'The *local pork loin steak with citrus salsa* sounds rather good. If I have that then I think I might start with the *mussels in a turmeric & dill broth with coconut.*'

'What? Are you sure about the mussels? The sauce sounds... well it isn't what you'd normally choose.'

'I know, but I thought I'd try something different for a change.'

She caught the slight warning in his words; the don't-presume-to-know my every flavour preference. No doubt his choice of the mussels was a flash of impulse and now, following her query, simple stubbornness. She was about to say something on the lines of her reserving the right to say *I told you so* when he didn't like the mussel sauce, but thought better of it. He'd probably had a tough day as well.

While he walked over to the bar counter to order their food she let her eyes trace the mortar running between the old bricks in the chimneybreast. It was like finding a route through a maze. There were stops and blocks to the mortar lines where the brickwork held an oak beam to span the open fireplace. They might as well have been the snags and hitches in trying to train an apprentice. It was just another bloody maze, although she could hardly liken Gayle to an oak beam.

'You never said if Gayle is going to restore the old box,' Clive said when he returned from placing the food order.

'The apothecary box? I don't know; she was a bit odd about it. She didn't even really want to touch the glass bottles, but I think she'll be fine with the box once we've removed all its contents and packed them away safely.'

'Why didn't she want to touch the bottles? Was she worried she'd break them? I thought they were fascinating when we collected the box from the auction house. Powders and spirits and the like. A pity a couple of them are missing. Hey - did she do chemistry at school? Maybe she had some kind of an accident? Did you think to ask her?'

'No, I assumed it was because she felt unwell having fainted. I never made an association between the bottles and how she was reacting.'

'Well there probably isn't one, but no harm in asking.'

Chrissie studied her wine glass. Was the scar on Gayle's forehead a chemical burn? She couldn't be sure and she wasn't an expert but wouldn't a chemical burn be patchier and less linear? Gayle's had been almost a mix of the two – star-shaped and angular but fine, very fine. She gave herself a little shake. It was time to stop obsessing about Gayle.

'So changing the subject from Gayle and my troubles, how about yours? Tell me, do you think there's a connection between Tuscan's and Jon Dareham's deaths?'

'Ah, now that's interesting,' Clive murmured. He glanced around before leaning towards her. 'Remember we were getting a cast of the tumble dryer rim, where the door opens to load clothes into the drum? Well the bruising on Jon Dareham's chest matches it. The pathologist tells me it would fit with him having been held down before he died. So it looks as if someone wanted it to appear like an accident but in reality the nitrous oxide overdose was forced on him.'

'A bit like gluing up Tuscan's balloons? Another overdose forced on the victim? The same hand at work, do you think?'

Clive smiled. 'I like that; the same hand at work. The pathologist said there were some marks on Jon Dareham compatible with a handprint, possibly as a result of a struggle. He found a faint hand-shaped bruise on one arm where someone might have gripped it and less specific marks on his back consistent with pushing him down while he lay on the rim into the dryer.'

'But if his chest was across the hard rim and someone was pushing down on his back, how could he breathe the nitrous oxide?'

'He'd have used his diaphragm for a bit. The pathologist said it's like an opera singer's technique to inflate the lower parts of the lungs without moving the ribcage.'

For a millisecond Chrissie imagined an opera singer in a tumble dryer and then shook her head and dismissed the image.

'The blood toxicology and the level of nitrous oxide gas in his body are still to come back.' Clive frowned in concentration, 'I can't recall the full name but the pathologist called it a headspace GCMS technique. I thought the headspace bit was some kind of sick medic's joke, but no, it's related to nitrous oxide's special properties; it has a very low blood-gas partition coefficient... I'm sure he called it that. Remember I tried to explain it to you before but couldn't very well because I don't really get it myself?'

'Kind of. You said the gas comes out of the blood into air spaces, fills the fringes of the lungs and stops the next breath of air getting absorbed.'

'Yes, I think that's right. Well remembered, Chrissie.'

'Thanks. But perversely you said that's why you also absorb it very fast and get a rapid high.'

'And that's the attraction. But there's no sign Jon Dareham was a chronic user. Not like Tuscan. He had changes in his red blood cells from chronic use. Megaloblastic, was the word used. Something to do with the nitrous oxide causing a vitamin B12 deficiency.'

'Really?'

'And apparently the gas can also damage the spinal cord and your nerves, makes it difficult to walk and gives you numb patches.'

'And they call it laughing gas? Now that has to be a sick medic joke, surely?'

'Yep, you laugh all the way to your death. But in answer to your question I'd say yes; the two deaths are murders and they are very much connected.'

'And they knew each other, in fact they were very close.'

'Hmm, so you heard all about that on the news this afternoon, did you? They've certainly stirred it up with the gay community now.'

'Well no, you'd already told me. And as I said, I didn't have the radio on driving home because of Gayle. I wanted to be able to know if she was about to faint again. So what did the news say?'

'Hey this looks like someone from the kitchen is bringing our food across. Sorry Chrissie, the news will have to wait. Hmm, I can smell the mussel sauce from here!'

CHAPTER 15

Two recent deaths have sent shockwaves through the local LGBT community. Two weeks ago, Suffolk man Toussaint Grabb a.k.a. Tuscan died unexpectedly near Eye. His partner, Dunwich resident Jon Dareham was found dead five days ago.

'What?' Nick didn't usually talk out loud to himself while driving, but hell; the morning newsreader had just mentioned the bloke he'd pulled out of the water. He slowed and turned up the radio.

The police are treating Jon Dareham's death as suspicious, and his seemingly motiveless killing is adding fuel to the fear this is a LGBT hate crime.

'Really? An LGBT hate crime?' Nick took a few moments to process the newsreader's words.

The police have also issued an alert to all recreational users of nitrous oxide, the so-called laughing gas. They are warned to be extra vigilant and to look out for any tampering of recreational user equipment.

At last something made sense. Jon Dareham had been found with canisters of nitrous oxide; Nick remembered hearing it on the radio five days ago. And Chrissie had hinted the laughing gas and Tuscan weren't all they appeared to be.

Nick drove, consumed by his thoughts. He barely concentrated on the road as he wrestled his demons for the rest of the journey. What exactly had he seen in the bottom of the boat with Tuscan? Yes, little silver metal canisters, but what else? Had there been any signs of tampering? If he wanted to picture the laughing gas paraphernalia, he'd need to summon the image of Tuscan slumped forwards with his head over the side of the boat and relive the bear hug again. God no! He'd spent his time suppressing the flashbacks, and now he was thinking of summoning one? Was he mad?

By the time he reached Needham Market and turned into the entrance to Willows & Son, he felt exhausted. This had to stop. He needed to prove to himself he could control the flashbacks. He drove past the showroom office and the forecourt for visitor parking, and headed along the side of the workshop unit to the delivery and secure parking area at the rear. He drew up outside the metal link fencing where there was space for staff cars and switched off the Fiesta's engine. Yes, he could do this.

'I can do this,' he muttered like a mantra.

He closed his eyes and let his mind travel back to the moment he first saw the boat with a body in it. He fast-forwarded to climbing in and stumbling towards the body. The bear hug... Tuscan's wet cold arms falling against him as he dragged him back... yes wet and cold from the moat. But wet and cold were OK. They were good. He could handle wet and cold. Breathe, that's good; now hum.

But what was in the bottom of the boat? Focus. Now he had it: the glint of sunlight on shiny metal canisters the shape of giant ampules; a valve mechanism, angular, dull metallic and attached to a shiny ampule; short lengths of plastic tubing; two rubber balloons – one red, one green. Neither balloon was inflated. They looked untouched. They'd never been inflated.

'One red, one green, and never been seen,' he murmured.

'Oi! Nick! Are you all right?'

Nick opened his eyes to see Dave's worried face staring at him through the driver's door window.

'Yeah, of course I'm OK.'

'Well you look bloody pale and your eyes were closed. Heavy night was it?' Dave ran a hand back over his thinning hair in a show of exasperation. 'It's only Wednesday and you look wasted. You know the boss has had a call from Victor Coady? He only wants us to construct a wooden footbridge to cross the moat.'

'What? But we're not bridge builders.'

'I know, but it's to be a gently curved walkway over the water.'

'Well I suppose we can construct a rounded wooden arch with a handrail.'

'He wants a prefabricated one and it'll rest on some concrete blocks on the bank.'

'What, like you can lift it on and off?'

'Something like that. Anyway, the dredgers have started work on the moat, so we can drive over and measure up, but we'll have to wait until they've finished dredging before we can erect it there.'

'And we make it here in the workshop in the meantime? So why the bridge?'

'I think it's for safety.'

'Poor Mr Coady,' Nick sighed.

CHAPTER 16

Nick was on Matt's mind. He wouldn't have described it as weighing heavy or troubling him exactly; it was more of a niggle, a Wednesday morning niggle as he sat in the Balcon & Mora office in Bury St Edmunds. Distant sounds of the market setting up on Cornhill and Buttermarket drifted through the open window. Somewhere far-off a trader shouted and crates crashed and rattled.

'Hey Damon, are you goin' to tell me who them blokes were? You must've identified them two Elmsett phone box callers by now.'

'I have but I don't want you telling Nick.'

Matt twisted on his plastic chair and viewed his boss. Damon's tawny eyes appeared hooded as he leaned back in the office chair and sipped his coffee.

'Yeah, but you're forgettin' them shots of the blokes and the Toyota Land Cruiser are on me mobile. I can always find out for me self, so you might as well let me in on it.'

'Ye-e-s, OK then. I can tell you the Toyota's registration number shows the registered owner is a lease car company. I've got the name of a leasing company, but not who they've leased the Toyota to. Your second caller didn't ring here, so we can rule him out.'

'Cool. And facial recognition? Did you get a Google match?'

'No. I think our bloke is either too internet savvy to have images of himself out there and tagged with his name, or not internet savvy enough to be using social media etcetera. I tell you what though – why don't you have a shot at getting the bloke's name out of the leasing company? I'll send you over what I've got. It's coming… now!'

'Cool!' Matt studied his screen. He'd done this before; not with this particular car leasing company, but with others and he'd got the patter down to a tee. The Toyota's named registered keeper, the car leasing company, popped up on his screen along with its address and phone number.

'It's in Sudbury,' he murmured. 'I reckon the bloke's home'll be within a fifteen mile radius of where he leases it from.'

He opened his file of private parking firms registered with the British Parking Association. If they were on his list it meant they had the power to get registered keeper details from the DVLA. He was going to pretend to be one of them, but he needed to decide with care. As long as he picked a small parking firm and location far enough away from the car leasing firm address, he figured his scam would work. The names this time were a gift. It was going to be OK.

'Right then.' He cleared his throat and tapped-in the leasing firm's number on the office phone. A flutter of angst caught him as he listened to the ringtone.

A woman's voice answered. 'Shuttlecock Cars. Zara speaking. How may I help?'

'Hello. I'm Dylan from Balcony Parking, Norwich. We've got you as the registered keeper for a,' he reeled off the car registration number, 'a black Toyota Land Cruiser parkin' in a Balcony Parkin' parkin' space without displayin' a valid ticket.' He paused, dropped his voice and added, 'It always gets me when I say parkin' twice like that – the Balcony Parkin' parkin' space.'

'Tell me about it. Shuttlecock Cars is bit of a tongue twister if you say it fast.' A brittle laugh sounded through his earpiece.

'Yeah, Shuttlecock Cars – I like that.'

'So the driver didn't buy a ticket? You know we get this all the time. Just because the car is leased they think they can break the speed limit and park anywhere. It's the same with the hire cars. It's a real pain for us. So when was this?'

'Saturday, 26th April at 10:17. Norwich Balcony Parkin–'

'Parking space,' she finished for him and laughed.

'Yeah, it were 4 days ago; well inside our 14-day requirement to contact you.'

'Right, I've just looked up the car and yes it was leased at the time. It's on a long lease.'

'Well I hope he aint goin' to make a habit of it, coz he squeezed past the barrier. Almost damaged it. We caught it all on CCTV. There were no intention of payin' for a–'

'Balcony Parking parking space?'

Matt laughed. He liked the sound of Zara. He hoped she was going to be a good sport over his next and most important question: 'Would it make it easier for you if I sent it direct to the lessee?' he asked.

'Well good luck with that, Dylan because it's leased to a business. SS Shinton Dredging. You'll be lucky if you get the name out of them, you know – the name of whoever was driving the Toyota.'

'Yeah, but it has to be worth a try. I'll save you the trouble an' send it direct to them, if that's OK with you. And thanks, Zara.'

'No problem. Good luck with it, Dylan. Nice talking to you.'

He ended the call. It was a killer app moment and he punched the air.

Damon's voice floated from his office chair behind, 'Nice one, Matt. Pretty neat. You're always slick with those calls.'

'What?' For a moment he'd forgotten Damon and the office. He'd been in his own world. 'Yeah, well it's like reading them speech bubbles in me comic-strip books.'

'Really?'

'Yeah, it is when I'm makin' a call I've done lots of times in the past. It's like a comic-strip and I'm one of them characters in it. I see it in me mind - the sequence of drawin's with them speech balloons and captions.' He thought for a moment and added, 'Talkin' to a real face aint like that. Talkin' to you aint like it, Damon.'

'Hmm, well I'm cool with that.'

'Awesome.' Matt glowed. He supposed if Damon had said he'd been pretty neat in an email he'd have added a smiley. Was now, face to face, a good emoji moment? 'Yeah, emoji! Hey but I aint heard of SS Shinton Dredgin'. Have you?'

'The name's vaguely familiar. I'll Google it.'

While Damon searched, Matt wiped his sweaty palms on his tee-shirt and swigged back some cola. A star-burst of gassy bubbles exploded in his mouth and stung the back of his nose. 'Malware!' he spluttered. 'Well, what you got, Damon?'

When Damon didn't answer, he typed the dredging company in his own search box. 'Blog Almighty,' he breathed as he read an article in the Eastern Anglia Daily

Tribune dated 24th April 2014. *Questions over Safety Surrounding Local Man's Death.*

Toussaint Grabb, a.k.a. Tuscan, was found dead in a boat on the 17th of April. He worked for the East Anglia-based dredging firm, SS Shinton Dredging LTD, and is believed to have been working alone while assessing the depth of silt build-up in the moat of a farmhouse near Eye. Dredging work is due to start there shortly. A spokesman for the firm said there were clear guidelines for safe practice and regular staff training in safety. The coroner has ordered an investigation into the circumstances surrounding the man's death. More information will be available at the inquest.

'DOS-in' hell! It's the dredgin' firm where Nick were workin' and pulled that Toussaint bloke out of the water. Remember you'd been searchin' the origin of the name Toussaint? Born on All Saints Day, more than like.'

'Yes, but that was in an earlier article than the one you've got up now. And laughing gas was mentioned in the earlier piece. I told you, no drug dealing, no murders.'

'Yeah, but Damon, laughin' gas aint mentioned in this one. An' anyhow this is different. We're findin' out who our client is, right? We want to know who's payin' us to find out about Nick?'

The hooded look descended on Damon's face. 'Then search some more on the dredging firm, Matt. But don't spend more than half an hour on it. There's real work to do that brings in money.'

'Right, then I'll start with the Companies House site.' Matt opened the gov.uk site and keyed the dredging firm in the search box. 'Yeah, the *Overview* tab says it's a private limited company and the registered office address is in

Elmsett. Well that aint a surprise, considerin' it were the Elmsett call box.' He clicked on the *People* tab. 'There's 2 officers listed: Silvia Shinton, secretary; and Shaun Simon Shinton, director. They both have the same address. I guess they'll be a Mr & Mrs, and the S and S of SS Shinton Dredgin'. OK, now for the *Filing History* tab.'

'Ah, the filing tab! Let's have a look at the accounts.' It was obvious that Damon was still following Matt's screen from the administrator view on his own computer.

A dropdown box appeared with a list of the annual *Total Exemption Full Accounts*. Matt clicked on the latest one. It was the PDF filed for the previous year ended March 2013. Scammin' hell, he'd need Chrissie with her accountancy skills to understand it.

'Look for employees. They'll be mentioned somewhere in that document because they're a cost which is exempt from business tax.' Damon's instruction sounded sharp but Matt recognised the tone; it meant they were closing in on the target.

He scrolled through the PDF document and found what he wanted on page 5 under *Employees*.

'*The average monthly number of persons (including directors) employed by the company during the year was 5*,' he read from his screen.

'So excluding Silvia Shinton, it leaves 4 employees who could have phoned from the call box,' Damon said.

'Unless there's more than one bird.'

'And of course one of them might have been Toussaint, the guy who died in the boat a couple of weeks ago. That's assuming he was working for them back in 2013. So it may only be three people to find and fit a name to. Try searching Silvia Shinton.'

'But why, Damon? I though you said it aint her.'

'Yes, but she's listed on the Companies House site as secretary to the dredging company. I'm guessing she'll be the computer literate one. Look on her Facebook page. There may be some selfies of her with some of the staff.'

'That's neat.' Matt liked it when Damon worked with him. In the early days it had been akin to a tutorial, but now it felt more like teamwork, and today there was another new trick to learn from him.

'Flamin' malware. You're right, Damon.' Matt scrolled through her public access Facebook page. Something soon caught his eye. It was a shot of a new hydraulic excavator fitted with a dredging bucket, but more importantly it also featured four men in high visibility jackets. They stood, smiling in front of the new yellow monster. The caption with it said *a little something new to add to the collection.* Underneath the photo Silvia had added *Will, Cliff, Dave and the shy one, my hubby.*

The picture was a little grainy when Matt expanded it, but there was no mistaking *the shy one*. He had partly turned away from the camera at the moment of the shot and it hadn't caught his face full-on.

Will, Cliff and Dave didn't look in the least bit like either of the men who had made the call from the Elmsett telephone box, but *the shy one* most certainly did. He had the same face, build and stature as the man who got out of the black Toyota Land Cruiser and made the call.

'The caller were her hubby, Shaun Simon Shinton,' Matt breathed.

'So it's Shaun Simon Shinton, the director of the dredging firm. He's our client. Job done, Matt! I'll put his name and address against our records.'

The rush of the hunt had left Matt feeling empty. He gulped more cola and pulled a face when the bubbles exploded in the back of his nose.

'I don't get why Shaun Shinton went to all that trouble to find Nick's address and number? Are you sure that's all he were after?'

'Maybe he just wants to thank Nick. Now come on, it's time to get back to paying work; we've contact details to find for the card company. I'm sending you the list of names… now!'

'Yeah but it don't make no sense,' Matt muttered, convinced Damon wasn't telling him everything. It was all very well to search for names, addresses and phone numbers but how to search what was going on inside someone's head? Damon's head? And Damon was the one who had made him promise not to tell Nick. Mind you, Matt reasoned, no one had mentioned anything about not telling Chrissie. Her name hadn't come up in any of the talks he'd had with Damon on the subject. He could talk to her about it. She'd know what to do.

CHAPTER 17

It was Wednesday lunchtime and Chrissie stepped back for a moment to get a better impression of the chair she had just unloaded from a customer's car. It was one of a pair. The customer, a chatty young woman from Sudbury, followed her into the barn workshop with the undamaged one. She had brought it so that Chrissie could copy the carved panel forming part of the damaged chair's back.

Watery sunlight streamed through the open door, spotlighting the chairs where they rested on the concrete. To Chrissie's eye the chairs were a contradiction in style and date. A bit of a mishmash, as Ron would say.

'So tell me about these chairs. What do you know about them?' Chrissie asked.

Ping! A text alert sounded from her pocket. She ignored it and concentrated on the customer.

'I don't know a lot,' the woman said. 'They came with the house. You know the kind of thing; elderly lady dies and relatives live hundreds of miles away and want a quick sale. They weren't interested in her furniture, so they were pleased to sell some of it with the house. A kind of job lot of stuff! You should see what they left in the cellar. So what can you tell me about my chairs? I'd be fascinated to hear.'

It was Chrissie's moment to impress.

'They're side chairs, meaning they don't have arms. They're mahogany and delicate – almost like bedroom pieces. The legs are square, slender and very slightly curved at the bottom. The back legs are undecorated and with no defined foot, whereas the front ones have pale wood inlay strips and short Spanish feet. The style and lines suggest Empire period to me.'

'I've not heard of Empire period before. When was that?'

'Early 19th century. It started in France and spread from there. Of course they could be a slightly earlier French style, a kind of minimalist neo-classicism. The point is, I'm not sure because I think I'm probably looking at a late Victorian or Edwardian copy of an earlier French style.'

'But what makes you say it's a copy?' The customer's voice rose in anxiety.

Ping! Another text alert sounded from Chrissie's pocket. She ignored it and forged on, 'The carving looks machined to me and the fineness of the inlay strips and inlay decoration make me think it's machine tooled.'

'Could they be French?'

'Yes, I suppose they could have found their way across from France. It might also explain a lot. They were expensive chairs to produce and were meant to be on show.'

'So not necessarily meant for the bedroom, then?'

Chrissie was conscious that Gayle had sidled over and was listening in. 'Hi, Gayle. Gayle is our apprentice, Mrs Dell.'

'Hi, Gayle. What do you say? Do you think my chairs are French?' Mrs Dell asked brightly.

Gayle's pale face flamed as she dropped her gaze.

'We'll have a better idea when I start working on it,' Chrissie said quickly. 'Was the old lady French, do you know?'

Ping! Chrissie thrust her hand into her pocket to silence her phone.

'Aren't you going to answer it?' Gayle piped in, surprise sounding in her voice.

'If it was urgent they'd call me. It can wait.' She could have added *I'm with a customer*, however customer etiquette was best talked about over a mug of tea and not in front of Mrs Dell. The girl's cheeks were blushing as it was.

'So Mrs Dell, do you think there was a French connection with the old lady?'

'I don't know. I've never thought about it but I've done a bit of a search into our family history, so it might be interesting to have a look into the old lady's. I mean I've got her name from the deeds, her date of death and the names of some of her relatives. It might be enough to get me started.' She smiled at Chrissie.

'Well that could be fascinating.'

'When you're in Sudbury next you must drop in and have a look at some of the other pieces that came with the house.'

'I'd like that. And your cellar sounds interesting. Perhaps when I bring the chairs back in a couple of weeks?' Chrissie said as she walked with Mrs Dell out of the workshop and back to her car.

She waited as Mrs Dell drove away. At last now she could check her text messages.

Ping! God! What was so urgent? She pulled her phone from her linen trousers.

'Why the hell's Matt sent me all these texts?' She scrolled through them. It was the same message sent several times, and on first glance appeared pretty wishy-washy.

Hi. I need to talk. This searching business is freaking me out.

CHAPTER 18

Nick's Wednesday lunchtime break felt peaceful. Dave and he were paying a visit to the moated farmhouse to see Mr Coady and take measurements for the footbridge. He sat with Dave on the bench, just as they had sat several times before. His mind drifted back to the first time, almost two weeks earlier, when they had eaten their fateful lunch. That had been the day when Dave had suggested they take a walk around the moat. The walk when they'd seen the boat on the water and... well the rest was history.

The panoramic view across the fields was just as awesome, but life and time had moved on and already the wheat and barley had more than doubled in height. Nick recalled it had been sunny that day; not cloudy with watery sunshine, like today. And silent, apart from the birds chirping and chattering; yes, it had been silent back then.

'I reckon they've stopped for lunch at last.' Dave's voice broke into his thoughts.

'What? You mean the dredgers? If we'd known they were going to make such a racket, we'd have been better off waiting till now to measure up.'

They'd driven straight over from Willows & Son that morning to discuss the exact siting and dimensions of Mr Coady's footbridge. They soon discovered it would entail measuring the width of more than one section of the moat. Mr Coady wanted a single bridge that he could move and position at different points along the bank.

'Wouldn't it make better sense to have more than one bridge?' Dave had reasoned. 'A single one might sound like a good idea but the design you're suggesting is in solid oak.

It's going to be heavy; not a portable walkway you can toss across by yourself. And if you want to move it you'll almost certainly need some mechanised lifting equipment. It's not a job for one person.'

It quickly became apparent that Mr Coady was torn between aesthetics, cost, practicalities and safety issues. He showed them a picture he'd found in a magazine illustrating a graceful wooden structure gently arching across a pond. Clearly aesthetics were winning.

'How much clearance do you want above the surface of the moat?' Nick had asked.

The eventual compromise was to have only one footbridge, constructed in western red cedar and arching high enough to allow a small rowing boat to pass underneath. It was also to be long enough to span the widest section of the moat.

'We can rest it on specially designed concrete blocks on the bank and technically it won't be a fixed structure, Mr Coady. But its weight and span aren't going to make it exactly portable.'

Mr Coady had walked the circumference of the moat with them and pointed out potential crossings where there were gaps in the overgrown banks.

The dredgers had been working there since Monday, initially setting up their equipment, but now dredging was well underway. 'What a din they make!'

'I know, Dave. It's deafening when you get up close,' Mr Coady had said. And they'd had to get closer when they started taking measurements.

The noise soon became a distraction and made verbal communication difficult. Even hand signals had been misinterpreted. So when Nick took his last bite of lunchtime cheese and pickle sandwich and said *we'd have been better off waiting till now to measure up*, Dave's response was predictable.

'Come on then, Nick. Let's get the measuring completed while they're still at lunch. What do you say?'

'You're on.'

Dave led the way. They skirted a bed of lily of the valley. Some of the white flowers were already beginning to dry and shrivel. They'd seemed so fresh and bursting with life when Nick had walked past them on the fateful drowning day.

'You know their leaves are poisonous. They do bad things to your heart,' Dave said.

They collected their equipment from the Willows & Son van parked to the side of the farmhouse. Nick carried a long carpenter's sprit level, a bit like a short plank of wood but made of metal, while Dave took the digital measurer and a writing pad to record the measurements.

'I'll go this side of the moat.' Dave peeled away and Nick followed the gravel drive bisecting a section of the moat.

The dredging firm had laid 3-metre width heavy-duty road mats across the grass to protect it and make trackways for their vehicles. They had also spread the mats along a short section of the bank, the same place where Tuscan had parked his dark blue 4x4 Defender and launched the small flat-bottomed boat into the moat. The bank there had slipped and collapsed a little, as if at some time in the past cattle had trodden it down to get to the water. It was the natural place for the dredgers to launch their pontoons.

Nick shortened his stride as he gazed at the array of equipment.

One pontoon was loaded with a skip. A hydraulic digger complete with its dredging bucket had been driven onto the second pontoon. Was it simply a floating platform or was it a pontoon boat? Nick wondered.

'We aim to minimise any damage to the edges of the moat.'

'W-what?' Nick gasped and spun round. Where had Shaun, the dredging boss appeared from?

'Sorry to startle you, but it's obvious what you must be thinking. Everyone always asks the same questions.'

'But I haven't asked anything yet.'

'But you will. So in answer to your inevitable question – we float the hydraulic digger instead of driving it along the bank. As you can see, all those trees and shrubs block our access to the water. We simply can't get at it from most of the bank, and we don't want to damage anything.'

'Right, so you keep the heavy equipment off the banks and float it on the water.'

'Except where we've protected our access area with the road mats.' Shaun smiled as if inviting more questions.

'That's cool. I'd stop to hear more but Dave's waiting for me. We're trying to measure up for Mr Coady's foot-bridge while you're all having lunch.'

'Good idea. But just one last thing before you rush off. You must've heard the recent warnings about laughing gas. Did you notice anything odd about Tuscan's stuff?'

'What?' for a moment Nick didn't follow the sudden change in direction.

'Tuscan's laughing gas stuff. Anything odd about it?'

'I-I, I'm not an expert, Shaun. I didn't even know what the stuff was at first.'

'Yes, but did anything about it strike you as odd?'

'I don't know.'

One red, one green, and never been seen burst into Nick's mind. 'The balloons,' he murmured, 'they looked… I don't think he'd used them.'

Shaun shrugged. 'So it all looked OK. That's something, at least.'

Nick hurried away. It was bad enough walking along the bank where the drama had played out, but to have Shaun bringing it all back was…. He didn't want to think about it. Tuscan and his paraphernalia were history and he had work to do.

Taking the measurements turned out to be more efficient without the distraction of active dredging work going on around them. Nick stood on one side of the moat, one metre back from its edge and held his long carpenter's spirit level so that it stood upright. Dave, across on the other side of the moat, also positioned himself a meter back from his edge of the water and used the digital measurer with its laser beam to aim at Nick's spirit level. It was a clever bit of kit, the way it could measure, calculate and tell you if you were aiming it flat or at an angle, horizontal or vertical. It was never going to be as millimetre-accurate as a surveyor's bit of equipment with tripods and telescopes in this situation, but it was a damned sight easier than throwing a length of rope across and using that to measure the width.

They repeated the measurements at the widest points along the moat, as well as concentrating on the spot Mr Coady had chosen for the footbridge.

'Shaun asked me if I'd noticed anything odd about Tuscan's laughing gas stuff. Did he ask you as well?' Nick dropped the question as they packed their equipment back into the van.

'Shaun would know better than to ask me.'

'Why?'

'Because on the day it happened we talked for ages while we were waiting for the police. You won't remember because you were in a kind of dreamy state so we left you to yourself for a while. But no, it was obvious I was hearing about this laughing gas craze for the first time. How'd I know if any of the stuff looked odd? The whole idea of breathing nitrous oxide from a whipped cream dispenser was news to me. I know nitrous oxide has been used for years in the automotive industry as an accelerant, but I'm pretty sure it comes with a trace of sulphur dioxide to stop people inhaling it for a high.'

'Really? Does the sulphur smell, or something?'

'It tastes foul. You don't want to breathe sulphur dioxide, it'll make you sick. It's a deterrent.'

'Do you reckon Shaun asked me because he thinks I'm a user?'

'Hell, Nick, how'd I know what he thinks? You're not a user are you?'

'Of course not.'

'There you are, then. Let's get back to the workshop. We need to draw up some plans and order some wood.'

CHAPTER 19

Matt felt as if he had been waiting an eternity for Chrissie to answer his Wednesday lunchtime text message, his *Hi. I need to talk. This searching business is freaking me out* message.

'Come on, Chrissie,' he whined, and sent the message again for the nth time.

Brrumm. His mobile vibrated in silent mode. At last! He opened Chrissie's text.

What's up? She'd texted.

I need to talk some. Can we meet? he thumbed, and pressed send.

Nags Head? After work? Chrissie fired back.

•••

When Matt pushed the door into the Nags Head early that Wednesday evening, it took him a moment to acclimatise his eyes to the dim light. The jukebox was silent and the air, heavy with beery fragrance, hit him like a wall. He knew Chrissie was already there; he'd spotted her yellow TR 7 outside in the pub car park.

'Hiya, Chrissie,' he called as he recognised the hobo style bag slung over her shoulder and her short blonde hair, almost the colour of wheat beer in the dull lighting. She stood at the bar counter talking to the barman.

'Hi, Matt,' she said, smiling when she saw him. 'I was just ordering another drink. Lager for you?'

They carried their drinks to the bench seat and table tucked to one side and facing the old fireplace.

'So what was so urgent you had to send me the same text a dozen times?'

Matt put his glass on the pine table, avoiding the cigarette burns, just as one might step over the cracks in a pavement. He glanced around; only five or so other drinkers filled the bar area and none of them were close enough to listen in. It was safe to talk.

'It's Nick,' he blurted, 'and I aint sent twelve messages.'

'Well maybe not twelve and I was exaggerating a bit, but you get where I'm coming from. Why all the drama? What's Nick done?' She sipped her ginger beer and rested back on the bench seat.

'A bloke's asked Balcon & Mora to get Nick's address and contact details. Not only that, the bloke's gone to loads of trouble to keep his ID from us.'

'How do you know he's gone to loads of trouble?'

'Coz he called from a telephone box. That's real puttin' yourself out just to get contact details and an address.'

'It doesn't seem a very big deal, Matt. Why all the angst?'

'Damon only said about it coz he knows Nick's a mate. He thought we oughta find out who the mystery bloke was.'

'And have you?'

'Yeah, the bloke turns out to be Shaun Shinton. He's only the boss of the dredgin' firm workin' where Nick pulled that drowned bloke out of the moat.'

'Really? What did Nick say when you told him?'

'Well that's the thing. Damon won't let me tell Nick.'

'What? That's odd. Are you sure?'

'Client confidentiality,' Matt said carefully.

'And that's all this Shaun Shinton bloke wanted Balcon & Mora to find?'

136

'I'm startin' to think maybe he asked Damon to get more stuff on Nick, but Damon aint sayin' nothin' to me about it.'

He watched Chrissie frown while he gulped some lager. Was she frowning because she was thinking? Was it because he'd just told her something odd, bad or questionable? Then again, was her frown simply her disapproving of the way he'd gulped his lager? The truth was he couldn't tell. It had always been like this for him and it had landed him in tons of trouble over the years. As a kid it was a case of detentions at school and being picked on by the other kids. But as an adult? He'd learnt to look out for mannerisms and gestures. So he did what he always did and waited for her to say something or make a gesture he could understand.

'You aint said much,' he finally prompted.

'What? No, I was thinking. Why don't I drop Nick a hint? I'll tell him to watch his back as far as this Shaun Shinton bloke is concerned. It's probably all that's needed and it saves you giving him the lowdown on it and crossing Damon.'

'Yeah, I'm cool with that.'

'And if you think about it, Nick and his band mates must be used to this type of thing. They probably get it all the time from their fans.' She sipped her ginger beer.

Was it the poor light or was she frowning again? He waited, but when she picked at the skin of her index finger and then bit her nail, he knew he was watching a sign. A bad one.

'What's up?' he asked.

'Do you think it's too far for Gayle to cycle from Stowmarket to the Clegg workshop?'

137

'What?'

'Well, I've been giving her a lift every day and it's getting to be a right pain. Take today. I couldn't stay on at the workshop without Gayle having to stay on as well. So something like meeting you here is… well it's why I was a bit early. It's a real nuisance there isn't a decent bus service.'

'If she aint into cyclin' that far, she could try a scooter. Me first one were pretty cheap.'

'A scooter? Hey that's an idea.'

'Yeah, well I know she's a bird – but why not? I could give her a ride on the back of mine as a kinda taster. See if she likes it. What do you say?'

'I'd say being a "bird" as you call her, shouldn't make any difference. Getting a scooter is gender neutral. And don't you go scaring her by showing off on your Vespa.'

'I told you she were an internet ghost didn't I?'

'Yes, and I doubt there's much on the internet about me either. And ghost or not, it doesn't mean she can't get scared on the back of a scooter.'

'No, I weren't sayin' it meanin' she couldn't get scared. I were sayin' it coz I'm wonderin' if you've changed your mind. You know, about tellin' me stuff. Clues to help me internet search about her?'

'No, I told you. I can't and won't give you anything from Gayle's personal record. Anyway, all the Academy gives me is her date of birth and NI number for her wages & tax forms.'

'Scammin' hell, Chrissie, aint you curious about her? Maisie were dead curious.'

'Of course I am, but I'm her trainer. It would be wrong. And creepy. How would you feel if old Blumfield or Damon were searching the net about you?'

Matt didn't know how to answer. He doubted old Blumfield even knew how to use a computer. And as for Damon - Matt had never stopped to think about how he actually felt when Damon used administrator mode at work. Feelings didn't come into it. And anyway, wasn't everyone's activity online or offline interesting to someone out there, otherwise why all the cookies and CCTV? It was a fact. He worked around it. He didn't need to have feelings about it.

Chrissie filled his silence. 'I suppose Damon was a bad example. Of course he'll have searched the net about you. It's what he does all the time. It's his job.'

'Yeah, reckon so. But about scooterin' – if Gayle's interested you can tell her I'm around in Stowmarket tomorrow. Thursday's me assistant demonstrator day.' He didn't have to say he'd be working in the Academy's computing and IT department. He figured it was obvious. 'Or I can give her a ride on me Vespa at the weekend,' he added as he remembered he was meeting Maisie on Thursday. 'Yeah, I better phone Mais.'

•••

Matt was surprised later that same evening when Maisie shrieked at him over the phone. He'd expected her to be pleased with him for offering to give Gayle a taster ride on the back of his scooter. After all, Maisie had been the one who'd said they should have taken Gayle to Nick's gig in Southwold because she hadn't got her own crowd for a bit of a bop. To his way of thinking, his suggestion of a taster ride was simply a way of trying to be helpful and matey.

'But I've already told you, Mais. It aint a date. It's only so she gets a ride on a scooter. Chrissie's hopin' she'll like it and get one herself,' he explained.

'Then why'd you say you'd be holdin' a copy of the Eastern Anglia Daily Tribune, like it's some kind of blind date?'

'Well aint that what you do when you're meetin' a bird you aint met before?'

'But we've met her at the open mic night. And if she aint sure what you look like, you don't need to hold a newspaper to mark you out. You'll be standin' next to a blackberry bubblegum-coloured Vespa.'

'Well you come – yeah why don't you come as well, Mais? You were the one itchin' to know more about her. Then you can ask her stuff yourself, coz I aint found nothin' on social media yet.'

'What? You been lookin' to see if she's got a bloke?'

'No. I been lookin' coz you said she don't add up and I thought you'd want to know about her.'

By the time the call ended Matt's ear felt bruised, but at least Maisie had stopped shrieking and they'd reached an understanding. Or rather, Maisie had got the picture.

It turned out Thursday didn't suit Maisie, so Chrissie arranged for Gayle to meet Matt on Saturday in the quiet Museum of East Anglian Life car park. It was in the centre of Stowmarket and next to the busy Asda car park. Maisie had said Gayle would easily spot him and his brightly coloured Vespa without the added identifier of a folded newspaper, so long as there weren't too many other cars around.

'We can all meet for a coffee in Costa after you've given her a taster ride. I'll have finished me shift in the retro shop by two o'clock. So see you both in Costa just after two. How's that sound?'

'Mega,' he'd replied.

Saturday when it dawned was cloudy with breakthrough sunshine. Matt had dressed with some thought. He knew it wasn't a date, but a bird was a bird and he had his street cred to consider.

He wore the Purple Hills tee-shirt. It gave him a splash of colour to match his Vespa along with a dollop of edginess for anyone in the know. Jeans and an old denim bomber jacket completed the look. He waited in the Museum of East Anglian Life car park at a little before one o'clock, as agreed. A handful of cars were parked at the end closest to the museum grounds. He pulled his scooter onto its stand where it was in clear view from the bustling shoppers' car park and the Saturday street market in the shopping precinct beyond. He eased his full face helmet off, smoothed his beard and scanned the throng.

'Hiya!' he called and waved when he recognised a girl with mid-brown hair and blonde highlights. 'Over here, Gayle!'

She looked pretty much as he remembered her, except this time her jeans were teamed with a grey sweatshirt and charcoal sneakers with white trim. Her pale square face made him think of a hunted animal. He couldn't think why. No one was forcing her to take a trial ride on the back of his scooter. He waited while she walked across to him.

'Hi, Matt,' she said in the small voice he remembered.

'This is me Vespa – special edition retro look. What d'you think?'

'Awesome.'

'So you aint ridden on one of them before, right?'

'No.'

'But you can ride a bicycle?'

'Yeah.'

'Well you won't need one if you get a scooter. Are you ready to have a go?'

She nodded.

'You'll need a helmet. I got Maisie's with me. I reckon it'll fit you OK.'

He watched her gather her hair back, and with a couple of deft moves secure it in an untidy loose knot with an elasticated ponytail holder. She didn't say a word as she took hold of the helmet and pulled it onto her head. It struck him as odd. He didn't remember her being so quiet in the Nags Head at the open mic night. When Maisie was quiet, he'd learnt it meant she was cross; a stage crosser than shrieking and nearly always because he'd done something wrong.

'You OK, Gayle?'

Again, only a nod.

'Right, I'm gettin' on me scooter first. Then you get on behind me. There's room for your feet on the footrest but you'll have to hold on to summut, so put your arms round me middle and don't go leanin' off to the side. You only lean if I lean, and then like you're glued to me, OK?'

'Where are we going?'

'I figured I'd do the route to the Clegg workshop an' back so you get an idea what it'd be like goin' to work on one.'

Matt was used to Maisie riding pillion, so he was surprised by how stiff and rigid Gayle was behind him. He eased onto the Finborough Road, riding slowly at first, and then gradually increasing his speed. By the time he rode back into the car park forty-five minutes later, he'd whizzed along lanes between untidy hedgerows and topped speeds of over forty miles an hour, leaned into corners and accelerated out of them, overtaken cyclists and slowed to a stop at road junctions. At some point, he couldn't have said exactly when, he became less aware of her arms like a tight band around him. He no longer felt her body like an awkward backpack, it was as if she had become at one with his scooter.

'Were that OK then, Gayle?' he asked as he parked the Vespa.

'It was awesome. Really awesome.'

He was pleased. He'd already sensed she'd relaxed on the ride and now her words explained her flushed face. He figured she'd caught the scootering bug.

'So d'you think you want to get a scooter then?' He didn't wait for her answer but continued, 'We'd best get goin' if we're meetin' Maisie for coffee.' He led the way from the car park and through the shopping precinct to Costa.

They found Maisie sitting at a table close to the plate glass windows at the front of the coffee shop. 'I were lucky to get these, seats,' she explained. 'You get the drinks, Matt, while I hear all about it from Gayle.'

When at last he set a tray on the table, he'd slopped Gayle's hot chocolate with cream and marshmallows into its saucer and Maisie's berry-flavoured cooler overflowed onto a paper serviette.

'Hey, careful!' Maisie squeaked as she rescued Matt's large cup of caramel cappuccino from where it rested, askew on the rim of the tray.

'So why aint you ridden a bicycle since you were twelve?' Maisie asked, obviously mid-conversation with Gayle.

'It was a kid's bike. I grew out of it and there wasn't money for another one.'

'How about skateboardin'? Ever get to try that?' Matt asked, thinking back to his own childhood, conducted on a tight budget after his father walked out. He'd only been five years old when his mum had been left to fend for herself.

'Or roller-skating?' Maisie added.

Matt sipped his caramel cappuccino, holding his cup like a comfort blanket against the pain of past skateboarding memories. He didn't know why he'd mentioned skateboards. He'd failed to master the skill on borrowed boards, and never owned one. He still resented the injustice of them; the unfairness that other kids could somehow balance on a moving platform but he couldn't. The eight-year-old Matt had been convinced those same kids must have tapped into hidden special powers; the kind of powers his comic-strip heroes possessed. It was only later, much later, when he realised it depended not only on balance and coordination, but also the distribution of weight, the lever effect of centre of balance, the size of the wheels and momentum. Now aged twenty-two, a scooter worked perfectly for him, but the pang of the injustice of skateboards still had the power to sting almost as much as the hardness of a pavement, or the humiliation of a fall.

'Yeah, but I reckon ridin' a bike's easier than skateboardin',' he murmured.

'I wouldn't know. I never got to try a skateboard,' Gayle said in her small voice.

'Do you miss Leicester?' Maisie asked.

'Sometimes.'

'Aint Leicester where that school kid stabbed a teacher last week?'

'No Mais, that were in Leeds,' Matt said, and sipped his soothing caramel cappuccino.

'Right, but you got some relatives in Suffolk? That's why you're here?'

'No. No one's here.' Gayle spoke quietly, and Maisie leaned forwards.

'But you gotta have a reason for Suffolk? I mean–'

'She were relocated, Mais.'

'Yeah, I know,' Maisie said slowly, as if speaking to a child.

'Look, I-I had to move. And here was the first good apprenticeship to come up.'

'Yeah, but you must have had a say in it?' Maisie persisted.

'Yes. Suffolk's one of my childhood dreams.'

'Well here aint Beatrix Potter and the Lake District. I reckon you might have some long lost relative here and you aint known it.'

Matt smiled. He'd read about this kind of thing, except it had been called subliminal advertising. He launched in; 'D'you mean like subliminal info? The things you've been told an' seen as a kid and forgotten about? Do you mean the stuff in your subconscious, Mais?'

'What you on about Matt? No, what I'm thinkin' is, wouldn't it'd be real cool to do one of them searches, you know, find your ancestors kinda a thing? You might discover you had long lost family here. What d'you say, Gayle?'

'No. No sorry, but it isn't my kind of thing. Look, about a scooter - how'd I get one and a licence, Matt?'

Maisie pouted, but Matt felt on more solid ground. This was, after all, the reason he was there.

'First you got to do the CBT. That's your compulsory bike trainin'. It takes the best part of a day but you can do it in Stowmarket. Go online and sign up.'

'But I haven't got a scooter yet.'

'That's OK. You can use one from the motorcycle school. That's what I done.'

'And a licence?'

'Yeah, you'll need a provisional licence. You can do that online as well.'

'And Matt an' me can give you a hand lookin for a scooter. Right; a selfie?'

'What?'

'Smile!' Maisie leaned closer, shot her hand up and trained her phone camera on Gayle and herself. 'I'll send it to you. What's your number?'

'No, I hate photos of me. I always look awful in them. You have to delete it, please.'

CHAPTER 20

It was late on Saturday afternoon by the time Matt phoned Chrissie to say Gayle's taster ride on his scooter had been a success.

'She's caught the scooterin' bug,' he said.

'Are you sure?'

It was almost too good to be true. At first Chrissie didn't dare to believe it in case Matt had misread Gayle's responses and signs. She was, after all, a girl of few words. But by Sunday morning Chrissie had decided Matt must have got it right. Why else had he told her when there were places still available for Gayle's Compulsory Bike Training? He probably looked with Gayle on the Stowmarket motorcycle school's website. On the other hand, he might have looked it up for himself and….

Stop, she told herself. Matt had said *she's caught the scooterin' bug*. It took one to know one. Trust his instincts. Relax. It was going to happen; Gayle would get her CBT and a scooter. Chrissie would get her freedom back.

For once, Chrissie felt totally at peace with her world as she took a leisurely Sunday morning shower. She'd had a lie-in, chilled out with a mug of tea in the kitchen and was ready to get into the day. Warm water splattered on her head and streamed over her shoulders as she luxuriated in her five minutes of inner calm. It was going to be all right. She would no longer be bound inexorably to Gayle's timetable, and if she looked at it from Gayle's point of view, Gayle would get independent travel. Giving her a day off as soon as possible for the CBT was a small price to pay for an all-round win-win solution.

Clive was still out on his morning run and for the moment she had the cottage to herself. It might only be the first Sunday in May, and the Ipswich half marathon scheduled for some time in September, but the months would fly and it was a distance he needed to train for. It was his way of unwinding. She understood all that, just so long as no one expected her to run a half marathon as well. She padded to the bedroom with its narrow sash windows and dressed with some thought; old jeans and old tee-shirt, clothes she hoped would be suitable for a mudlark. She was going to try her hand at mudlarking, the ancient practice of searching around in tidal river mud for discarded objects like old coins, pottery and clay pipes.

By the time she heard the front door open and Clive's footsteps in the hallway, she was already dressed and back in the kitchen with a map spread out on the kitchen table.

'Good run?' she called.

'Yes thanks,' he said, putting his head round the kitchen door. 'I'm going to take a quick shower. Why the map? I thought it was Pin Mill for lunch and then the Stour and Orwell Walk? Old discarded bottles, right? You haven't changed your mind, have you?'

'Yes, sorry. I've just checked the tides. We'll have switch to dry land and hunt in old rubbish tips instead.'

'What?'

'Only joking. High tide was a couple of hours ago, so the water will be well on its way out by the time we've had brunch and start walking. There'll be lots of freshly exposed tidal mud. Now hurry up and have your shower.'

It was cool and breezy as they loaded Clive's car with his backpack, a bucket, plastic carrier bags, a pointed trowel, walking poles and wellington boots. Chrissie threw in a change of clothes in case the worst happened and she accidently sat in the mud.

'You know we aren't going to find any bottles to put in that apothecary box of yours, don't you?' Clive said.

'Yes, I know, but my cousin Angela told me about mudlarking and I wanted to give it a try. I know this isn't the Thames and I'm not going to find a Viking torc, but I still thought it might be fun.'

'So how is Gayle now about the chemicals and bottles?' he asked as they eased onto the slip road to join the A14.

'I don't know. She doesn't say much about herself and she always clams up if I ask her something she doesn't want to talk about. I don't think she's taken a look at the box's contents since the time she fainted. I'd guess she's still avoiding them.'

'But otherwise she seems all right?'

'Well as I said, she doesn't give anything away. No – sorry, she let slip she liked a song on the car radio. Counting Stars. Yes that's right, OneRepublic; they're an American band.'

'So from what you're saying she's a closed book. One she's not letting you open. Honestly Chrissie, you and your nosiness. It doesn't automatically mean she's hiding any secrets. You already know she had an unfortunate experience in her last apprenticeship. Surely that's the obvious explanation?'

'I know, except she shuts down about nearly everything in her past. Not just her recent past.'

'There are plenty of people out there who appear more interesting if they create a little bit of mystery about themselves. And the easiest way to do that is to keep quiet about yourself. Have you ever considered she might not have a lot to say?'

'Well you could be right about that. Matt says she's an internet ghost.'

'Now that's unusual.'

'Is it? Why?'

'Well, you told me she's nineteen. She's part of the generation living life through social media. It's easier to be an old ghost than a teen ghost.'

'Meaning?'

'It's interesting, that's all. Stop reading things into what I say.'

They lapsed into silence as Clive took them off the A14 and followed the road under the Orwell Bridge to trace the southern banks of the Orwell. At first Chrissie caught glimpses of the estuary mud and sand, still sodden, glassy smooth and reflecting the sky close to the outgoing tidal water. It looked drier and more obviously sandy closer to the foreshore. Irregular stones, muddy grey and the size of bricks, peppered the exposed surface. If she was painting it, her palate would have been a shade card of dull blues and greys fading into wet sandy browns. And then she lost sight of the water as the road turned inland.

The road led them through the quiet village of Woolverston and then busier Chelmondiston. 'The church here took a hit from a V2 rocket in 1944,' Clive said as he turned into a lane barely wider than his car.

'Really?'

Trust a bloke to know a snippet of information like that, Chrissie thought. 'It seems a bit off target for London. Were they aiming for Ipswich or Felixstowe and Harwich do you think?'

'After London, Norwich was targeted by V2s the most times in the UK. I don't know how accurate the rockets were. This one might have been heading for Ipswich, but could have been off target for Norwich or London '

'But how do you know this kind of stuff?' Chrissie asked, wondering if Matt and Clive had more in common than she'd thought.

'You're forgetting; I went to school in Norwich and my dad was a teacher at the Norwich School. Not during the war, of course. He was only a small kid at the time. But I'm from there. It's part of Norwich's history.'

'Right.'

The lane twisted down between trees and cottages. She sensed the water ahead.

'I'll park in the car park. It'll be easier than on the road here. It always gets half blocked with parked cars by lunchtime.'

They ate fancy bacon butties sitting at tables outside the Butt and Oyster, and gazed at the small boatyard with its crane. A concrete walkway stretched across the sand to the receding water's edge. Small yachts and dinghies lay beached by the retreating tide. Further out in the estuary a Thames barge glided past, the gentle breeze filling its rusty-red sails. The smell of salt water, sewage and seaweed blended into a distinctive scent, the breath of the estuary. It conjured up childhood memories for Chrissie; holidays spent catching crabs with string and bait dangled from boardwalk moorings in a smaller estuary between South-wold and Walberswick.

'You look relaxed,' Clive said.

'I feel relaxed. This,' she swept an arm expansively, 'this is good for the soul.'

'I can't decide if those old boats, the disintegrating wooden wrecks being swallowed by the mud, are picturesque or depressing,' Clive murmured.

'I'd say atmospheric. Come on, I'm itching to get started. It's going to be almost as exciting as crabbing with string and bait.'

They followed the shoreline and ambled across the sandy mud eastwards towards the mouth of the estuary.

When they returned to the car several hours later, they were tired and muddy, and there weren't any treasures in the bucket.

'All we've got are fragments of old roof tile and bits of brick. And the broken glass looks modern to me. In fact, looking at this lot we could have been litter picking,' Clive muttered as he gazed into the bucket.

'Stand it in the boot. I'll look through it more closely when we get home. I think there's a nail hole in one of the bits of tile. If it's a square hole I think it means it's pretty old; possibly Tudor. So, did you enjoy mudlarking, then?'

'I think I'd class it as a slow walk looking at the ground.'

'Yes, but did you enjoy it?'

'It gave me lots of time to think and mull things over.'

'And?'

'It occurred to me while we were out on the estuary, that dredging must be like mudlarking. Mostly you don't find anything of value but very occasionally you find something the equivalent of a gold torc. It got me wondering about Toussaint and Jon. I figure their connection was more than sexual. I think they had a bit of a business partnership going on as well.'

'Really? Why do you say that?'

'Well there must be the occasional bit of treasure dredged up from moats and rivers and ponds, don't you think? And who could be better placed than Toussaint to snaffle them away and then with Jon's help, sell them undeclared?'

'But what about all the other people involved with the dredging firm? Any one of them could do that.'

'Yes, but we have access to Toussaint's bank accounts. We're still waiting for Jon's but there are some interesting payments into one of Toussaint's accounts.'

'Interesting? In what way?'

'Well there's his regular wage from the dredging firm, and small payments in from a web-based selling site for old bottles. But more interestingly there are occasional large amounts. And I mean really quite large amounts - several thousands of pounds each time and usually in cash. It's not clear where the money came from.'

'Could he have been blackmailing someone? There's the LGBT side of things to consider.'

'No, I don't think it's blackmail. The amounts vary and they're irregular. I need to see Jon's accounts. His business was fine arts, remember. I'm guessing Jon had the contacts. He could have sold some dredged-up artefacts and spilt the money with Toussaint–'

'Hey stop. Remember I was an accountant. Toussaint doesn't have to be selling through Jon. And he doesn't have to be the only one up to those tricks. There could have been others involved; in fact as I said, anyone in the dredging firm. You need both Toussaint and Jon's accounts and the business books to draw the conclusion you're suggesting. The sequence of events and the timing would have to fit.'

'I know. We made the initial request for Toussaint and Jon within days of their deaths, but it seems to take forever. God save me from red tape and bureaucracy. So far we've found big payments to Toussaint, and all I can do is guess what they're for. I'm sure I'm onto something with the artefact theory, but it's so frustrating.'

'Sometimes in forensic accounting... well you have to know what you're looking for before you can find it. The thing that gets me is - on today's evidence, finding valuable artefacts doesn't happen.'

Clive laughed.

'Well, not very often. I think you police need to widen your net. Only last week I had to warn Nick to watch his back with those dredging guys. Shaun Shinton; yes, that was the name.'

'What?'

'It was a tip-off from Matt.' She caught Clive's raised eyebrows and soldiered on, 'He'd been asked to do an internet search, you know – find Nick's contact details for the guy. It sounded a bit odd so we agreed I'd tell Nick to watch his back. No specifics – just watch your back.'

'God! What is it with Nick? Why is it always him? You know the saying; if a name keeps coming up, it's got to mean something.'

'Yes, but Nick hasn't done anything. He's just got caught up in it all.'

'Are you sure, Chrissie?'

CHAPTER 21

Nick liked to think of his lodging as a first floor apartment, a bijou garret and something his mates envied. It was his own space; somewhere to retreat. It might only be a room squeezed into the roof space above his landlady's double garage, but at least it had its own staircase. Admittedly it was only an outside flight of wooden steps, but they were for his room alone. They led down in all weathers from the small, railed wooden platform outside his door to the gravel driveway at ground level.

'Hey, Nick! Are you up? What the hell's going on?' His landlady's voice cut through his door.

Of course he was up; not fully dressed yet, but he was up. It was Monday morning and he was due to leave for work in another five minutes.

Thud! Thud! The door vibrated. 'Hey, Nick! I know you're in there.'

He checked his watch. 07:25.

'OK, OK, Sarah. No need to beat the door down. Hang on a moment.'

He pulled on his fresh tee-shirt and work jeans and hurried to let her in. 'What's up? Has something happened?'

'You're asking me what's up like you don't already know? What the hell have you been doing in there?' Sarah, already dressed for work in a pastel accordion pleated skirt, filled the doorway as she edged to get a glimpse inside. Her angry face didn't give any clues. He tried to see past her as she stepped back and gestured at the staging.

'I don't get what you're on about,' he said, struggling to make sense of the early morning intrusion.

'Then come outside and remind yourself.' The accordion pleats swayed and swirled with each furious step.

He followed onto the wooden staging, stumbling as his toe struck something. It rolled away. Light glinted on shiny steel. He concentrated, pulling outlines into focus. The forms morphed into familiar objects; small ampule shapes. In a flash his brain registered them just as he'd seen them in the bottom of Toussaint's boat. But here there were hundreds, and just as in the boat, each was three, maybe four inches long. God, there'd been a hailstorm of whipped cream chargers. The little canisters of nitrous oxide were everywhere. They littered the staging and peppered the staircase. They'd even collected in heaps on the bottom step and under the staging. Some had spilled onto the gravel driveway.

'What the hell?' he breathed.

'No – you tell me.'

'But this isn't anything to do with me.'

'That's hard to believe.'

'But they weren't here when I came back last night.'

'No, and then you tipped a sack load of them outside your door. Are they what I think they are?'

'What? No! They're nothing to do with me. I've never seen them before. I mean I've seen things like this, but they aren't mine.'

'But they're what I think they are, right? I've seen things like this lying around near the playing field car park. They're canisters for whipped cream dispensers and inflating bicycle tyres. It's laughing gas, isn't it?'

Nick's head spun. He sat down heavily and sent a heap of canisters hopscotching down the steps. 'But it's not me. Someone else has done this. You have to believe me.'

Sarah barely paused for breath as she let fly, 'Drugs! I won't have it - not here; not from a lodger; not in my home! I know what you've done. You've locked yourself away in your garret – no, *my* garret, and taken God knows what. Judging by this,' she waved her arms, 'you were so high you don't even know what you took. Of course you can't remember throwing this lot around because at the time you were probably out of your mind on drugs. I won't have it, do you hear!'

'But it wasn't me. I don't smoke. I don't use nitrous oxide. You know I drink, but I don't do drugs. I just don't. You've got to believe me, Sarah.'

'I haven't *got to* anything. Now clear this lot up. We'll talk about it this evening, but I think you should start looking for a new lodging.'

She pushed past him and down the wooden stairs, her footfall sending canisters tumbling in all directions. A breeze lifted her black, feather-cut hair, broadening the shape of her head. It reminded Nick of a dog raising its hackles. Had the world gone crazy? He watched her stride to her car, slam the door and accelerate away, her tyres spitting gravel. He glanced at his watch. 07:30. It had taken a mere five minutes to turn his world upside down. His Monday morning was in shambles.

He took slow breaths and hummed; it was a technique he used when his nerves got the better of him. They gripped his stomach, caught his diaphragm and forced his breath to come in sharp shallow bursts. *Watch your back*, she'd said. Yes, Chrissie had warned him, but she couldn't have predicted something like this, could she? Breathe slowly; hum. Think. He needed to make a call. The tidying up could wait.

His mobile was exactly where he had left it on the floor by his bed. Things might be kicking off around him, but no, he wasn't going mad.

'Hey, Chrissie. Have you left for work yet?' he rushed when she picked up his call. He struggled to steady his flaky voice against the pulse in his ears.

'Hi, Nick. I've just got in my car and about to head to Stowmarket... God, it's Monday, apprentice release day isn't it? I don't have to pick up Gayle. Why do you want to know?' She sounded distracted.

'Something odd's happened. Here; outside my door. You said to watch my back. And... can you drop by now; on your way out of Woolpit? Please, it's important.'

'What? What's happened to your door? Are you OK? You sound a bit....' Engine noise took over.

He guessed she must have started the TR7's 2 litre engine.

'I'll be round your place in about four minutes,' she said and ended the call.

Nick slipped his phone into his pocket and put on his work trainers. 'Keep busy and hum,' he chanted like a mantra. 'Right; now for a bin liner.' The more he thought about it, the more he realised the canisters must have been "placed". A theatrical act, not just sick, but kind of spooky as well.

Armed with a bin liner, he walked onto the platform just as he caught the unmistakeable sound of Chrissie's thirty-three-year-old TR7 drawing into the drive. She leapt out of the car.

'What are those things? What the hell's happened here?'

He winced. She sounded like a re-run of Sarah.

'They're canisters of laughing gas. It was like this when I opened my door this morning. Someone must have dumped them here during the night. Sarah saw it when she left for work, came up my stairs shouting. She went ballistic.'

'I bet she did. But you must have heard something during the night?'

'No, I didn't hear thing.'

'What do you mean? Weren't you here?'

'Yes, but I'd been cycling all day in Thetford Forest with Jake and Adam. I got back late, had a couple of beers and went to bed. I was dead to the world.'

'Could Jake or Adam have done this? You know, like a joke?'

'I don't think so. We hired bikes in Thetford. They didn't come back here afterwards.'

'So someone else did this. But why?'

'You tell me. You said to watch my back. You told me everything wasn't quite as it seemed with the laughing gas.'

'OK. Calm down. Do you want me to call the police? Or Clive?'

'No! I'm in enough trouble with Sarah. I don't need any more aggro.'

'Right; take some photos and then put some gloves on and get the canisters into your bin liner there.' She walked around her car and opened the boot.

'You don't need to take them away for me, Chrissie.'

'I wasn't going to. I've got some silicone gloves in here for when I check the engine oil.'

159

He smiled. The ever-practical Chrissie; he should have known. 'So why do I need gloves?'

'There's a hell of a lot of canisters out here. It feels… well you could have been set up. If this ever becomes official, you don't want your fingerprints all over the canisters.'

Suitably gloved, he bent to pick up handfuls of the silvery metal ampules. Something seemed odd. The end seal had been broken on a fair number of them, but not all. So why the mix of used and unused? And who had got through such a stockpile of laughing gas? A bakery? A caterer? A rave?

'You don't need to hang around, Chrissie. I can do this on my own.'

'OK, if you're sure. Now for God's sake remember this is about drugs. So watch out for syringes and needles. Anything you find that's not one of those canisters – put in a separate bin liner or a clean plastic bag. And keep it, OK?'

'God, have you been moonlighting as a SOCO or something?'

'No, but you pick up the patter when you've been around someone like Clive for a few years. Look, I must go. I'll call you later. Bye.'

He only half listened to her drive away. It was time to focus on collecting up the canisters. They hadn't got there by themselves. They must have been carried in some kind of container, and the new ones were likely to have still been in boxes. So were there any traces of boxes or containers?

He found what he was looking for on the ground behind the garage. A torn piece of lightweight cardboard nestled against the bricks. He reckoned it must have blown there from under the platform. It looked slightly damp from the morning dew. When he picked it up and turned it over, he caught his breath.

The words *144 Cream Chargers* were printed in bold black letters across the once glossy white card. It seemed pretty careless on someone's part to let a bit of packaging escape like this. But then when he thought about it, if someone was trying to incriminate him, did it matter? Any evidence spread around his garret would only stack against him, not the mystery perpetrator. So where would they have put the rest of the box?

'The bins,' he muttered and strode to the large wheelie bins standing near the entrance gate. They were coloured black, green or brown to indicate the type of rubbish to go in them. He flipped back the lids. God, it was in the green bin, in full view and begging to be seen by Sarah or anyone who cared to look.

He pulled out the rest of the *144 Cream Chargers* box. What? Crushed in underneath was a second complete but empty box. It too was labelled *144 Cream Chargers*.

'Just bag it, and hum; hum a tune,' he told himself. Luckily he remembered the photo just in time and took a quick snap first.

Action calmed his nerves. He forgot his anxious stomach and breathy chest; one unwound and the other breezed away unnoticed as he gathered the canisters. On impulse he stashed the bags in his car. He was late for work. He had to leave.

CHAPTER 22

It was Monday lunchtime by the time Matt opened the text from Nick. It was so odd he had to read the message twice just to be sure he hadn't skipped any vital words.

Did you dump a shitload of cream chargers round my place last night?

'Is everything all right?' Damon asked as he put a can of cola on Matt's table desk. 'Is it work related? You know the rules.'

'It's a text from Nick. He were the subject of one of our client's searches. I reckon that makes him work.'

Damon made a face, drawing his eyebrows together and pursing his lower lip. Matt watched, trying to make sense of it. Damon raised one eyebrow, titled his head slightly sideways and shrugged.

What the blog did all that mean, Matt wondered.

'Well?' Damon followed.

'Well what?'

'Well let me see, then.'

'Oh right. You should 'a said.' He held up his phone so that Damon could see.

'Did you dump a shitload of cream chargers round my place last night?' Damon read out in staccato fashion. 'Cream chargers? They're little canisters of nitrous oxide, aren't they?'

'Yeah, laughin' gas.'

'Is Nick into weed and drugs and stuff, then?'

'Nah, he don't smoke and he don't vape. A shitload of cream chargers sounds weird. But s'posin' it were anythin' to do with that Shaun Shinton bloke, how'd he get Nick's address in Woolpit? You said you were only givin' out his parents' address in Barkin' Tye.'

'Hmm.'

'No, Damon. This aint fair. You got to say what you passed on.'

The look came again; the one with the drawn eyebrows and pursed lower lip followed by the eyebrow flicker, sideways head-tilt and a shrug.

Matt waited. He needed words. This was no place for ambiguity.

'OK, I'll tell you. I didn't give the Woolpit address. So either our client used the other details I'd given to find it, or this is nothing to do with him.'

'It's still weird, right? Who'd bother to cart them cream chargers all the way out there?'

'From Nick's text, I'd say you.'

'Well it aint.' He smoothed his tee-shirt across his belly. The worn cotton had once been white, but a decade of washes with his mixed coloureds had turned it a confused grey. The letters across its front and tatty sleeves were barely legible. What had once started out as **R.E.M.** and their album **OUT OF TIME** now looked more like P T V – OVE R TIME. And as for their megahit single **Losing My Religion** printed on both sleeves, well it could have said any number of things.

'Do you like R.E.M.? Is the tee one of your nineties collection?' Damon murmured as if changing the subject.

'Nah, it's me....' He wanted to say Maisie had bought it for him from the retro clothes shop where she worked, but it would have been a lie. It had been his older brother Tom's. The older brother he'd looked up to; the person who should have been a friend and father figure despite their seven-year age gap. But Tom had been a tease and a bully, even before their dad left home. And after he'd gone? Well Tom just got worse. The small scars on Matt's arm were a reminder.

'Nah, it's me brother's. Yeah, Tom left it behind when 'e moved out a few years back.'

'Well, I used to follow R.E.M. They're a great band. If I didn't know better I'd think your tee said **Using Nitrogen** on the sleeve.'

'Yeah - almost like in them cream chargers. Cool. But it don't mean I dumped any on Nick.'

Damon didn't comment but headed to his own desk and office chair. 'I've been thinking.' He leaned back against the faux leather and half closed his eyes.

'Yeah?'

'I think we should branch out a little. You know, do something related to what we're already doing, but with a different emphasis.'

'Branch out? Killer app!' So he was right. The Balcon & Mora leaflets, spread out like a fan on the waiting room table were an omen after all. 'Yeah, I'd guessed you were hatchin' somethin'. It aint a marketing drive, is it?'

'Family histories. People are interested. They'll pay to find out,' Damon announced.

'Cool.'

'And using some of the family history and genealogy websites could help our other searches.'

'Yeah, but aint you got to join some of them sites, first? And don't that mean payin'? I mean Balcon & Mora payin'?'

Damon sat more upright. 'True. So we need to do some initial research.'

'We?' Matt inwardly glowed. Happy.

'Yes, I reckon we see how far we get with the free sites. Then we'll know what we want from the paying ones. So how about some lunchtime fun? Have a go tracing your family history with the free stuff.'

'Yeah, but you said we. What'll you be doin' then?'

'I'll do mine as well. Now come on, I don't want us to spend too much time on this; there's paying work to finish this afternoon.'

Matt didn't feel a burning desire to research his relatives. He was curious, but his curiosity didn't stretch to his distant kin. He already knew of his mum, dad and older brother; his so-called nuclear family. He didn't need to look them up on a family tree. Their part in his life could be defined by their pervasive disinterest. Take his dad. Was it possible to show more disinterest than to leave when Matt was five? So wouldn't his more distant relatives be just that – even more distant and just as indifferent? It almost made him shudder.

No, the family kin he dreamed of were the superheroes in his comic-strip books. When he was eight he'd liked to imagine a grandfather who'd come from Krypton; what was to be gained by discovering he really came from Ipswich?

'But Damon, I don't 'ave to do me family, do I?'

'No, just choose anyone. A random name, but I think you'll need a date of birth. It's only to see how the site works.'

'Mega. So how's about doin' it the other way round? Usin' a date of birth and seein' if it fits the name? You know like that Toussaint bloke you guessed about?'

'The French name? Toussaint? I reckoned November 1st, didn't I?'

'Yeah, an' I reckon if he were 33 in the newspaper report this April, then....' Matt did the maths, 'then he'll 've been born in November 1980.'

He opened the free birth, marriage and death site *FreeBMD* and went straight to the search tab and chose *births*. He entered Grabb and settled for T as a first name, and after some thought selected the *phonetic search surnames* option. The rest he had to leave blank. He had no idea for *mother surname*, and as for *districts* and *counties*, he chose the *all* option.

Damon's voice butted into his thoughts, 'Hey, Matt – you do know don't you, that when the General Register Office records a birth, marriage or death, they record it on their index under the date the event was registered with them, not the actual date of the event. You need to allow for that in the *date range* boxes.'

'So what's the point of the FreeBMD site if it don't give you the actual date of birth?'

'It gives you the mother's name and the district and date where the birth was registered.'

'Yeah, but not the dad? And no addresses?'

'No, but it gives you the GRO volume and page number where the name is recorded on the GRO index.'

'And then I get to see what's on the birth certificate.'

'No it says on the blurb at the start you have to use the GRO site for that. We give them the name along with the GRO volume & page number so they can retrieve the birth certificate and copy it for us.'

'An' I bet they charge for doin' that, right?'

'Exactly.'

'Are you watchin' me search?'

'Yes, it's on my screen alongside my own search. Now put the date range in and click *find*.'

Matt wanted to object, but he was torn. Curiosity took the upper hand and he clicked *find*. 'Scammin' DOS! That were fast.'

'***Births Dec 1980:*** *Surname:* Grabb; *First name(s)*: Toussaint; *Mother*: Martin; *District*: Coventry; *Vol/Page*: 7 / 288,' Damon read out.

'Martin don't sound very French for his mum's surname,' Matt muttered.

'Well he can't be the other Ts: *Taya-Marie* Garbe, or *Thomas* Graff, or *Timothy* Grubb, can he?'

'S'pose not.'

'Right, let me check on the name Martin.' Damon tapped across his keyboard. 'There, I knew it. In France it's a very common surname. According to this it's based on a popular French saint; Saint Martin of Tours.'

'Another saint? Phishin' hell! His mum sounds like she got religion bad. So, any more we can find out 'bout Toussaint from the site?'

'We could try his mum's marriage certificate using Martin for her name and Grabb for his dad's. It might give us more details about his dad's full name.'

'OK, but we aint got their date of marriage so what you reckon I put in them date fields?'

'Leave them blank and see what happens?'

Matt couldn't believe his eyes, 'DOS-in' amazin'! We got three!'

'Well it's not going to be the marriage in 1881 or 1910. I'd go with the 1978 result. William C Grabb in the district of Coventry.'

'Cool. This is awesome. Let's try another name. How about....' He racked his brains trying to think of a name with a date of birth. 'Hey, I know. How about Gayle Corby?'

'Who's Gayle Corby?' Damon's voice sharpened.

'I s'pose you'd call her a kinda mate. I got her date of birth when I were helpin' her with the DVLA website on Saturday.'

'What?'

'She wants to ride a scooter but she's got to apply for a provisional drivin' license first.'

'Hey stop there a moment. Is she a client? Are the police after her? Don't tell me she's mixed up with Toussaint's death? You know you're like flypaper if there's someone dodgy out there?'

'Dunno about Gayle; didn't think to ask.'

Flypaper? It didn't sound like a compliment to Matt as he filled in the fields to search for Gayle's birth certificate index.

'Try putting her age in and leaving the years blank,' Damon said when the FreeBMD site found no results.

Again there were no search results.

'But I know her date of birth coz of helpin' her with her application on the DVLA site,' Matt moaned as he selected the *phonetic search surnames* option.

The phonetic search didn't throw up Gayle Corby.

'It may not be her real name, or at least not the name on her birth certificate,' Damon said, his voice losing its edge and gaining animation. 'She's starting to feel like a name we're tracing for one of our card clients. In fact it sounds like your flypaper effect.'

'Most of the one's we're tracin' just move to disappear. Do you reckon she done it by deed poll?'

'That'll mean the National Archives or the Royal Courts of Justice records. That's if she ever enrolled the deed poll. You could look on the Gazette website, it might be easier. Yeah, it'd be a project for you; design an app.'

'Really?' Matt wasn't sure about the flypaper analogy, but designing an app had street cred. Even the Utterly Computing & IT department would recognise it. He pulled his thoughts back on track. 'Most deed poll changes aint public, right? I read only 10% get enrolled an' even then some get blanked if it's a kid and the court deems 'em sensitive,' Matt murmured, remembering something he'd touched-on during his many hours of internet surfing.

'True.'

'And she aint got a passport. Otherwise the DVLA site would have used her passport mug shot for the photo card licence.'

'Interesting. Have you got a photo of her?'

'Maisie took a selfie with her on Saturday. Yeah, it were a nice one of Mais. She WhatsApp'd it to me.' Matt pulled out his mobile and opened WhatsApp.

'Nice shot,' Damon said when Matt pushed back his chair and lumbered over to show him. Gayle and Maisie filled Matt's phone's screen. 'Is Gayle the one with…?' Damon's voice trailed.

'Maisie's got the blonde hair with pink streaks. Gayle's kinda….'

'Mid-brown hair, I'd say. And blonde highlights. Lucky for us her hair is pulled back and we've a nice full front shot of her face. It shows her square jaw nicely.'

'Hey, but you aint doin' a Google reverse search usin' this photo. Gayle don't want it on the net.'

'I'm not going to post it, Matt. But if Gayle's used a previous name, it might come up with different names for this same face on a Google reverse search. I'll need to edit Maisie out of it first, of course.'

'I don't reckon Maisie'd like that.'

'She won't know and as I said, I'm not posting it up anywhere. Anyway, I'm not sure how reliably Google recognises the same face in different photos. It may only be able give us the exact same photo back.' Damon murmured.

Matt waited. His problem was that he'd read so much about facial recognition and the algorithms that he wasn't always sure what was currently available, what was in development and what was mere aspiration.

'Blog on, Damon! Look, Google's found a whole bunch of photos.'

'Hmm, they've given us five girls: Jade Formby, Roxanna Marshal, Cami Martin, Sarah Smith, and Eva Townsend. They're all facing the camera with a similar pose; no one's smiling and their hair is drawn back in the same kind of style. And young, they're pretty much the same age. They could all be related, until you look closely, and then you can see they're all different.'

'So, what d'you reckon?' Matt asked, confused by the identikit of faces.

'I'd say Google hasn't got it down to an exact science yet, but my eye is drawn to Cami Martin. Her jaw's the most like your Gayle Corby. And the name Martin jumps off the screen.'

'You mean she's another French bird?'

'Maybe, but Martin is also a very common English surname. She doesn't have to be a French Martin.'

'Yeah, but as you say, coincidence aint no coincidence when you're searchin'.'

'Exactly.'

'So now I reckon I should enter the name Cami Martin in the FreeBMD site. If her birth registration date is a match for Gayle's date of birth, then it could be her, right?'

'Except, time's up. We've real names to search and money to earn. It can wait till tomorrow.'

'Fraggin' hell!' Matt breathed, 'sometimes you're just phishin' unreasonable.'

CHAPTER 23

Monday was turning into a difficult day for Chrissie. It had been impossible to keep focused on work after leaving Nick. Her thoughts kept harking back on a continual loop - had Nick found anything more when he cleared up the cream chargers? Was he even safe? She'd told him she'd phone later, but would calling him reinforce his fears and fuel his anxiety? She wanted to call Clive, but Nick had said no.

She had hurried to the old barn workshop, keen to lose herself in work and nail down her inner turmoil. Mrs Dell's mishmash chairs with their Edwardian take on an earlier French style were going to save her. They had to. They would engage all her brainpower, the hours would fly by and Nick's problem would resolve. Or would it? Was he even safe? Oh God, back on the loop again.

She surveyed the scene. Mrs Dell's intact chair, the one brought along for reference, lay on her workbench, its intricate back panel ready to be traced. She was going to use it as a template so that she could make identical pieces to replace what was missing from the damaged chair's back panel. She had already sourced a suitable piece of mahogany from Ron's store, his collection of broken furniture set aside over the years for harvesting. But first she needed to check the thickness of the chair's back panel and then she'd pass her harvested mahogany through the thickness planer.

'Six millimetres,' she murmured.

'How's it going, Mrs Jax?' Ron said as he limped past with a rag and pot of stain.

'Early days, Mr Clegg. I know I'll need to re-glue where the joint has come loose just here.' She laid her hand on the damaged chair next to her and then ran her finger to one of the wooden bars connecting the back panel to the back's upright. 'I'm hoping I can do it without having to take half the chair apart.'

Ron smiled.

'What? Why are you smiling?'

'I was just remembering you talking about it to Mrs Dell; the classification tour through bedroom piece, Empire style, French neo-classical, Edwardian copy and finally - not a bedroom piece after all.'

'I know. Thanks for not saying anything. I'd have felt really stupid in front of Gayle.'

He nodded. 'You are allowed to say when you don't know. We'll have more idea once you've started working on it. People respect honesty too.'

It was her turn to smile. She liked his use of "we", as if he didn't know either, although she suspected he was on-ly saving her feelings.

By lunchtime she had planed her section of mahogany to an eight millimetre thickness; the extra couple of milli-metres would be enough to allow for sanding the wood smooth. She had traced the sections she needed to replace and had pasted the tracing paper onto her planed wood. The scroll saw was set with a new blade and she was ready to start on the intricate cutting. She should have been totally absorbed but instead she found herself listening for text alerts, or her mobile's sudden ring.

The call, when it came, was unexpected.

'Sarah?' she breathed when she saw the caller ID. 'Hi, Sarah. Is everything OK?'

'Since you ask; no. Everything is not all right. Did you know Nick was a bloody addict when you recommended him as a lodger?'

'What?'

'Not only is he an addict, he's made my home look like a vaping parlour... an Amsterdam coffee house with a drug dealer's back yard. He has to go. I want him out.'

'But Sarah–'

'Luckily there's someone else who can move in by the weekend.'

'But what about–'

'It's a complete coincidence of course, but Utterly Academy rang me an hour ago – I'm on their approved list to take lodgers and they wanted to know if I had a vacancy. It seems they've got a student who's desperate to move from her current lodging. I think you may know her. Goes by the name of Gayle Corby. I gather she's your apprentice.'

'What?'

'She doesn't like dogs. That's why she wants to move.'

'What?'

'So I'm calling to ask... and I know it doesn't mean a lot, judging by how wrong you got it about Nick, but is this one into drugs?'

'I don't... you can't–'

'Is she into drugs, Chrissie?'

'I don't' know, Sarah. But then I didn't know she doesn't like dogs.'

Chrissie stifled the words ready to slip from her tongue; the remonstrations, the calls for her friend to calm down. The truth was she'd had no idea Gayle was unhappy with her lodging. The girl, as Clive had said, was a closed book. The last she'd heard it was full steam ahead for a scooter and commuting independence.

'Hey Sarah. Sarah?'

Silence; Sarah had ended the call. The only sound was Ron's bench stool scraping back on the concrete floor as he stood up.

'Tea?' he asked.

'What?' she said, her thoughts elsewhere.

'Tea – I'm going to put the kettle on. It might be a good idea to have a break before you start on that fine scroll saw work.'

He was right of course, but she didn't want to hear it. The earlier restless loop of questions erupted in her mind. And as if that wasn't bad enough, a whole heap of new ones landed there as well. Loops upon loops; they could have been a spinning gyroscope, except nothing was holding steady.

'Did you know Gayle was unhappy with her lodging?' she asked, putting voice to a question flitting past.

'No, I can't say that I did.'

'Did you know she doesn't like dogs?'

'Dogs? I don't think she's ever talked about them. Why, has she been attacked by a dog?'

'I don't think so. It just seems… but if Gayle doesn't tell us, how are we supposed to know? We can't be expected to read her mind.'

'No… but slow down. And explain, Mrs Jax. I can't read your mind either, at least not before I've had my lunch.' He moved stiffly as he set out a couple of mugs and flicked the kettle on.

She took charge of making the tea. It was something to occupy her hands.

Ron appeared to focus on his lunch, as he unwrapped his customary white bread bap filled with thick cut ham. Chutney had escaped the layer and stained the side of the soft white bread with rivulets of grainy brown.

'I don't suppose you'd want a jar of Verity's pear chutney? Her tree had a bumper crop last year. It's been hard going trying to get through the extra jars.'

'Who's Verity?' Chrissie asked, momentarily distracted and curious.

'A neighbour – but she'll want her old jars back for this year's chutney.'

He sat and ate his bap while Chrissie perched on her bench stool and nursed her mug of tea. 'Aren't you going to eat anything?' Ron asked.

'I'm not hungry. I thought it was just my head churning, but Sarah's call has... well I've lost my appetite.'

Ron didn't say anything. She knew he was giving her space, waiting for her to explain in her own time and in her own way. And explain she must. He was Gayle's trainer too. But if Ron was to fully understand then she'd have to tell him about Nick's early morning call and the cream chargers. It was a confidence and she wasn't sure if Nick was ready for her to break it. Mind you, Ron was hardly the police.

She made a decision and took a deep breath. 'It started this morning, or rather, things probably started during the night,' she began.

He was a good listener, his eyes on her face while he sipped his tea. And calm; he didn't interrupt as her words kept rolling. Out it all came: the early morning call, the cream chargers, Shaun Shinton and the dredging firm, and finally Balcon & Mora and their client wanting information on Nick. By the time she finished, her mug was still full and her tea was lukewarm. 'So what do you say, Mr Clegg?'

She waited; the scent of linseed oil and wood dust pervasive, the age of the old barn weighing down, oppressive.

'Nick is a friend and of course you care, but he has to make his own decisions. How he squares this with Sarah is up to him.' He spoke slowly, his tone weary.

'She'd soon melt if he launched a charm offensive. Sarah's always had a bit of a soft spot for him.'

'Well, I'll take your word for it. But it begs the question, what has he got mixed up in? I don't imagine we have the full picture.'

'Do you think he could be in danger?'

'Why? Because someone asked Balcon & Mora to trace his details? Or because someone dumped… what did you call them? Ah yes cream chargers, outside his door? I'd say the chargers sound more like a prank.'

'Yes, and one that's about to get him chucked out of his lodging, unless….'

'You aren't responsible for him, Mrs Jax.'

'No but….'

'Gayle however is our responsibility, or rather her apprenticeship with us is our responsibility.'

'Yes, and I know things like her lodging aren't down to us, but don't you think we should have known she was unhappy?'

'Possibly. But we have tried to create a….'

'Supportive environment?

177

'Yes, certainly at work. It's up to her what she chooses to tell us.'

'That's what I thought, but… not happy with her lodgings? You'd think she'd have said, or I'd have noticed something.'

'She's good at keeping things close. I reckon she told the Academy while she's there today, Mrs Jax. Accept it and… well we shouldn't compensate by asking more questions.'

Chrissie caught the barb. He was saying what she'd said to herself often enough; she needed to curb her curiosity. And not interfere. Yes, *keep your nose out of it* was definitely part of his message. God, if only she could be a more passive person. She swigged back her cold tea.

CHAPTER 24

'You haven't said much today.'

'We've been busy, Dave. There hasn't been time,' Nick murmured.

They stood for a moment amidst the Monday bustle of the Willows & Son delivery area. In front of them, the wide roller shutter doors were open, giving them a view directly into the modern workshop with its large table saw, thickness planer, pillar drill and band saw. A myriad of tools and equipment filled space against the side walls, and looping above it all and close to the ceiling were the extraction pipes, worming their way to the cyclonic dust extraction unit.

Nick wasn't being strictly accurate about not having time to talk. Dave and he had briefly talked through how they were going to use the planks of western red cedar delivered that morning from Frosticks, their wood supplier. They had agreed which of the lengths of two-by-four cedar were to be cut to make the frame between the four-by-eight arched support beams that would span the moat; which pieces were to be cut into floor planks, handrails and rail posts. The curved support beams were to be laminated using a bending form which they would need to construct. Mr Coady's fancy arched bridge couldn't be transformed into reality without talking. It was just that today, there was no place for small talk.

Dave must have sensed it.

'You aren't usually as quiet at this,' Dave said, but then Dave hadn't known Nick as a kid. How could he have imagined the present-day 6'3" Nick as anything other than standing tall amongst his peer group? But Nick had been a small and weedy child before a growth spurt shot him to a height above the bullies. Quietness and solitude were a place he had learnt to escape to as a youngster. And today he needed to escape the bin liners packed with cream chargers.

They were stowed in his car boot. He could see them from where he stood, or rather he could see his blue Ford Fiesta parked the other side of the chain link fence; beyond the secure delivery area and alongside the protected parking for the Willows vans.

If he could sense the presence of the cream chargers, then surely it must be apparent to others. Worse still, his guilty secret must be written across his face. If he chatted with Dave it would be obvious he was hiding something. Sarah's brutal tirade had already infiltrated his mind with the accumulative ease of each hostile accusation. If he spoke, he knew he'd give himself away. And knowing it only seemed to tempt him in the way that a fear of heights might draw one over a precipice.

He groaned and headed back into the workshop.

'Aren't you going to stop for a cuppa?' Dave said, somewhere behind him.

'No, Dave. I think I'll get on with grooving and cutting the floor planks.'

The day passed quickly while Nick forced himself to concentrate on work. Each time Sarah's harsh words surfaced in his awareness, or the cream chargers muscled into his imagined eye line, his stomach lurched.

By four o'clock it was time to pack up and go home, except he wasn't sure where home was anymore. Who the hell had done this to him? And why?

He drove out to Woolpit, thinking all the way about the cream chargers a few feet behind in the boot. They clutched the back of his mind and however fast he drove he couldn't get away from them.

He saw the blue flashing lights in Sarah's driveway just as he slowed to turn in.

'Oh God, it's the police,' he breathed. His guts twisted and he drove on past. What the hell could he do? Cut and run to his parents' home in Barking Tye, the other side of Stowmarket? It would only be a matter of hours before they came looking for him there.

He pulled into the side of a road next to the village cricket pitch. Panic felt a single breath away. 'Hum... and think,' he told himself.

He didn't actually know the police were at Sarah's because of him. He feared it, but he couldn't be sure. And he couldn't keep running. If he was going to face this and get through it then he needed to act as natural, surprised and innocent as possible. But first he had to lose the cream chargers.

Fired with a plan he drove to Chrissie's end of terrace cottage. It was only a couple of minutes away. He was in luck; her car wasn't parked outside and nobody seemed to be around. After a glance up and down the lane, he opened his car boot and carried the bin liners along the short path to her front door. A trellis with fresh young honeysuckle leaves softened the brickwork on one side. He walked past it and then a couple more strides took him abreast the end wall. A section of rough hedge separated a strip of side garden from the handkerchief-sized front garden and lane. It was the ideal spot. He simply lifted the bin liners over the hedge and dropped them on the other side. It was done.

Back in his car he felt liberated. He was free of his burden; he could do this. Hum; keep humming. 'Think of it as a performance,' he whispered.

He drove back to Sarah's house, and this time indicated and turned slowly onto the gravel drive. A police car was parked at an angle in front of the double garage, its blue light still flashing. Was it an obstruction or a statement he wondered as he drew up to one side.

Nick got out of his Ford Fiesta and took a deep breath. He could do this, but only if he emotionally separated from it; he could act the performance.

A uniformed police constable stood talking to Sarah, her concertina skirt billowing in the light breeze.

'Hi, what's going on?' Nick asked.

The constable didn't answer, but Sarah let forth; 'It's a drugs bust!'

'What?'

'Some kind of anonymous tip off.'

'What? What do you mean, a "drugs bust"? Did you just say a "tip off"?'

'I'm not at liberty to say,' the constable said.

Nick sensed the staleness in the words; well-rehearsed but delivered with boredom.

'He says he's following up some lead. Something ridiculous like a warehouse full of drugs, no doubt. Apparently it's your room up there.' Sarah briefly jerked her head to indicate the platform at the top of the wooden steps.

Nick frowned. He wasn't acting now; he was genuinely puzzled. What the hell was Sarah doing? He'd assumed she was the one who'd called the police. Now she was all outrage and innocence. Was this a case of the pair of them versus the police? An attempt to protect her reputation in the village?

'Please would you give me your name, sir?' The constable's voice was even, his expression neutral.

'Nick Cowley. I'm Nick Cowley.'

'And is that your room? Up there above the garage?'

'Yes, I'm the lodger. Why?'

'Would you mind showing me?'

'I've kept telling him I won't show him without your say-so.' Sarah butted in.

'You want to see my room? But why?'

'We've had a complaint... an incident has been reported. I'm just following up on it. An initial response; a formality.'

'What kind of complaint? What kind of incident?'

'If you could just show me your room, please? It won't take a moment.'

'Don't you need a search warrant or something?'

'Not if you're showing me, but it's easy enough to come back with the paperwork.' His manner was mater-of-fact, unemotional. 'We get a lot of this kind of thing. It's a process, distinguishing the genuine from the hoaxers and malicious time-wasters. Why did you mention drugs just now?' His question was directed at Sarah.

'I just assumed.' She almost spat the words.

'And what makes you assume this is about drugs?'

'I-I don't know.'

'Perhaps if you wouldn't mind showing me?' the constable said and glanced up at the platform.

Nick led the way. Something told him the sooner this was done, the less likely things would escalate. He comforted himself with the thought that if this was about drugs, wouldn't there have been a pair of police constables and a sniffer dog at the very least? Oh God, what if the prankster had visited again?

In the event, it didn't take long. His room stretched above the garage and the ceiling sloped, following the pitch of the roof. It might look spacious, but it was an illusion. Three adults, Nick tall and Sarah in a concertina skirt, quickly made the room feel crowded. Nick watched the constable take a cursory look around the room, peer under the bed, glance into the cramped shower unit, flick the worn rug back with the toe of his shoe, pull open a couple of drawers and run his hand along the clothes hanging from a short rail.

'Thank you. Now if you wouldn't mind showing me the inside of your car and boot, please, Mr Cowley?' The constable flipped up the lid of a small bin near the basin as he spoke.

Once again Nick led the way. His car was already un-locked, but he opened the boot for inspection, and then lift-ed the flap in the floor to show where the spare tyre and jack were stowed. The constable seemed to lose interest.

'One last thing; I'd like to take a quick look in your waste bins, please. I think I saw them by the gate as I drove in.'

'Oh for God's sake,' Sarah murmured under her breath as they headed for the bins. She shot Nick a look of accusa-tion and blame. It was clear what she was thinking.

The bin check turned out to be unpleasant and pro-tracted. Nick stood and watched as the constable donned a pair of gloves and lifted each plastic bin liner out for Sarah to untie. He peered and rummaged inside. They went through the same routine for each bin: the landfill, recycling, garden waste and finally the trug for glass bottles.

'Good, thanks for your time and for co-operating,' he said as he peeled off his gloves.

Afterwards, after the constable and the flashing lights had gone, Nick faced Sarah.

'What the hell made you call the police?' he asked, his voice holding steady.

'I didn't.'

'Well somebody must have, and if you didn't, Sarah, who did? You'll have been gossiping, right?'

'No I haven't. This is all down to you.'

'That's crazy. Why would I want the police to come here? Don't you see? If you haven't told anyone, it can only be the person who dumped the laughing gas cream chargers outside my door in the first place. Who else would know about them?'

'You - it comes back to you, Nick.'

'No, I've already said. I don't do drugs or that kinda crap. Someone's done this to cause me a shitload of trouble.'

'You? Trouble? What about me? I feel so embarrassed. And humiliated – yes humiliated. It'll be all round Woolpit. They'll be saying *did you know Sarah was busted for drugs*? This is where it ends. I'm not prepared to go through this again. I want you gone.'

'What? But I haven't done anything. All I've done is clear up someone else's mess. Nitrous oxide isn't even illegal. They were only cream chargers, Sarah. Sarah?'

'I want you out by Saturday. You've got until the end of the week.'

'But Sarah–'

185

'I've got a new lodger moving in on Sunday.' She turned on her heel and walked back into the house.

CHAPTER 25

It was a little after six o'clock when Chrissie opened Nick's text message. It was still Monday and she was still in the Clegg & Jax workshop.

Her phone lay on the bench near the kettle and mugs. A new message banner lit up when she absentmindedly checked the phone as she cleared away. *Message sent 17:05. Nick.*

'What? Nick sent this an hour ago?' How could she have missed it? But then after her talk with Ron she'd been concentrating on the intricate scroll saw work and engrossed in starting the delicate carving. There wasn't time to feel guilt or anxiety. She opened his message.

Police came round to my place this pm - anonymous tip off. Nothing found (it's at your place now). Sarah kicked me out. Got till Saturday to move my things. What the hell's going on? Staying with Jake till I find somewhere.

'What? An anonymous tip off? A police search?' It took another reading before the implications of *it's at your place* also sank in.

'My place?' she gasped. 'It's all at my place?' And then a thought gelled in her mind. An unseen hand was playing Nick. He'd been well and truly set up. It was crazy, but how else could she explain it. Something rather calculating and malevolent was behind all this.

The sound of Ron's old van starting up in the courtyard broke into her thoughts and pulled her back to the practical. It was time to finish clearing away and lock up.

The lane running in front of 1 – 3 Albert Cottages was quiet when she arrived home and Clive's black Ford

Mondeo was parked opposite her front door. She drew up and jumped out, eyes scanning for any sign of Nick's bin liners or silver metal cream chargers. The road surface and gutters were clear. There was no black plastic or the glint of metal canisters in the shrubby rough hedge facing the terrace from across the lane. The short path to her door looked the same as when she'd left in the morning. So where had Nick put them, she wondered.

She opened the door with her latchkey half expecting to stumble over a couple of black plastic sacks, but her hallway was clear.

'Hi, Chrissie,' Clive called from the kitchen.

She slung her keys onto the narrow hall table as she passed.

'Have you been back long?'

'About five minutes. I'm just making myself a coffee. Do you want one?'

'Yes please,' She cast around the kitchen for tell-tale signs of Nick's laughing gas rubbish. Nothing. The scrubbed-pine kitchen table was neat and tidy with her closed laptop, and the work surfaces looked pretty much as she'd left them.

'Everything all right? Have you lost something?' Clive asked as he fiddled with the cafetière.

'No. You haven't moved any sacks of rubbish, have you?'

'Sacks of rubbish? No, why?'

'Nothing.'

'Nothing?'

'Well maybe something. Nick texted to say he'd left something round here.'

'What kind of something?'

'I'm not sure but I'd guess it'll be in black bin liners. You haven't chucked anything like that into our bins, have you?'

She watched Clive frown. He seemed genuinely puzzled.

'God, has someone taken them? Was he followed here?' she breathed.

'Taken what? Was who followed here? What's going on, Chrissie? You've got that look.'

'I-I'm not sure if I should say. It's not my....' It felt spooky.

'If this is about Nick, then... just tell me. Is this to do with what you said yesterday? Remember, about warning Nick to watch his back? Matt's tip off about Shaun Shinton, the dredging guy?' He stood facing her.

'Yes, and you said if a name keeps cropping up it has to mean something. Well Nick's isn't the only name. What about Shaun Shinton?' She knew the defiance showed in her voice, and as if to prove her point, she handed Clive her phone with the Nick's message.

Clive read it out; '*Police came round to my place this pm - anonymous tip off. Nothing found (it's at your place now). Sarah kicked me out. Got till Saturday to move my things. What the hell's going on? Staying with Jake till I find somewhere.*'

She waited for him to say something, make a comment, but instead he seemed happy to hang fire while he digested it.

She soldiered on, 'Matt referred to Shaun Shinton as the "mystery bloke", so I reckon if he can be Balcon & Mora's mystery bloke he could have also made the anonymous tip off to the police. The anonymous caller; right, Clive?'

'Now stop, Chrissie. First things first; what were you expecting to find round here? And what were the police tipped off about? I know you know because why else would you be talking about bin liners?'

She closed her mouth. Stubborn.

'Think about it, Chrissie. As soon as Nick dumped whatever it is round here, he involved us. And that includes me. If he's dragged me into it, then I have a right to know what the hell I've been dragged into. Do you understand?'

She nodded. But… if she could first find the stash of nitrous oxide canisters, then explaining would be so much easier. She closed her eyes and tried to imagine what Nick would have done. She put herself in his place: the door was locked; he was at the front of her cottage, No. 3. It was the end of the terrace. There was only one way he could have gone.

'Of course, I bet he's put it over our hedge!'

'What?'

She brushed past Clive and hurried through the hallway. Outside, she traced the front of her cottage to the end wall. A hedge separated her modest side garden from the front, and she stood on tiptoe and peered over. 'Yes!' she shouted to Clive, who stood at her front door.

She left it to Clive to go round into her side garden and retrieve two bulging black plastic bin liners. Back in the kitchen he stood them on the floor, his face expressionless.

'Wait, I'll put on my cleaning gloves to open them. I know there'll be cream chargers in there, but God knows what else Nick found when he cleared it all up.'

Her fingers were awkward in the heavy-duty rubber gloves as she untied the tops of the bags. She held each wide open in turn for Clive.

'Christ, Chrissie! What the hell? Is he dealing in these or something?'

She stared down at the sliding heap of canisters. 'Nick found this lot tipped all over the platform and staircase outside his room this morning. Or rather Sarah found a load of them strewn across the driveway when she was leaving for work.'

'What? I assume they're his,' Clive muttered.

'No; he says they're not and I believe him.'

'But if they're not his, whose are they?'

'I don't know.'

'So you're saying someone else left them there? Why? Why would anyone want to chuck this lot around outside Nick's place?'

'I don't know, but it didn't stop there, did it? What about the anonymous tip off to the police? Someone wanted to cause him a lot of trouble. What if it's related to this spate of nitrous oxide deaths? I wouldn't be surprised if some of the canisters have been tampered with, you know – to try and point a finger at Nick.'

'But why assume whoever dumped them round Nick's also called the police? What about Sarah? She could have been the one to call the police, Chrissie.'

'No, Clive. I know Sarah, at least I thought I knew Sarah… but even she wouldn't have wanted the police round to teach Nick a lesson.'

'So what do you suggest we do with this lot now?'

'I don't know. But I'm worried about Nick. You could at least start by finding out who the anonymous tip off was from.'

'But it was anonymous, Chrissie. That's the whole point.'

'Yes, but aren't all calls recorded? You'll be able to find out the number the call was made from, along with the time. And also if it was Shaun Shinton's voice, right?'

'Yes but–'

'And the one thing the person who did this doesn't know, is that Nick's prints won't be on any of the stuff other than maybe the outside of the bags. I told him to wear gloves when he tidied up the mess. If he's telling the truth, there won't be any of his prints on the canisters.'

'What d'you mean, you told him to wear gloves? When was this?'

'He called me this morning before I'd left Woolpit for work. I dropped by; saw all the drama.'

'For God's sake, Chrissie. Now you're telling me. Why couldn't you have said that at the start?'

'Because just before I got home I'd only just read Nick's message about him dumping the stuff round here. And then I couldn't find it, remember?'

'OK, but are you now suggesting I turn this in as evidence? Forensics will take weeks to examine it. There must be hundreds of canisters in here.'

'But if they've been tampered with it could be vital evidence. People are dying out there from nitrous oxide.'

'Hmm, I suppose… yes, I could hand them in. Hmm… organised crime or log it under the Jon and Toussaint murders?' Clive frowned.

The smell of fresh coffee filled the kitchen and with it a perverse sense of homeliness and normality descended. Chrissie felt calmer but it was clear from Clive's face that he was still struggling with it.

'Well, while you chew over which department picks up the bill, I think we need a drink as well as coffee. Then I suggest we tip all the stuff into new bin liners. That way we'll definitely keep Nick's prints out of this, right?' Chrissie reasoned.

'No, I think we'll decant the stuff into fresh bin liners now, before you start drinking wine, Chrissie.'

She laughed. He seemed to have lightened up a little, judging by the way he stood with his back more relaxed and the tension gone from his shoulders.

Transferring the contents from Nick's bin liners turned out to be straightforward. Chrissie pulled a couple of black plastic ones off the roll she kept in the cupboard under the sink, and still wearing the heavy-duty gloves, held the new bin liners while Clive tipped the contents in.

'What about the sealed plastic bags amongst this lot?' Clive asked.

'Cut the knots and tip the stuff in with everything else – he won't have touched what's inside them.' She watched as Clive shook out crushed and torn packaging. It tumbled into the sack. '*144 Cream Chargers*,' she read out, squinting at bold black letters printed across the larger pieces of grubby white card.

While Clive took the new bin liners outside to stow in his car boot, Chrissie carried a tray with coffee, a beer and a glass of wine through to the cosy living room. She was happily ensconced on the sofa by the time she heard Clive's footsteps returning along the hallway.

'Sorry, I haven't asked how your day went,' she said as he sat down beside her.

'Well, some of Jon Dareham's toxicology tests are back at last.'

'That's good. Any surprises or just high levels of nitrous oxide as you expected?'

'Yes, the same as Toussaint, the nitrous oxide level in his brain and other tissue was way up here,' Clive said, holding up his hand as if marking a level above his head. 'The surprise with Jon is that he had fentanyl in his system as well.'

'Fentanyl? I've heard of it but I can't think why.'

'It's a fast-acting narcotic. Intravenous drug users shoot up with it. Trouble is they kill themselves because of the lethal combination of strength with rapid effect. The pathologist tells me it's been around a long time for anaesthetic use but now it's on the street it's a killer.'

'So Jon liked fine art and fast drugs.'

'I don't know about the fast drugs. The pathologist was surprised because there were no needle tracks or signs of injection sites.'

'Perhaps he just swallowed it?'

'It doesn't work if you do that. Apparently you can absorb it through your skin using a skin patch, or a tablet under your tongue or even stuck to the inside of your cheek. But there wasn't any sign of that. But remember I told you Jon Dareham had some fresh blood in his nose? Now the pathologist wonders if the fentanyl was administered as a nasal spray. They're looking into it.'

'A nasal spray? Like a hay fever spray?'

'Yes, but with fentanyl in it. The nasal sprays aren't as easy to get hold of as the fentanyl skin patches, but apparently it's absorbed much faster, so – a quick squirt or two up the nose and whoosh – a woozy compliant Jon Dareham is led happily to the tumble dryer.'

'So you don't think Jon sprayed it up his own nose?'

'We'll have to wait and see what the pathologist finds. Lucky for us, they haven't released his body yet, so I expect they'll take a closer look inside his nose.'

'And how does that add anything to what you already know? I mean... you already knew he'd been murdered... both Jon and Toussaint were murdered.'

'It opens up more possibilities, Chrissie. It only needed one person to kill him and the killer didn't need to be big or strong; someone just needed to get close enough to spray something up his nose.'

'Someone he knew?'

'It's the most likely. You can see how it starts to build a picture; how it could be the breakthrough moment in the case for me. It has to be the clue the killer didn't think they'd left behind. Things like this are... well it's the moment that gives me a buzz. It's what being a detective is about. That moment when you know they've slipped up and you're going to get them.'

'Aww, that's wonderful, Clive.' She gave him a hug and kissed him. 'It's difficult to imagine how a nose bleed could be a defining moment. There's more wine in the fridge if you'd like a glass, as well as your beer.'

'Coffee, beer and then wine, eh, Chrissie?'

'I know, and it's still only Monday.'

CHAPTER 26

Matt braked gently and turned into the Utterly Academy main entrance. His Vespa smoothed to just above idling speed as he headed for the student and staff car parks. It was Thursday and the morning light seemed to enhance the red chequered pattern running through the pale Suffolk brickwork of the main building, the old Utterly Mansion.

For once, he wasn't filled with his usual excitement and anticipation. Yes, it was Thursday morning and so he'd be spending it assisting the students in the computer lab, but somehow even the prospect of eating in the canteen after-wards or a making a visit to the library didn't raise his spir-its. Today he felt burdened. He didn't like the conundrum he was carrying in his head about Gayle Corby.

She might not have a scooter yet, but he'd said he'd help her look for one. It made her a scootering mate; his first scootering mate. So what, if she'd changed her name?

Would it matter if he discovered Cami Martin, the girl with a face most like Gayle's, had a date of birth registra-tion compatible with Gayle's date of birth? Should he wor-ry because he couldn't find any record of a Gayle Corby's birth registration? It didn't prove Gayle and Cami were one and the same bird. He'd first have to request a copy of Cami Martin's birth certificate from the General Register Office. But what if Cami was a shortening for Camille, or a myriad of other first names beginning with the letters CAM on a birth certificate? He could end up making, not just one, but several requests. If it was going to cost him money, he wasn't going to do it.

Damon hadn't appeared overly surprised or inquisitive when Matt talked about it at the end of their busy Monday at Balcon & Mora. By then Matt had finished the paying work, as Damon called it, and wanted to slip back onto the BMD website.

'What do you expect? You tell me she's been relocated from Leicester. It follows she might have changed her name as well,' Damon had said.

'But why'd she relocate?' Matt had asked.

'As long as neither Cami Martin, nor Gayle Corby is on our clients' lists for contact details, then it's none of our business.'

'Yeah, but Damon, aint you even curious?'

'The poor girl's probably been trolled or bullied. So, as I said – as long as it isn't about card repayment debt to our clients, which it doesn't appear to be – then I'm not interested. Not at the end of a long Monday.'

And so it had been left to moulder in Matt's head. But of course it wasn't just the small matter of Gayle's name change; he'd also had a call from Nick to say he was temporarily staying with Jake.

'Sarah's chucked me out because of the cream chargers. Now, Sarah's found another lodger. I reckon it's Gayle, Chrissie's apprentice. Are you sure you didn't have anything to do with dumping the chargers round my place? Some kind of crass joke?' Nick had said.

'Bloggin' Trojan! Course it weren't nothin' to do with me,' he'd said, but it had unsettled him. And it was Gayle again. Her name kept cropping up.

Matt dragged his mind back to the here and now, stowed his helmet, and chained the Vespa to a bike stand. He sauntered past the parked cars, his backpack slung across one shoulder, and headed to the modern front entrance. Massive glass doors in a square glass porch gave a contemporary feel to the three-storey Edwardian façade. He stepped into the entrance hall, the elegance of the pale marble floor momentarily transporting him to his imagined Italy and the Motherland of his Vespa. He glanced at the imposing staircase leading to the first floor. Should he head straight up to the student accommodation office and ask about accommodation available on the Academy's approved list? He was sure he could swing it to find out how Gayle came to be the one who was offered Nick's lodging.

He fingered the ID card hanging around his neck; the one with his mug shot and *Matt Finch, Assistant Demonstrator, Computing & IT Department* printed across it. Should he go directly to the computer lab instead of the admin floor? If he was serious about developing the app, as suggested by Damon, then he'd need to talk it over with Mr Smith, the head of the department. But the whole trigger for the app had been Gayle and the difficulties of tracing deed poll registrations.

She'd done it again. Gayle's name had come up, churning the conundrum in his head. But he needed to make a decision right now, while he was still at the foot of the staircase. Should he go straight up the stairs to the admin floor, or should he thread along the ground level corridors and out to the computer lab?

'Hi, Matt. You're looking very thoughtful.' Rosie's voice caught him by surprise.

'Hey Rosie! I didn't see you comin' in.' It was hardly the slick greeting he would have prepared for his favourite library assistant.

'The stairs aren't going to bite you,' she said, brushing past him.

'N-no, I know that, Rosie. I-I were thinkin' if it were worth goin' up to admin. Don't know if anyone'll be there yet.'

'I came on the bus and I'm pretty sure I saw Glynnis coming in through this door when my bus drew in. I guess she must've walked past you and you didn't notice. I reckon you'll find her in the office by now.'

A group of students meandered in, untidy with backpacks. They moved like a loose herd towards the main stairs and headed up to the canteen on the first floor. The movement drew Matt with them, his 'N-no, I'd've noticed Glynnis if she'd…' was lost in the hustle and effort of climbing the stairs.

By the time he'd reached the first floor, Rosie had disappeared. He toyed with the idea of following her into the library, but thought better of it and lumbered up the smaller staircase to the second floor.

The door to the main admin office was open.

'Hiya,' he said hopefully and walked in.

Glynnis stood at a bank of filing cabinets along one wall. One of the drawers was open and she looked briefly at Matt, before turning her attention back to the drawer. She extracted a slim file and pushed the drawer closed with her hip.

'It's Matt isn't it?' she said.

'Yeah.' He reckoned she was in her mid to late twenties, and her pink fashion-statement glasses made her look schoolmarmish.

She walked over towards him and put the file on her desk. Her pink nail varnish was a couple of shades darker than her fashion-statement frames; less schoolmarm, more sex kitten. Mixed messages. Matt felt confused.

'I'm l-lookin' for somewhere in Woolpit,' he stammered.

'What do you mean, looking for somewhere? I'm not a Google map, you know.'

'No-no… I meant to say I'm l-lookin' for somewhere to stay in Woolpit. You know, a flat or as a lodger.'

'Ah right, I've got you now. You need the accommodation officer. She should be here in a moment.'

The open plan office felt hot and claustrophobic. 'I can come back,' he mumbled, his mind filled with the lure of the canteen, only one floor below.

'No, Deidre really will be here; in fact, here she is now.'

A middle-aged woman with short chestnut hair strode in.

'H-hi, Deidre. I was askin' Glynnis here about accommodation in Woolpit.'

'In Woolpit? Give me just a moment and I'll have a look.' She sounded slightly breathless.

He felt her focus on his ID card hanging from his neck. He dropped his gaze and concentrated on the scuff marking her white leather trainer. Her foot moved but he kept his eyes on the ground while she settled at her desk and signed in to her computer. She spoke as she clicked on menu options and scrolled through lists.

'Let me see… yes, Stowmarket… here we are, Woolpit. Now what have we on the list in Woolpit?'

He looked up, transported to his childhood; a kid handing in copied schoolwork. He shifted his weight from one foot to the other. Why hadn't he simply phoned the accommodation number? That way neither of them could have read each other's face. It would have evened the odds for him.

'You're the second person this week asking for Woolpit, and it's still only Thursday.' Deidre appeared to be addressing the screen, narrowing her eyes as she read.

'Crazy,' he murmured. 'See the thing is, Deidre I reckon... yeah it's called Spice House, a place with a room over the garage. See, that'd be OK for me.'

'The other person asking was interested in Spice House as well. Funny how word gets round. Sarah the landlady sounded nice when I spoke to her on Monday.'

'Yeah, well I only know about it coz I were talkin' to Nick, the current lodger. But how else I s'posed to know? How'd this other person get to hear it were available?'

'I don't know. She asked me about it, so I phoned the landlady. It had literally just become available.'

'So this student, is she takin' it? Coz if she aint, then I got a chance, yeah?'

Deidre frowned and pursed her lips by way of an answer.

'Aint she got back to you, Deidre?'

'It was only three days ago. Too soon for me to follow up on.'

'But you can call Sarah now. Tell her there's me interested. You can do that for me, yeah?'

'Yes, but she, I mean the student, was having problems with her current place. She seemed distressed. I don't want to put any pressure on her.'

He waited. Matt knew using silence on a Balcon & Mora call-phishing exercise didn't work, but on a face to face, silence got results.

Glynnis's voice sounded to one side of him, 'Did you say Nick told you? Did you mean Nick Cowley? The Nick who sings in a band? Tall bloke, nice smile. He's cool.'

'Yeah.'

'Maybe he told her as well? She probably fancies him.'

'Well that don't make sense, Glynnis. If she fancies him, then why'd she want to move in if he's movin' out?'

'I don't know. I guess if she's a fan, it'd be like collecting memorabilia. Imagine sleeping in Ed Sheeran's old bed?'

Matt opened his mouth, realised he'd lost the thread of what she was saying, and waited.

'Hmm,' she sighed.

'Well if she don't like her current lodgin', aint she got no home to go to?' Matt said, hoping to bring the talk onto something more solid.

'She's not from Suffolk,' Deidre said, her voice taking control.

'Norfolk then?

'Look, if someone chooses Utterly Academy, and comes all the way from Leicester, then the least I can do is get their accommodation right for them.'

'Don't she like Leicester then? Why'd she want to come all this way?'

'I didn't ask.'

'You were sayin' it could be coz she fancies Nick?'

'No, Glynnis said... hey look, I don't know why she moved from Leicester. So how about you? Why do you want to live in Woolpit?'

He'd guessed she'd ask. It was his moment; 'Well, I been distressed as well. It's what livin' at home done to me.

Real pressure; like crushin' me. And there's a cricket pitch in Woolpit. I wanna play cricket.' He paused, conscious of Deidre looking at his paunched stocky physique.

Seconds passed before she said, 'I think… yes, she said she's allergic to dogs. And there's a dog where she's staying. That's right… hay fever and dust; she's got lots of allergies, she said.'

'Well I don't mind dogs. What about where she's been stayin'? I could move in there.'

'Ye-e-s, except it isn't Woolpit. You wanted Woolpit. You said you play cricket.'

'Nah, I said I wanna play cricket. Look Deidre, I'm real distressed. Anywhere'd be better than Tumble Weed Drive.'

'Ah, Tumble Weed Drive. I suppose I could put you in touch with the landlady, but I'll need to find out from the student first. You know it's a room in central Stowmarket? If central Stowmarket is ok, there are other properties on our list.'

'Nah, I'd prefer Woolpit.'

It was left with Deidre to get back to Matt once she'd made a few calls.

He mulled over the allergy thing as he shambled down the staircase. He didn't remember a red-eyed Gayle sneezing or talking as if her nose was blocked. She'd hopped up behind him on his Vespa without a word about hay fever. There'd been no request to avoid riding past the flowering rapeseed fields or the hedgerows filled with blossoming hawthorn. And if she was allergic, how did she cope with the dust and wood dust in the old barn workshop? Surely Chrissie would have mentioned by now if Gayle was constantly having to wear a breathing mask, or sneezing and coughing and wheezing? There was dust extraction for the various power tools and ventilation if the doors were left open, but Chrissie would have said if there'd been an allergy.

'Has to be like me sayin' I wanna play cricket,' he muttered.

•••

By early afternoon Matt was safely ensconced in the Academy library. He had chosen his favourite computer station near the wall; a vantage point giving him a clear view of the door, photocopiers and the library assistant's desk. Old wooden floorboards stretched the length of the room and if he cared to look upwards, gothic styled beams spanned the high ceiling. The smell of wood, books and printer ink tickled his nose while daylight streamed in through tall windows. A handful of students worked at tables with tablets and laptops while others had taken up residence at the computer stations.

Matt pulled his focus back to his screen. He'd held off for as long as he could, but curiosity had finally got the better of him. He opened the FreeBMD site, clicked *births* in the search tab option and entered Martin as the surname and C for the given name. He chose Leicestershire for *counties*. He left the *mother surname* blank but put the *date range* for a six-month period after Gayle's birthday, nineteen years ago. There was no match recorded. He widened the search to the *all* option for *districts* and *counties*.

'Yeah, a result! Recorded **Births Sep 1995**: *Surname*: Martin; *Given Name(s)*: Camille; *Mother*: Vern; *District*: Coventry.'

He'd expected Leicester. But Coventry was only 26 miles from Leicester. It was pretty much the same distance as between Bury St Edmunds and Ipswich, about thirty minutes via the A14 on his 125cc Vespa, if he stepped on it a bit. Not very far. If Gayle said she was from Leicester, she could easily have been born in Coventry and subsequently moved to Leicester. She could still be Camille Martin, or Camy for short.

The poor girl's probably been trolled or bullied.

Damon's words echoed in Matt's head. But trolling would have played out on social media sites and if she'd changed her name to escape, she'd have also closed her accounts. It was a no brainer. And anyway, there were literally hundreds of Camille Martins on Facebook. He figured he'd give the social media sites a miss, at least to begin with. He needed to narrow his search.

'Scammin' dongle! What about the local news rags?'

It didn't take him long to discover the Coventry Tribune and Leicester Times. He reckoned they would be good sources to mine. Minutes stretched into an hour as he scrolled through date parameters along with name combinations. He'd got back as far as 2007 before he sensed he was onto something.

'Hi, Matt.'

'Hey Rosie! I didn't see you comin'.'

Inwardly he winced. DOS-in' hell, he'd said the same thing when he'd seen her in the entrance hall earlier that day. And here she was again, her pale rust-coloured blouse worn like a short tunic over slim-fit cropped jeans. He tried to turn his attention back to the screen.

'I'm starting to think I'm invisible.'

'No. No, Rosie you aint. Honest you aint.'

'So what are you so interested in?' She stepped closer and peered at the screen. Stands of auburn hair had escaped from her loose ponytail. '*Horror for Twelve-Year-Old Girl Trapped with Dead Father for Whole Weekend*. Wooah – what are you looking at, Matt? That's heavy.'

'I only just found it. Aint really read it yet.'

'*Yesterday, young mother Sippy Martin arrived home from a weekend away to find husband Gaspard Martin dead upstairs in their bedroom. Their twelve-year-old daughter had been locked in the house. "If I hadn't had my key on me, we'd have had to break the door down," said a tearful Mrs Martin.* Where'ds this happen, Matt? Stowmarket?'

'Nah, Coventry. And it were in 2007.'

'What?' Rosie continued reading from the screen; '*No one else was found in the house. The family, according to a neighbour, is already known to Social Services. The girl was led away in shock. Her mother said that she didn't appear to know that Daddy was dead. Mrs Martin said her husband didn't suffer from depression and had seemed normal when she'd left on Saturday morning. The police are treating Mr Martin's death as unexplained. The case has been initially referred to the coroner.* That's kind of spooky, Matt.'

'Yeah, fraggin' horrible.'

'So what happened? Was it an overdose?'

'I don't know, Rosie. I only just found it. I got to track it through on the local news site first.'

'Wooah, I can see how people-tracing work is interesting.'

'I aint people tracin'.' His skin flamed underneath his beard.

'This isn't anything to do with any students here is it? You know they're strictly off limits. You could get yourself chucked out.'

'Yeah, Rosie. I know. But how can Gaspard Martin, a stiff discovered seven years ago in Coventry be anythin' to do with students we got here now?' Matt hoped he sounded confident, but blog Almighty, Gaspard and Sippy's daughter had better not be called Camille. It didn't bear thinking.

'Well Matt, I finish here at four o'clock and my bus is at twenty past. So, if you've got an end to this story, tell me before I leave. I usually pick up a quick coffee from the machine in the canteen on my way to the bus stop.' She turned on her heel and pushed a book trolley over to a bank of bookcases.

He watched her, distracted for a moment. Rosie looked closer to thirty than twenty, and had always had this confusing skin-flaming effect on him. Had he just received an invitation to join her for a coffee? Was *I didn't see you comin'* a slicker opening than he'd thought? He had no idea.

Back on the Coventry newspaper site Matt found what he was looking for. It was dated three months after the piece announcing the discovery of Gaspard Martin's dead body, locked inside the family home with his daughter.

'Yeah, the report of the coroner's hearin',' he muttered.

Part of it had been held in open session to the public and the rest had not, complete with reporting restrictions. It made it difficult for Matt to get his head around all the facts. Some he had to guess, such as the reason for the reporting restrictions and closed session.

'So *Gaspard Martin's death was unnatural and unexpected*. That's like sayin' he were killed.'

Matt read on: *the post-mortem tests found raised blood alcohol levels along with 19.4mg of propranolol per litre of blood in Mr Martin's system. The pathologist explained that propranolol is a prescription drug belonging to a group called beta blockers, and blood levels of propranolol above 4 mg per litre can be fatal. The overdose slowed Mr Martin's heart and lowered his blood pressure to a level sufficient to kill him. The family doctor said that propranolol is used in the treatment of various heart and circulatory conditions, tremors and other problems such as controlling migraine. However, Mr Martin wasn't known to have suffered from any of these conditions and hadn't been prescribed propranolol. Mrs Martin confirmed that he didn't take any regular medications.*

So where'd he get hold of the stuff, Matt wondered.

Mr Martin's father-in-law Mr Vern told the coroner that his propranolol tablets had gone missing a couple of weeks before Mr Martin died. He had no idea where the tablets could have got to but said he thought it was unlikely his son-in-law Mr Martin had acquired them, as he never visited. When asked if his daughter and granddaughter visited, he said yes, his granddaughter always came for tea after school and stayed for a couple of hours until his daughter Sippy collected her after work.

Detective Inspector Oaklands reported that 2 empty blister packs of propranolol tablets were found in Mr and Mrs Martin's kitchen waste bin along with an empty carton labelled with Mr Vern's prescription details. A child's chemistry set and pestle and mortar were also found in the kitchen and testing identified traces of propranolol on the pestle and mortar and in a test tube from the set. DI Oak-land confirmed that the front and back door had been locked from the inside and the keys were found in Mr Mar-tin's trouser pocket.

Both Mrs Martin and the police said that no note from Mr Martin has been found in the bedroom or the rest of the house. Mrs Martin told the coroner that she did not believe her husband was depressed or suicidal.

Further evidence from the police, social services, fam-ily doctor, paediatrician, child psychologist, Mrs Martin, and her daughter was heard in closed session. The coroner ordered reporting restrictions.

'Blog Almighty!' Matt breathed.

He caught Rosie's voice from across the library ex-plaining something to a student by the photocopier. For a moment he watched her, his eyes not seeing as his brain sorted and juggled the public access part of the coroner's report.

Rosie looked up, smiled and walked over. 'How did the story end, Matt?'

'Oh hi, Rosie. Yeah, how'd it end? I were goin' to say, weren't I?'

'Well?'

'It don't say, but I s'pect his wife done it... or his daughter. But see, that bit were heard in secret.'

'Secret? Then it probably means... well they do that when kids are involved. Was the wife charged with any-thing?'

'It don't say.'

'Hmm.' Rosie nodded slowly and walked back to the library assistant's station.

What the blog did Rosie mean by that, Matt wondered.

CHAPTER 27

Nick felt exhausted, both physically and mentally. Thank God it's Friday, he thought; the end of a busy week. He'd spent it drinking and composing with Jake late into the evenings, sleeping fitfully on a put-you-up bed, and knuckling down at Willows & Son to make Victor Coady's footbridge. But he reckoned it was the injustice of being kicked out by Sarah that had really got under his skin and drained him.

He banged the side of the Willows van as a signal to Dave. He'd loaded the post-hole digger and bags of concrete mix. He'd also put in the steel rods they'd use to reinforce the concrete and hold the two support beams when they spanned the moat. The doors were securely closed. 'Yeah, ready to roll,' he shouted, and stepped up to the passenger seat. It was time to drive over to the moated farmhouse near Eye and put in the specially designed concrete posts as footings to hold and rest the bridge on.

'You've been a moody bugger all week,' Dave muttered, 'Let's hope you find your bonhomie once you're outside and working in some fresh air.'

'Bon-om-ee? We're not crossing the bloody English Channel to Calais are we?'

'Ha, that's more like it. So what the hell's been going on, Nick?'

Dave revved the engine, let the clutch in with a jolt and accelerated out of the Willows & Son loading bay. The van lurched as they turned onto the road taking them under the low railway bridge near Needham Market.

'So what's wrong, Nick? Aren't you going to say? Has the devil got your tongue?'

'Why d'you always ask questions just as you slam the van into gear?'

'Still a bit tetchy then,' Dave murmured.

'*Slam into gear*,' Nick echoed sensing the rhythm of the lurch and the road.

The words joined lyrics hiding in his head. *Don't scream in my ear* surfaced minutes later as Dave steered out of a roundabout and joined the A140.

'I've been writing songs with Jake,' Nick explained. He didn't bother to say their latest working title was Early Monday Hello, the words conjured by Sarah's angry face and furious rant on Monday. Dave didn't need to know all the details behind why he was staying with Jake while he cleared his room over Sarah's garage. Any mention of the cream chargers was bound to be misunderstood. He leaned forwards and switched on the van's radio.

OneRepublic's hit record Counting Stars filled the cab.

'This is catchy,' Dave said and started to hum along.

'Yeah, they're an American band. Pop rock… or you could say folk pop with a disco beat.' Nick's mind flicked to the music video. Wasn't there a crocodile crawling through the basement of a house in it?

The music filled the space and took away the need for further small talk. Dave drove and Nick settled into his own thoughts, but a newsreader's voice soon brought him back.

And finally a very rare gold aestel believed to date from the mid-9th century and dubbed the Dunwich Jewel has been discovered for sale on an internet auction site. It is claimed to have been found last year in Suffolk near

Greyfriars, the ruined Franciscan priory close to Dunwich. A sharp-eyed expert from the British Museum Antiquities Department became suspicious when a record of treasure declaration and validation along with the findspot grid reference could not be found. The police have been informed. And now for the weather....

'What's an aestel?' Dave asked.

Before Nick could answer *how the hell would I know*, the eight o'clock voice for the BBC Radio Suffolk morning programme drifted across. *Thank you to the listener who has just texted in after the news and asked, "What is an aestel?" Well, someone's handed me the description to share with you. An aestel is something used by a monk or holy person. It's a kind of gold pointer to go on the tip of a wooden cane, or walrus ivory or even perhaps a finger. It was used to point at holy texts or manuscripts without touching them. Wow, it's a 9th century equivalent to a cursor or latex glove.*

'Isn't Dunwich where that bloke who died, lived?' Dave said, cutting across the presenter's voice.

'What are you on about, Dave?'

'Tuscan, or Toussaint or whatever he called himself. His boyfriend or partner, or whatever he liked to refer to him as, lived in Dunwich. He dealt in fine goods. And he's dead.'

'So what? It doesn't make him connected with this astebel thing on the news.'

'Aestel. It's an aestel, Nick. I reckon I'll ask Shaun. He'll likely be tidying up round the moat. I know the dredging's supposed to be finished by today but the last of their equipment will still need to be collected and trailered away.'

'Yeah but why ask Shaun about the thing on the news?'

'Because I expect dredging and metal detecting are similar and are both small worlds. He'll know about undeclared treasure. Word like that gets around. Ear to the ground and all that.'

'Hmm. Shaun always makes me feel uncomfortable.'

'Why's that then?'

'I don't know. It's like he's saying one thing and meaning something different.'

'What? You think he fancies you?'

'No, nothing like that. It's just that he makes me feel kinda wary, on my guard.' Nick wasn't going to say Chrissie had told him to watch his back.

The rest of the journey was filled with the radio. It seemed the aestel had generated huge interest. *And we have another call from a listener. So, Jim, you don't think it could be associated with the Franciscan Priory at Dunwich because the aestel predates the priory by about 400 years?*

A different voice drifted from the radio, *"Yes, we're talking 1277 or 1290 for the construction of the priory. The aestel dates around 850. There's no reference to a sacred building being there back in the 9th century."*

'It sounds from the radio like it wasn't really found near the priory,' Dave said as he turned onto the winding gravel driveway to the moated farmhouse, 'I wonder where it was found.'

'Or stolen,' Nicked added.

'Yeah, as you say, or stolen. I bet all this Dunwich Jewel stuff is just to cook up a spoof provenance.'

'Do you think the astebel is a fake, then?'

'Aestel, Nick. It's an aestel. Hey, isn't that Shaun's Toyota Land Cruiser parked ahead?'

'Yeah. Let's edge off the drive just here, then we won't have to carry everything so far.' It also meant they wouldn't have to keep walking past Shaun's black Toyota, but Nick wasn't going to say that.

Dave pulled off the driveway and Nick opened the van doors. 'What d'you reckon? We make the footing holes on this side and concrete them in before we start on the other side of the moat, or do we dig all four first?'

'No, Nick. We'll dig all the holes first. Get the depths and heights right with the form tubes and then concrete each in turn.'

'Right. Lucky I remembered the laser leveller, then.' He unloaded the long carpenter's spirit level and digital measurer along with the mallet and stakes to mark where to dig each footing.

Nick, being the tallest, landed the job of working the petrol engine post-hole drill. It took longer than he'd expected to bore each of the four holes with an 8-inch bit, but with Dave's help they had then enlarged and deepened them with a handheld post auger and spades. The four finished holes were sizeable; they had 10-inch diameters and were twenty-four inches deep.

Nick was pleased to stop for lunch. He sat with Dave in the front of the van, the doors open and a light breeze cooling him while they ate. He gulped more bottled water and took another bite of his ploughman's sandwich.

He gazed across the rough grass at the bush-like hazel bordering the moat. Already the elm had shot tall, and the hawthorn dominated the spotlight with its blocks of white scented blossom. Nature hadn't stood still, not even for the few weeks since he'd first come to the moated farmhouse.

'Uh oh, I wonder what he wants,' Nick murmured mid chew as he caught sight of Shaun's stocky figure walking towards the van.

'Morning,' Shaun called as he approached, 'Sorry but we may need to ask you to move your van. We've got the last of the road mats on the trailer, so we'll be on our way after lunch. Hey, you two looked as if you were digging deep. Did you find anything interesting?'

'Afraid not, Shaun. No hoard of coins today,' Dave answered.

'How about you? Did you find anything interesting in the moat?' Nick asked.

'A few old bottles, nothing much.'

Dave leaned across Nick and towards the passenger door. 'Hey Shaun, have you heard about the Dunwich Jewel? It was on the local news this morning. It's supposed to be a 9th century gold aestel.' The conspiratorial tone in Dave's voice was obvious.

Shaun looked at them in a rather blank way.

'Well,' Dave persisted, 'it seems from the radio it's either a fake, or undeclared treasure. You must've heard something about it. So, what's the word out there? You know, among the metal detecting and dredging fraternity? It must be all anyone's talking about.'

'The Dunwich Jewel? Now there's a catchy name. Early medieval Anglo-Saxon aestels are unbelievably rare.' Shaun's shock of dark hair obscured most of his forehead, but the frown was still obvious.

'So you have heard something, then?'

'There's always a bit of a shockwave if treasure isn't declared. But until it's authenticated, who knows what it all means.' He shrugged; it was a kind of full stop to further discussion.

'Glass bottles are OK though? They aren't going to be judged as undeclared treasure, are they? You see I've a friend who wants some bottles for an antique apothecary chest.'

'You should be on safe ground with bottles.'

'Great. Do you know where I can get any?' Nick asked on impulse.

'Ah, you need to talk to my wife Silvia. She's the expert. We dredge up so many bottles; we give them to her to sort. How about I give you my office number and then you can call and ask her? I'm sure she'd be happy to help. Your name is Nick, isn't it? I'll tell her to expect a call from you.'

'Cool. Does she work for the firm as well, then?'

'Yes, we're a family business.'

As long as he was only dealing with Silvia, Nick reckoned he'd be all right.

The afternoon proved to be a hard graft. Nick had hoped the really physical work of the day was finished once they'd dug the holes for the concrete footings. He hadn't accounted for mixing, carrying and pouring the wet concrete, nor the fussing over the forms to get them positioned so they were just right to fill with concrete.

They needed to make the height of all the concrete the same level. And that was before they'd positioned a long, thick steel rod down the centre of each wet concrete footing so that it protruded about 4 inches above the surface.

'Now, Nick; one last trick. We measure the span of the bridge, but from steel rod to steel rod. Then we know the exact distance between where we drill into the underside of the long span beams.'

'Neat. Then we just slot them down over the rods?'

'Mmm, but not until Monday. The concrete will have had plenty of time to set by then.'

'Monday? It'll be nice to have the place to ourselves. I wonder how long it'll take to recover. I know the dredgers put down road mats to stop all the tyre and tread ruts, but the grass still looks a bit... flattened,' Nick said as they carried their tools back to the van.

'And the moat water's still pretty muddy. A good dose of rain and a couple of weeks will sort it. Do you fancy a pint once we're back?'

'No thanks, Dave. I'll give it a miss, if that's OK. I've done enough drinking this week.' It wasn't strictly true. He was planning to meet his mates in the Nags Head later.

For the first time, he dozed off in the passenger seat as Dave drove the van back to Willows.

CHAPTER 28

Chrissie raised her voice against the sound of the orbital sander and held her phone closer to her ear. 'Sorry, Clive, but it's a bit noisy in here at the moment. Ron's sanding the top of a chest.'

'I said it's Friday. Are you dropping by the Nags Head after work?' Clive's voice came across richer rather than louder.

'That's better. Yes, I'd hoped to hear the latest on Nick's move to a new flat. Do you want to meet at the Nags Head? We could eat at the Chinese and then the Regal isn't far, if you fancy watching *The Amazing Spider-Man 2*. We've missed *3 Days to Kill*. It's the one with Kevin Costner.'

'Umm....'

'Or if you prefer, I could pick up a takeaway for us? What time will you be home?'

'That sounds nicer. I should think by eight.'

'Chinese then? Beef and water chestnuts in black bean sauce, for you?

'Yes please. And fried rice. Oh, I nearly forgot. That anonymous call you asked me to trace? Well it was a female voice from the BT call box in Elmsett. The time on the log was 13:55, Monday. OK then, see you this evening. Bye.'

She barely had time to say goodbye before he'd gone.

'A female voice?' Chrissie frowned across the barn workshop. Gayle stood planing a piece of mahogany held firm in a bench clamp. *A female voice* she repeated inwardly as she focused fleetingly on Gayle.

It wasn't what she'd expected. Shaun Shinton sat at the top of her list of anonymous calling suspects but she had never heard his voice. Could he have slipped into falsetto to disguise himself?

And of course there was her friend Sarah. She'd thought they knew each other pretty well, but it hadn't stopped Sarah lambasting her and accusing her of knowing all along that Nick was some kind of acidhead junkie. In fact not only knowing it, but deliberately concealing it from Sarah. The hurt cut again as she remembered Sarah's tone. It had been unjustified as well as a surprise. Could Sarah have phoned the police in a fit of pique? The old Sarah she thought she knew wouldn't have. But this new Sarah? She'd certainly been cross enough.

'You're frowning, Chrissie. Am I doing something wrong?' Gayle asked, her voice small in the workshop now that Ron had stopped sanding the chest.

'What?' Chrissie dragged her mind back to where her gaze had rested.

'You were staring at me. Am I planing it wrong?'

'Oh no, not at all. Sorry, I was miles away. Something Clive just said.' She gave herself a metaphorical shake and walked over to where Gayle was working.

The drawer from the apothecary box was in pieces on the workbench and Chrissie absentmindedly picked up one of its sides. 'Well done; you've got all the old glue out of the joints. By the time you've finished and re-glued, it'll be stronger than when it started out. Remember to run your fingers and eye along the edge you're planing. That'll tell you when you've got it right.'

'Yeah, I think I've got it straight and flat now.'

'Good. Is it for the drawer dividers?'

Gayle nodded, her jawline seemingly belligerent in its squareness.

'Remember – don't cut the dividers to the exact length until you've got your drawer together and glued. There's always a fine adjustment.' Chrissie looked up and caught Ron's eye as he changed his sanding paper to a finer grade. He cast a glance heavenwards, smiled and almost imperceptibly shook his head, before returning to his sanding.

'I learned that lesson the hard way,' Chrissie shouted above the noise of the sander.

A little later, during the last tea break of the day, Chrissie was secretly relieved when Gayle said she was busy that evening. 'I'll give the Nags Head a miss, thanks. I need to pack.'

'To pack?' Ron said mildly.

'Yeah, I'm moving to a new place. Where I am at the moment is… well Clare is nice an' all that, but…,' Gayle's voice drifted.

'Who's Clare?'

'She's my landlady. She's always asking what I'm doing, where I'm going, what time I'm eating? I'm sure she's been in my room and through my things.'

'But,' Chrissie bit back the *wasn't there supposed to be something about a dog?* Uh-oh, Gayle had just told her, in not so many words, to mind her own business, keep out and stay away. She took a deep breath and mentally regrouped.

'But you've found somewhere else, I hope?' There, that was bland enough she decided.

'Yeah, somewhere a bit separate. Even has its own stairs.'

'Good. Do you remember Mrs Dell, the customer with a load of furniture left behind in her house by the previous owner? Her chairs are ready to take back. I was thinking Monday, but if you want to come along with me and help go through the furniture, then I'm sure she won't mind waiting until Tuesday for her chairs.'

'She lives in Sudbury, doesn't she?' Ron said, putting his mug of tea down on the workbench, his arthritic knuckles reminding Chrissie of the gnarled head of a walking cane.

'Sudbury? I haven't been to Sudbury before.'

'So is that a yes for Tuesday, Gayle?'

She nodded.

It occurred to Chrissie that this business of not asking questions could make her seem uncaring and disinterested. Shouldn't she have asked Gayle if she needed any help moving, or how she was going to get all her stuff to the new place? And while she was on the subject, was the new place Nick's soon-to-be old place? And if it was, did she want Chrissie to pick her up from Woolpit to give her a lift to work? The string of questions was lengthening by the minute. The frustration of holding her tongue was almost unbearable.

•••

Chrissie parked in the Nags Head car park. She had already spotted Matt's blackberry bubblegum-coloured Vespa. It was on its parking stand near the maxi-sized plastic waste bins, but it took her a moment to notice Nick's old Ford Fiesta. Its blue paintwork looked tired in the cloudy evening. She locked her car and hurried through the heavy door into the bar. It felt as if, in the blink of an eye, she had exchanged the dusty barn workshop with its scents of wood and oils, for the dimly lit bar with its smell of beer, and a jukebox standing in for a pillar drill. It was only six o'clock, but the small sash windows and beamed ceiling made it feel darker inside, and later.

The main bar area was starting to fill with the usual after-work Friday crowd. She glanced around, searching out her friends.

'Hi, Chrissie!' Nick's voice carried from where he sat with Matt at a small table close to the wall. They both looked as if they had plenty left in their glasses, but nevertheless she mimicked raising a glass and then shrugging, her eyebrows raised in a question. Nick mouthed *we're OK*, and Matt frowned and looked confused.

'A ginger beer and ice please,' she said to the barman. A notice pinned near the dartboard announced the next match in the Head Pub Quizzing League.

'Do you quiz?' the barman asked, catching her glance as he dropped ice into her glass.

'A Head Pub Quizzing League? What's that?'

'Any pub with *Head* in its name. You'd be surprised how many Saracens', Kings' and Queens' Heads there are round here.'

'Not many Nags, I imagine.' She laughed and carried her glass over to Nick and Matt.

'God, what a week,' she said and slumped onto a chair. 'Have you found somewhere to live yet, or are you still camped on Jake's floor? And Gayle – what am I supposed to say to her? She told me she was packing this evening. I can't let on I know she's moving into your old attic room, or that I know Sarah, or that Sarah rang me to check Gayle isn't the blatant acidhead junkie that she's decided you are, Nick!'

She had started by directing her question at Nick, but as she launched into her string of angst, Chrissie might as well have been addressing the whole bar.

'Hey, keep your voice down,' Nick hissed.

'D'you reckon Gayle's into drugs?'

'No, Matt.'

'And neither am I. And thanks, Chrissie. I owe you for getting rid of the canisters.'

She focused on her ginger beer. She hadn't told him about Clive helping her re-bag them for forensics. Her duplicity felt uncomfortable but she knew he'd freak out if she said anything.

Matt filled her silence 'Hey Nick, d'you reckon Gayle fancies you?'

'What, Matt? Why'd you ask? I don't think I've seen her since that first Friday in here.'

'N-no, I were just wonderin', that's all.' Matt frowned. Chrissie knew that frown.

'Look you two; Gayle came here to get away from Leicester. Give her a break. Don't either of you go upsetting her. And you know half the girls at your gigs fancy Jake or you, Nick.'

'Yeah, but it's only fan stuff. Hey, but Jake and I have seen this cool place to rent in Bury. We figured we could afford somewhere better if there were two of us renting.'

'Killer app, mate!'

'It's above a shop, St Andrews Street South.'

'That's bloggin' central.'

'Do you need a parking permit for your car round there?' Chrissie asked, ever practical.

'Yeah, but there's street parking after six.'

'You want to get a scooter, mate. No trouble parkin' one of them. I'm helpin' Gayle look at scooters tomorrow.'

'Great! But what about the CBT thing she has to do?' Chrissie asked before taking a long slow mouthful of ginger beer.

'It's tomorrow, Saturday. She were real lucky she got a cancellation on the CBT course. Saturday's right popular. She'll be done by four, so we'll go lookin' after that.'

'And Maisie?' Nick asked, 'is she going to get a scooter soon?'

'I don't s'pose so. It aint Maisie's kinda thing.'

Matt seemed to slip into his own thoughts while Nick told Chrissie about the Dunwich Jewel, a.k.a. the 9th century pointer; the so called Saxon aestel discussed on the radio that morning.

'So are you saying it's some kind of fake? Or is it un-declared treasure that's surfaced on a selling site? Either way it's fraud.' Chrissie was pleased to have a new puzzle to chew over.

'They hinted on the radio it wasn't found in Dunwich.'

'Really? Mudlarking – I wonder if it could have….' Her thoughts raced on. 'Of course medieval Dunwich slipped into the sea.'

'True, but don't forget metal detecting or dredging. Woah – I'd forgotten about Walberswick! It isn't far from Dunwich.'

'Walberswick? What are you on about, Nick?'

'Shaun's lot were doing some dredging at Walberswick. I remember Shaun telling Dave and me. It was soon after Toussaint died. He'd come over to finish off assessing the depth of silt in the moat.'

'Well if you're suggesting Shaun's firm dredged up a 9th century aestel in Walberswick, you have to be off beam. Walberswick only really got on the map after Dunwich slipped into the sea in the 13th century. Before then it wasn't big enough or important enough for anything much, let alone a Saxon aestel.'

'It sounds like you'd get on with Jim, the listener who phoned in to the radio programme. He said it couldn't be Dunwich because the town wasn't big in the 9th century. Yeah, and the priory wasn't built until 400 years later.'

'In the 13th century,' Chrissie said, sliding through the maths.

The door swung open and a couple of blokes in paint-spattered trainers sauntered into the bar. She was momentarily distracted.

'Well I don't get what you're on about,' Matt muttered. He hadn't spoken for a while and his voice pulled her back into the conversation.

'The aestel thing? I wouldn't have known what an aestel was if I hadn't been reading up about old bottles and mudlarking and treasure.'

'Yeah, they said on the radio. It's a Saxon gold pointer, like a cursor but only for holy texts,' Nick added. 'Are you still interested in old bottles for your apothecary box, Chrissie?'

'Yes, but I want ones with the original labels on them.'

'Cool, I think I may be able to get some for you. Anyone want another drink?'

'Ta, mate. Another half of Carlsberg, if you're buyin'. An' while you're up there, Nick – why don't you ask the barman to sign Chrissie for the Nags Head quiz team?'

CHAPTER 29

Matt waited for Gayle outside the motorcycle school. He cast a glance along the road leading back into Stowmarket. It was half past three. He hoped to spot a handful of scooters approaching in single file with an instructor on a motorbike bringing up the rear. He reckoned it wouldn't have changed much from the time when he took his CBT. The small group would be linked by a radio connection, with an earpiece to wear inside their helmets and the instructor giving directions from his vantage point at the back. It was quite the opposite approach to a mother duck leading her ducklings, with the weak and wayward ones dropping unnoticed from the end of the line.

A mild gust of wind caught at his legs. Saturday was proving pretty much the same as Friday, with the May sunshine weak in a cloudy sky. He turned his attention to the motorbikes and scooters lined up outside the shop-fronted motorcycle school. The ones at the far end were for sale, and those clustered nearer to where he stood were waiting for collection after servicing and repair. The next gust decided him; he locked his Vespa and sauntered into the showroom.

Inside and surrounded by the smell of new rubber, polish and leather, Matt relaxed and let his mind drift. He ran his hand over the seat of a spanking new step-through Honda SH125 scooter. It stood sleek and black at the end of a stand of new motorbikes.

He'd tried to banish the Gayle conundrum, but it was ever ready to surface in his mind. When he'd first walked into the Nags Head the evening before, he'd intended to give his mates a hint that Gayle might not be Gayle. Or rather, Gayle might not have started her life with the name Gayle. However, when he thought of it in those terms, it seemed unimportant, almost trivial. So what, if she had been recorded at birth with a different name, such as Camille Martin?

His problem had eased as he drank his pint of lager. Nick saying he hadn't seen Gayle and hadn't chatted her up, meant Nick didn't need to know about the identity puzzle. And when Chrissie said Gayle wasn't into drugs and to lay off her because they all knew she'd had to leave Leicester – well, it made it all right. But that had been yesterday.

The sound of the returning CBT group drifted through the door linking the servicing and repair unit. The noise pulled him back to the here-and-now and his attention returned to the Honda SH125, the glossy step-through scooter in front of him.

'It has excellent fuel economy.' The salesman looked young in charcoal grey jeans and smart tee-shirt.

'What? Yeah, I'm sure it do. I were more interested in the Honda PS scooter, or should I call it a PES125 scooter? Its stylin' looks like this SH one.' Matt hoped he sounded cool, and then added, 'It aint for me. It's me mate lookin'.'

'Yes, I saw you ride in on the Vespa. A classic. I'm afraid Honda is discontinuing the model you're interested in, so there aren't many new ones left in stock any longer. I can take a look on our computer, if you like.'

'Yeah but if you still had one for sale, then it'd be kinda obsolete and it'd kill its resale price, right?'

'Not for a year or two, and of course there's always the rarity value to consider.'

'Yeah, 'ventually!'

227

Matt was pleased. It was something to tell Gayle; some ammunition to knock down the asking price of a three-year-old Honda PES scooter. Gayle had seen the 125A advertised for sale in Lavenham. But where was she? Then he remembered she'd still be with the rest of the group completing the paperwork with the instructor, that's if she'd passed her CBT.

He went outside to unlock his Vespa. He didn't have to wait long before a smiling Gayle joined him. Her pale face radiated pink. Excitement? Pleasure? Matt couldn't tell, but either way he hoped it was good news.

'Hey, how'd it go?' he asked.

'I passed.'

'Killer App!' he hooted and punched the air.

'D'you know – I haven't passed much before. Passing feels kinda good.'

'Yeah, y'nailed it, Gayle. So, d'you want to look at the Honda scooter you had your eye on in Lavenham?'

She nodded.

They took the back route leaving Stowmarket on the B road as far as Hitcham, before turning onto quieter roads bordered by hedges of blossoming hawthorn and seemingly endless fields of wheat and flowering rapeseed. Matt slowed his speed as he approached Lavenham. He wanted to avoid the tourist trap of the sloping High Street and old Market Place at the top of the hill. Both were crowded with old beamed merchants' houses and weavers' cottages; many of them had been turned over to shops, and all jostled for pavement space and the sky. Instead Matt nipped onto Lower Road, cutting several streets behind the High Street.

It was like scootering on the other side of a coin where the 21st century residents lived. These houses had mostly been built in more modern times, detached with small gardens and spaces to park a car.

'Here it is; number 184,' he shouted over his shoulder as he turned off Lower Road and into a modern cul-de-sac. He stopped outside the house with a silver coloured Honda scooter parked in front of closed garage doors. 'Were you OK with all them pollens?' he asked as he got of the Vespa.

She didn't answer, but instead pulled off her helmet and gazed at the scooter.

'C'mon then. Let's take a closer look,' Matt said. Gayle was beside him in a moment, eyes only for the scooter as the front door opened.

'Hello. Are you Gayle? I'm Steve. We spoke on the phone.' A man in his late forties smiled from the doorway. 'My daughter will be really sorry to see this go, but she's passed her driving test now and… well she tends to drive the car instead.'

'So, only one owner?' Matt asked.

'Yes, my daughter. A couple of superficial marks on the front plate, but it's not been involved in any accidents and it's mechanically sound. It had a new front tyre and MOT in January.'

'And does the top box come with it?' Gayle asked, her voice tiny.

'Yes, you'll need that for your helmet.'

The 125cc single cylinder four stroke engine sprang into life on the first try. Gayle sat on the scooter with one foot resting on the ground. Matt talked mileage and fuel economy with Steve while Gayle played with the instruments, then switched off the engine and pulled the Honda onto its parking stand. She walked around the scooter slowly.

'I love it,' she said. 'It'll be my first scooter, my first–'

'No-no, you aint s'posed to say that Gayle. You're s'posed to say *but they're stoppin' makin' these. How'm I goin' to get me money back if it aint got no second hand value?* And them scuffs – you should be right upset 'bout them scuffs.'

Steve pursed his lips and frowned. Gayle's face flamed.

'You gotta try it Matt,' she whispered.

'Yeah, sure.' He rode it at crawler speed around the drive. 'It's seems OK. Can we look at its paperwork?'

Half an hour later the deal was done. Money and insurance would still need to be organised, but Steve seemed to have taken a liking to Gayle. Something to do with reminding him of his daughter, he'd explained. It was after six o'clock by the time they rode back into Stowmarket.

'Nags Head and meet up with Maisie, OK?' Matt shouted over his shoulder.

Matt had enjoyed the ride back from Lavenham. Gayle sat more stiffly on the Vespa than Maisie, but it was still cool to have a bird on the back. Maisie always wrapped her arms tightly around him and pressed close. But then Maisie was a warmer kind of bird, more immediate and chatty. He knew where he was with Maisie. With Gayle he had to watch what he said. Watch what he asked. Even watch what he thought, just in case she was able to read his mind. This time he wouldn't ask if she was OK with the pollen.

Matt didn't say much as he pushed his Vespa onto its stand and walked with Gayle from the car park into the bar. It wasn't busy; just a sprinkling of Saturday shoppers, mainly couples with carrier bags resting close to their feet on the pine floorboards. He spotted Maisie immediately.

She was standing in front of the jukebox and appeared to be choosing a selection of singles.

'Hi, Matt! How'd it go?' she squealed when she saw him, and hurried over to give him a hug.

'Yeah, it went good. She's now Gayle Corby, CBT, official like.' He kissed Maisie's head lightly through her riot of blonde hair and pink highlights.

'Good on ya, Gayle!' Maisie shouted. The whole bar must have heard.

Gayle dropped her gaze. 'I'm getting the drinks; it's a thank you for taking me to Lavenham.'

'Oh right then, a half of lager for me, thanks.'

'Well, if you're buyin', mine's a rum n' cola.' Maisie slipped her arm through Matt's and guided him away from Gayle to a table close to the jukebox.

'So how'd the viewin' go? What you talk about?'

'Yeah, it went OK. What you mean "talk about"? There aint much talkin' when you're scooterin'. You know what it's like, Mais. The wind and visor take what you say.'

She nodded slowly. 'So you went all the way to Lavenham?'

'Yeah. She wanted to look at the Honda scooter she'd seen advertised there.'

'Did she buy it?'

'You ask her. She's bringin' the drinks over now.'

'Cool tractor-treads,' Maisie said, eyeing up Gayle's heavy-soled shoes, almost biker boots. She got up to help her carry the drinks.

'Yes, well they said to wear sensible shoes without steel toecaps for the CBT,' Gayle murmured in her quiet voice.

'Cool.' Maisie rescued the glass of rum n' cola and took a sip before leading the way back to the table and Matt. 'So tell me all about it Gayle. The scooter in Lavenham; did you like it?' She settled next to Matt, leaving the chair opposite for Gayle.

'It's awesome. I'm going to buy it.'

'Yeah, but you've looked at loads, right? The Lavenham one were the best deal?'

'I don't know. It's the first one I've really looked at. I liked it. If I'd looked at more and liked them, how'd I know which one to get?'

'Well you wanna make sure you get the best deal. Aint that right, Matt?'

'Yeah, but I figure this were a good deal, Mais.'

'Yes and we knocked a couple of hundred off what the man was asking.'

'Yeah Steve, he were the bloke sellin'. He kinda took a likin' to Gayle. I reckoned he thought she were a bit like his daughter. The scooter used to be hers.'

'What? You think...?' The colour in Gayle's face drained.

Bloggin' hell, she was turning a shade of death. Was it something he'd said?

Matt hadn't meant anything beyond his words. But was she reading his mind, reading deeper than his superficial statement? Did she know he'd read the newspaper article? The one mentioning Camille Martin; the daughter locked in a house with her father on a Saturday morning and by Sunday evening the house was still locked and the father was dead? Had telling Maisie that Steve *kinda took a likin' to Gayle* sounded like a reference to all that?

'Gayle? Are you OK? Are you gonna faint?' Maisie screeched, and leapt to guide her as she flopped forwards. Gayle bent almost double with her head between her knees while Maisie held her shoulders.

'Faintin'? Is Gayle faintin', Mais? Thank blog for that.'

'What? Why you sayin' *thank blog for that*? How's faintin' good?'

'N-no. Sorry, I aint meant it like that. Shouldn't we be layin' her out on the floor?' Matt stood up and sent his chair clattering.

Gayle began to crumple sideways off her chair.

'It aint nice - it's all sticky and beery on them floor-boards,' Maisie wailed.

Matt took the weight of Gayle's upper body, breaking her fall as she slithered onto the beery boards.

'That's better, you'll be all right down here,' he soothed.

'Not if she knew she were down here. It's manky on this floor.'

Gayle's eyelids flickered. She half opened her eyes but they were blank, as if unseeing. Matt watched, barely daring to breathe as Gayle seemed to re-inhabit her face.

Someone hurried over from the bar. Matt noticed the man's trainers and frayed jeans near the heel. A gruff voice, 'Are you OK? Do we need to call an ambulance?'

'S-sorry - I came over light-headed,' Gayle breathed, the sound so soft they had to bend closer to hear.

'She's only fainted. Give her some space,' Maisie said and then added, 'A girl at work's always faintin' like this.'

Nobody said anything for a moment as they gazed down at Gayle and waited as if they were part of an out-of-season nativity scene.

'No, no; really I'm fine,' Gayle murmured as she struggled to get to her feet.

'Careful! Don't try standin'. Just sit on the chair for a bit,' Maisie said, and with her words, the drama was over and normality restored.

'Your colour's comin' back. It weren't anythin' I said, were it?'

'Do you faint a lot?' Maisie cut in.

'It were a faint though, weren't it?' Matt had to know.

'Yes, yes. I'm always fainting. How could it be anything you said?'

'I don't know. I just want to be sure it weren't me.' He caught Maisie's look. He didn't know what it meant but he knew she wasn't smiling at him.

'Drink up, Matt, an' then we can walk Gayle home. She aint goin' on the back of your Vespa; not if she's goin' to flake out.'

'No, please no. I can walk by myself.'

He gulped his lager. 'We're still goin' to catch the late showin' of *The Amazing Spider-Man 2*, right Mais?'

'Look I don't want to make you late. Anyway I must get back. I've got to finish packing.'

'Ah right. You're movin' aint you?'

'How do you know, Matt?' Gayle's voice sounded sharp.

'I-I'm not sure. You must've said.' Deidre's voice came back to him as he remembered the call from the accommodation officer. It had been brief and to the point. Gayle, although she didn't mention Gayle by name, was going to be the next lodger at Spice House in Woolpit. Matt would have to look for somewhere else.

Matt dropped his gaze. It must be something to do with the eyes, he reckoned. He didn't want Gayle reading his thoughts and knowing he'd paid a visit to the accommodation officer.

'I thought you said it were too noisy on the scooter to do much talkin'.' Maisie' voice was strident.

'Yeah well Gayle must've said when she were talkin' to Steve,' he lied.

Bloggin' hell, he'd mentioned Steve. Was she going to go funny again? He felt Maisie slip her arm around his waist. 'C'mon. Drink up an' let's walk Gayle home. You can tell us all about the new place on the way, Gayle.'

'I think I'll leave the rest of mine.'

'Right OK,' Matt said. A quick glance told him she hadn't gone deathly pale. 'Let's get goin' then.'

He stopped at the bar counter on the way out and lowered his voice to whisper to the barman, 'You know you gotta ask Chrissie Jax to join the Nags Head quiz team. She'd be like your secret weapon; a killer app.' He indicated over his shoulder with his thumb, a kind of backward thumbing-a-lift motion aimed at the Head Pub Quizzing League notice pinned near the dartboard.

'Thanks mate. Can you write the name down for me?'

CHAPTER 30

'Did you have a good weekend? Because I hope you're in a better mood than you were last week,' Dave said to Nick.

It was Monday morning and they were in the Willows van, loaded with pieces of the wooden bridge and driving the long stretch of the A140 before turning east to Thorndon and then north towards Eye.

'Yeah, I s'pose it was a good weekend. I've found somewhere to live, which is brilliant, so it's only another week on Jake's floor. And it's not so bad when you know there's an end in sight. Except now, of course I can hardly move for all my stuff. I spent Saturday shifting it out of my last place.'

'Why didn't you say before? How long have you been sleeping on floors?'

'About a week at Jake's.' Nick wasn't going to say more.

'And the new place?'

'It's an unfurnished flat in Bury. Jake's coming in with me. It's on St Andrews Street South.'

They lapsed into silence as Dave drove. Nick let his mind drift, his thoughts moving between fragments of song, concrete footings, fixing the beams and the last time he'd sat in the van on his way to the moated farmhouse. There'd been the Saxon aestel on the radio; the so-called Dunwich Jewel.

'The Dunwich Jewel,' he murmured. 'It'd make a good title for a song. Any idea why's it's called a jewel, Dave?'

'That aestel thing? I looked it up after I got home on Friday. It's got a blue glass cabochon on it. Yeah, and before you ask, cabochon means a precious stone polished smooth, in other words it's not been cut with facets to catch the light like a modern diamond.'

'But a blue glass cabochon sounds kinda cheap.'

'Or very old, more like, and obviously considered very precious at the time.'

'Talking of glass, do you think I should follow up on what Shaun said, and ring his wife? You remember him saying? You know, to ring her about some old bottles?'

'Yes, why not? I guess Shaun and his crew must come across loads of interesting stuff. You'll probably find Silvia can tell you a lot, if she has a mind to.'

'Are you suggesting I chat her up then, Dave?'

Nick wasn't averse to the idea of flirting with Silvia, but he figured she would likely be hitting forty and much too old for him. Girls closer to his age of almost twenty-four were far more attractive. He understood them; knew how to read them. It was why he was able to keep his post-gig one-night stands fun, with no hurt feelings and a fan base intact. It was a generation thing.

Damn! The train of thought had taken him to Sarah, now his ex-landlady. How old was she? He supposed early forties. He'd sensed she'd always fancied him; after all, her innuendoes had been blatant enough. But he'd thought it was her idea of a game; only fun if the line wasn't crossed. She was allowed to flirt outrageously because it wasn't meant, and he, understanding, hadn't flirted back or crossed that line. So why had she reacted so excessively over the cream chargers? Why hadn't it been a wink wink, nudge nudge and *clear them up, love*?

237

Was it possible that she had genuinely fallen for him? Oh no, how could he have misread the signs? But it could explain why she'd been so passionately cross. Someone really hurting might want to hurt him back. And... did she call the police? He hadn't thought so, but now he wasn't sure what to think.

'Yeah, but she chucked me out,' he breathed. That wasn't the act of someone who'd taken a shine to him. It summed up his problem with the age group. How to interpret the response? How to anticipate the reaction? Contradictions and ambiguity; they could trip one up.

'Sorry, I didn't catch that. What did you just say?' Dave asked as he turned onto the gravelly track to the moated farmhouse.

'Time to get this bridge built. Time to get out.'

Dave parked the van on the rough grass as close as he could to the concrete footings. Nick flung open the van doors and started unloading the wood.

'Hey, tie some rope around one end of this arched support beam, Nick.'

'I suppose that means you want me on the other bank?'

'Yep, thanks for volunteering.'

The rest of the morning passed rapidly as they both focused on assembling the footbridge. Dave flung one end of the rope across the moat, and Nick caught it from the other side. He used it to take the weight of the arched support beam as Dave fed it across the water to him.

'Yeah, bloody hell! The steel rods we set in the footings fit exactly into the holes we drilled. How cool is that?' Nick shouted as he lowered the beam onto a rod.

'Precision measurement.'

With both arched support beams held on their respective steel rods set in the concrete footings, Nick walked back to Dave's side of the moat. They worked, side by side, first fitting the strengthening frame between the ends of the support beams. Next they attached the first pair of posts for the handrail. It was Nick's job to screw each piece of decking board into place on the support beams, kneeling on the ones he'd just fixed as he worked his way across the span.

He felt a bit precarious as he knelt; if he looked ahead there was nothing but air between the arched support beams and if he peered down, there was the drop into the water. It was only a short drop, but he knew what the water could do. He'd pulled Toussaint's head out of it.

Board by board the footbridge took shape. By mid-afternoon the decking was finished and the handrail and its support posts were secure.

'It looks better than I ever imagined,' Victor Coady said when he came out to admire the completed project.

'Come on then, let's see you walk across it!' Dave coaxed.

'Did you say you're coming over tomorrow to give it a coat of wood preservative?'

The drive back to Willows & Son felt more relaxing than the outward journey. Dave was leading the conversation, which meant little was required from Nick beyond the occasional yes, no and hmm.

'Mr Coady was damned pleased with his footbridge,' Dave said for what seemed like the hundredth time.

'Hmm.'

'I wouldn't be surprised if he asks us to make another.'

'Hmm.'

'Hey, did you call Shaun's wife? You know, about the bottles you were after?'

'Hmm.'

'So what did she say?'

'What did who say?'

'Silvia, Shaun's wife. Come on, concentrate. We can't have you dropping off in the van like you did on Friday when I drove back.'

'Ah, you mean the bottles. I thought I'd call her once we're back at Willows.'

He'd forgotten about Silvia. He'd been too focused on constructing the footbridge to give her another thought. But now that his mind had been dragged back, he reckoned if he was going to launch a charm offensive, then he'd make the call from the privacy of his own car.

•••

Nick took a deep breath and keyed in the number for SS Shinton Dredging. He imagined the office, deserted at the end of the day. He held his mobile to his ear. How many rings before the answerphone cuts in, he wondered.

He had driven his old Ford Fiesta out of the parking area reserved for the Willows staff and headed onto the quiet road running in front of the office showroom and workshop. Another hundred yards and he'd be at the junction onto the main road. He'd stopped alongside a silver birch, its catkins and young leaves shifting and swaying somewhere high above with the breeze.

The gentle rustling of their movement drifted through his open windows as his ringtone repeated and repeated. The whooshing roar of a train burst the peace as it hurled along the main line close by. He guessed it was hurrying through Needham market, its next stop Stowmarket Station, 4:45.

'Shinton Dredging. Silvia speaking. How can I help?'

The words were almost drowned by the noise of the train and for a moment he felt wrong-footed. He'd expected to hear the expressionless tones of the answerphone, not the warmer vibes of a living voice.

'Oh h-hi,' he stammered, 'I was told to… to give you a call about collecting old glass bottles. I'm Nick, from Willows & Son.' He paused, not sure if she'd heard him against the retreating express.

'Yes, Shaun said to expect a call from you.'

'Oh good, so he's told you. I'm looking for something specific. Old apothecary bottles.'

'Do you mean pharmacy bottles? The ones with labels on them for lotions and chemicals?'

'Yes, I guess so.'

'Any particular labels? And the size? Are they for a travelling case or the kind of bottle you'd stand on a shelf in a chemist's?'

'What? No, I don't know the size.' He felt stupid. What was he doing looking for bottles when he had no idea how big Chrissie's apothecary box was?

'That's OK. If you could tell me more exactly what you're after, then I can look for a closer match. I have lots of contacts and dealers I sell to, so if I haven't got anything suitable, I should be able to find something through my connections.'

Her voice soothed and the implied efficiency reassured.

'Look, I hope I haven't wasted your time, but I'll find out more and get back to you. I want to give the bottles to

241

someone as a kind of thank you. It's for an old apothecary box she's repairing.' God, what was he saying? He was supposed to be getting Silvia to talk and here he was dribbling stuff like a broken spout. Use her name, he told himself; that usually helps to smooth the way.

'No really, Silvia, I'll get straight back to you with the details,' he added.

'That's all right Nick. You're very welcome to come over and have a look at the selection here. The office is near Elmsett Airfield. Not too far for you to come across from Woolpit, I hope.'

'Woolpit?'

'You do live in Woolpit don't you?'

'Oh yeah. It's a great place. How did you know I live in Woolpit?'

'I suppose Shaun must have told me.'

'Yeah, of course. OK then Silvia, great talking to you. I'll get back to you soon.'

'Goodbye, Nick.'

He slipped his mobile into his pocket. How the hell did Silvia know he lived in Woolpit, or more accurately, used to live there? He was pretty damned sure he hadn't told Shaun, unless of course Dave had been shooting his mouth off.

And how the hell was he going to find out more about the size and number of bottles he needed for the apothecary box without asking Chrissie? He'd wanted them to have an element of surprise for her. After all, they were meant to be a gift. Unless, of course....

The idea came to him as he restarted the Fiesta and headed to the junction. Out of habit he indicated right, but right was the direction he'd turn if he was driving back to

Woolpit. For a moment he felt rootless and nostalgic for his old room above the double garage. He hoped Gayle would be all right there. She'd certainly fit into the tiny shower better than he ever had.

'Yeah but Gayle's the apprentice. She's been working on the apothecary box. If anyone knows the dimensions of the compartments for the bottles, it'll be her,' he murmured.

Better still, she was in the age group he understood. What could be more natural than to drop by and suggest a welcome drink and wish her good luck in her new place? He could ask her about the size of the bottles at the same time.

Fired with his plan, he drove to Woolpit. He cut through the back lanes, avoiding the ancient triangular village marketplace with its old water pump, and headed for Sarah's house. He parked in a side road where he was sure his car couldn't be seen from the house. If he'd had Gayle's number he'd have sent her a text warning her he was on his way back from constructing the footbridge at the moated farmhouse. But of course, if he'd had her number he could simply have asked her to send him the bottle information.

He got out of his car and walked as quietly as he could up the gravel drive. He cast around for any sign that Sarah might be home, but it seemed too peaceful and her car wasn't visible.

He made sure his footfall was heavy as he climbed the outside wooden steps to his old room over the double garage. If Gayle was in, then it was best if she heard him approaching. A disembodied tapping on the door might spook her.

'Hi, Gayle.' He knocked and then stood back on the staging, so as not to crowd her if she opened the door.

He heard her footsteps; picked up the sound of a key turning in the lock.

'Hi, Gayle,' he said again as she opened the door. He caught her surprise and the mild flush of her pale cheeks. Instinctively he read the faint signals and picked up her instant attraction to him. He needed to tread carefully with this one.

She didn't say anything, so he filled the silence; 'I'm Nick. I was one of the crowd Chrissie introduced you to in the Nags Head a few weeks back. I'm sorry if I look a mess but I'm literally on my way back from working near Eye, constructing a wooden footbridge. I don't know if you knew it, but I moved out of this room only a couple of days ago.'

She dropped her gaze and shook her head.

'Look, I figured I should call by, say hi and kinda wish you good luck here and give you the lowdown on Sarah, your landlady.' He smiled and turned on his heel, as if he was about to walk back down the wooden steps, his message delivered and matey duty completed.

'No, don't leave. It's nice of you to come round.'

He stopped, one foot still on the staging, the other on the first step down, and his hand on the rail. 'Look, to be honest, I don't want Sarah to see me here. Would you… shall we catch a drink in the White Hart?'

'The White Hart?'

'Yeah, it's one of the local pubs, good beers on tap. Chrissie tends to drink there, so… if you want avoid meeting your boss we could try one of the other pubs in Woolpit.' He raised his eyebrows and shrugged. He didn't want to smile too much. She might read it as creepy.

'How far is the White Hart?'

'A five-minute walk back into the centre of the village.'

'OK then.'

He waited while she gathered up a white denim jacket. It occurred to him, as she locked her door and followed him down the steps that she was more solid than her small voice suggested.

'So how are you settling in?' he asked.

She ignored his question and instead murmured, 'I remember you from the Nags Head. You sang with Jake on the open mic night.'

'Yeah, Jake's an old mate from school days. In fact I'm staying with Jake until we get into our new place.'

'Yes, I remember Jake looking up the words for your song on his iPad.'

'Yeah, we were probably singing version two of *A Last Laugh*. We're on version...I don't know, four or five now.'

'That's right, it was *A Last Laugh*. There'd been another laughing gas death. Matt read out a news flash from Jake's iPad. And someone mentioned Tuscan, yes Tuscan was mentioned.'

'Yeah, you know his real name was Toussaint?'

'Hmm.'

They walked in silence along the lane past hedgerows of shrubby elm and hazel, mixed with crab apple, prickly dog rose, blackthorn and white blocks of flowering hawthorn. Nick didn't want to think about Toussaint; didn't want to bring on a flashback.

'So what happened? Somebody said you'd pulled him out of the water?'

'Yeah, something like that. You know your white jacket makes you almost invisible against the hawthorn?'

'Does it?'

'Hmm.' It was his turn to nod.

Another fifty yards and beamed cottages and Suffolk-brick houses began to hem the lane as they approached the old centre of the village 'There's a fish & chip shop in that direction, but it's this way for the White Hart.' After a couple of dozen more paces, he took a sharp left around a half-barrel planted with a riot of purple coloured primulas and a solitary surviving daffodil.

'Here we are,' he said and led the way into the White Hart. He headed straight for the bar counter and sat on one of the bar stools. He knew she would follow suit. He had deliberately chosen a spot that wasn't intimate and didn't suggest anything beyond a quick polite drink.

She asked for a lime and soda and he selected a half of the Earl Soham Victoria bitter from the specials board.

'Things to watch out for with Sarah,' he said, and tasted the bitter. 'She tends to come to your room with an excuse to ask you something and then barges in to take a nosey around.'

'Right.'

'Oh yeah, and something else to bear in mind. Sarah is a friend of Chrissie's. So watch what you tell her as it could get back to your boss!'

'I'm always careful about what I say.'

'Yeah, I'd noticed. Hey there is something you could help me out with. It's… well it probably sounds silly, but I want to get Chrissie an antique bottle to add to her apothecary box. I want it to be a bit of a surprise.'

He glanced at Gayle, but her face was expressionless. He pressed on, 'The trouble is I don't know what size. If I give you my number, would you be able to text me with the size and the labels on the bottles still in the box? I don't want to double up on anything she's already got. Yeah, and in case I find more than one bottle, you'd better tell me how many are missing.'

He watched her over the top of his glass. The light hoppy bitter was starting to suit his mood. He relaxed, but Gayle seemed to tense and the set of her square jaw hardened.

'I don't want to talk or even think about chemicals or the apothecary box, just like I suppose you don't want to talk or think about pulling Toussaint out of the water.'

It wasn't the answer he was expecting. He held fire and waited.

'I tell you what; I'll trade information with you.' She appeared to contemplate her glass of lime and soda.

Nick was genuinely intrigued. He hadn't expected sophisticated flirting from her.

'Go on then. But I get to ask the first question. It's pretty obvious why I don't want to talk about Toussaint, but why don't you want to talk about chemicals and the apothecary box?'

'Because it brings back painful memories. Now my turn. How did Toussaint die? I've read all the stuff in the news but... what really happened to him?'

'I've read the same stuff as you, and I don't know. He... he had his head over the side of a boat and his face was in the moat. There was... well he had laughing gas paraphernalia in the boat with him. That's all I know. My turn now.'

She shifted a beer mat on the counter and avoided his gaze.

'Why does talking about chemicals and the apothecary box bring back painful memories?'

'Something bad happened.'

'Like an experiment going wrong in class at school? An accident, or something someone else did?'

'I don't... just talking about that kind of thing makes me feel odd. And now it's two extra questions you've just asked,' she said in a rush.

'OK, then. Your turn.'

'Tell me about Jake.'

'Jake? He's kinda cool – but you met him in the Nags Head. He's from Stowmarket. Works in Bury selling advertising space in the newspaper.' He caught her look, 'He's just split with his girlfriend. So yeah, unattached if you're interested. Hey, my turn now; why the interest in Tuscan?'

'Someone I know, knew him.' It sounded rehearsed to Nick. As if she had anticipated the question.

'A friend of a friend?'

'Hmm, something like that.'

'Right.' Nick wondered if he should ask more, but something held him back. He sensed she was uncomfortable when asked about herself, despite being the one who had initiated the trade in answers. 'Look, I better give you my number before I forget,' he said and drained his glass with a couple of last mouthfuls.

They walked back to Sarah's house, retracing their steps. 'I'm not being rude, I just don't want to bump into Sarah,' he said as he paused beside his car, parked out on the lane and hidden from the house.

'Thanks for the drink, Nick.'

'Hey, don't forget to send me the bottle info. I'm counting on you.' He raised his hand in a goodbye gesture as she walked back along the drive.

CHAPTER 31

'Right Gayle, I think we're all loaded up now,' Chrissie said as she closed the van door.

'Why the yellow stripe?' Gayle asked.

Chrissie frowned. Her mind was on Mrs Dell's chairs, the pair they had just that minute loaded into the van. 'Why the yellow stripe?' she echoed.

The workshop's van was an ex-Forestry Commission green. It had *Clegg & Jax. Master Cabinet Makers and Furniture Restorers* printed in black lettering on a yellow stripe along the side.

It took a moment to work out what Gayle was talking about. 'Oh I see. The stripe. I suppose because the van came with one. I rather liked it so we kept it but changed the writing from *Forestry Commission.*'

She glanced up at the old barn. Black weatherboarding covered it like a shabby coat, a little ragged at the edges, rather like the brick outhouse off to one side. To her eyes it looked part of a set of buildings, typical of a past era and telling a story. Not like the workshop's Citroen Berlingo van. It hid beneath its Forestry Commission green; a vehicle the size of an average saloon car but originally destined for Scotland and equipped with deceptively good ground clearance and off-road capability.

'It's got a slip differential, so there's decent traction off-road. You'd never guess just looking at it from here,' she said, voicing the end of her train of thought.

Gayle nodded. 'Do we have to go off-road to get to Mrs Dell's?'

'I hope not. I've never been to her place before. No, I was just thinking how you can't always know what's going on, by only looking at the outside of things. So, did your move go all right?'

'Yeah, thanks.'

Her tone didn't invite further enquiry. Chrissie tried to remember if Ron used to ask her about her release days and what she'd learned on them. She suspected he'd waited for her to tell him, but then she was a communicator. Gayle wasn't.

'How was the release day teaching, yesterday?' she asked as she started the van.

Beside her, Gayle appeared to focus on fastening her seatbelt. Chrissie left the question hanging in the air, but the air soon became heavy and oppressive with the silence.

'Look Gayle, you've hardly said a word this morning since I picked you up from your new place. I don't need to know any details, but I do need to know if you're not OK. You would tell me if there was anything wrong, wouldn't you?'

'Yes. But I'm... I'm not good at talking. That's all,' she said in her small voice.

'Right, but sometimes it's good to try.' Chrissie eased past Ron's battered old van parked near her TR7, resplendently yellow in the courtyard. She drove at low speed along the rutted entrance track and away from the workshop, mindful of the chairs loaded in the back. Her route took her down into Bildeston, nestling in its shallow valley, and from there over into Monks Eleigh.

'It's Lavenham that way. It's where I'm getting my scooter,' Gayle said, breaking the silence.

'I could have dropped you off to pick it up on our way back if you'd got your helmet with you, if we'd been organised. OK, Sudbury's this way.' They turned off the main road and crossed an ancient narrow bridge over a tributary of the River Brett. She concentrated on driving as the road twisted and turned between small copses and wild hedgerows.

'I've scribbled down the directions from Mrs Dell. Can you read them out when we get nearer, Gayle?'

She had noticed how Gayle was more confident when working on a task. She seemed to have less trouble finding her tongue if the subject matter covered the job in hand; just so long as it didn't involve personal preferences, or past history. Where did shyness and natural reticence cross the line and become secrecy and rudeness, Chrissie wondered.

She let her mind stray as they neared Sudbury, the countryside now flattening into rolling fields of rapeseed and wheat.

'*Go through the centre of the town and then follow the signs as if going to Bulmer,*' Gayle read from a sheet of paper. Their van was carried with the traffic in a one-way system past the old marketplace with its imposing church and a statue of Thomas Gainsborough. 'Left, bear left here,' Gayle squealed as the flow tried to take them around to the right.

'Thanks, Gayle.' It was the loudest Chrissie had ever heard her speak. She didn't know if she was pleased or shocked as they veered to the left.

'*Over the bridge and first turning to the right,*' Gayle added.

'Wow.' It felt as if the bridge floated on the River Stour as a panoramic view of lush water meadows stretched into the distance, restoring peace after the frenzy of the old centre. 'Wow,' Chrissie said again when two wrong and one missed turning later, they drew up outside Mrs Dell's house. Chrissie got out of the van and gazed up at a three-storey house built of pale Suffolk brick and fronted by a yew hedge. She guessed early or pre-Victorian, sometime around the turn of the 1800s.

'Come on, Gayle,' she tossed over her shoulder and opened a wrought iron gate. A path, three paving stones wide, led several yards to the front doorstep. Stuccoed cottages closed in on either side.

Before Chrissie had time to ring the bell, the black front door opened with a whoosh and Mrs Dell stood in the doorway beaming a welcome. 'Hello, good morning. I'm so excited. Please, you must bring the chairs straight in.'

Five minutes later, when both chairs stood side by side in the wide hallway, Chrissie felt a surge of anxiety. She watched, trying to read the signs as Mrs Dell ran a hand over the repaired back panel and down one of its legs, stooping to take a closer look before walking around the chair. Finally she stepped back to gaze at it next to its pair.

'Well?' Chrissie asked, unable to bear the suspense any longer. Was she or wasn't she pleased?

Mrs Dell smiled. 'You've done a wonderful job. I can't really see where you've mended it. Thank you so much. Now, I was going to show you some of the furniture the last owner left, wasn't I? But first you must see the jumble I found in the cellar. You might want to take some of it, if the price is right.' She led the way through the hallway.

'Did you ever discover if the old lady was French? You said you were going to look into her family history.' Chrissie said as she followed with Gayle.

'Ah, that's right, yes.' She opened a door under the stairs. 'The cellar,' she announced and stepped into the gloom of descending steps. 'I found a pile of old frames down here and some of them still had the photos in them. Sad, really. There was one of her on her wedding day.' The words floated up from the gloom, 'Now where's the light switch?'

'So was she French?'

'Yes, she was. She was married in Sudbury. I discovered it all from an old photograph. But because she married in Sudbury, the marriage was registered in the General Register Office records. I'd have fallen at the first hurdle if she'd married in France. Anyway, I had the date of her marriage from the photo and her husband's full name from old papers she'd left here relating to him buying this house. And I already had her full name, of course, from the sale of this house. Well - I had enough to find her maiden name in the GRO records using the FreeBMD site.'

'You make it sound easy.'

'It's fun; you should try it. Anyway, she was French, and her name was Bisset. Apparently it's French for a weaver. So you were right. It explains her taste in furniture and the French connection.'

'And why she might have come here to a silk weaving town and then met and married a wealthy man. OK Gayle, are you coming down to see the cellar?'

An hour later Chrissie and Gayle loaded the van with some of the castoffs cluttering the cellar. 'Not bad for a tenner,' Chrissie murmured as she went through the list. 'A damaged ornate antique French gilt mirror, a pair of rickety French Louis style bedside cabinets, a broken antique French farmhouse glacière cupboard and... this is my favourite, a very slightly chipped antique Limoges porcelain plate. I love its hand-painted gold trim.' She didn't bother to mention the pile of old photograph frames covered in dust and spotted with mildew now filling every spare corner in the van.

'And she paid you for repairing the chairs,' Gayle said, as Chrissie started the van.

'Yes, Mrs Dell has worked out well for us. You didn't seem very comfortable in the cellar. Thank you for coming down to help me carry things up.'

Chrissie wondered if a strategy of chatting without requiring answers might draw Gayle out. 'My brother used to be claustrophobic. I think it stemmed from him getting shut in a cupboard when we were kids. We were on holiday at the time and no one noticed Simon was missing. My parents assumed he was off catching crabs with me, and I thought he had one of his headaches and was with them. Yes, the creek between Southwold and Walberswick. I was the independent one, even then.'

'Left, we bear left here,' Gayle said as the central Sudbury one-way system caught them again.

Memories of Simon and her childhood filled her mind for a moment. He had been the needy one, someone she'd protected when he was a kid. Is that what had shaped her and made her feel she had to look out for Nick and Matt? Of course Simon had grown up, found a bossy girlfriend and was now a family man living one hundred and eighty miles away in Southampton. Their parents had followed him and the grandchildren.

'Have you ever thought about tracing your ancestry?' she said, meaning it more as a statement than a question.

Gayle didn't answer. She appeared to be looking out for road signs and traffic directions.

'I've never felt the need to know if my great-great-grandfather was a war hero somewhere, or a criminal. It'd be just my luck to find a load of dodgy skeletons lurking in the cupboard. How about you Gayle? Are you going to follow Mrs Dell's suggestion and try using the FreeBMD site?'

'No,' she said in her small voice.

•••

'So what do you think of the plate?' Chrissie asked as Clive turned it around in his hands that evening. The delicate gilt paintwork caught the light, as if to say look at me, look at me!

'It's a bit ornate, isn't it?'

'Of course it is. It's antique Limoges porcelain. Marie Antoinette and all that kind of thing. I've got to look up its mark and date it properly, but don't you think the pale blue is glorious? And the hand-painted flowers are works of art. It's like....' She was, for once lost for words.

'It's splendid. So how much did you say this set you back?'

'A few pence, maybe one pound. Mrs Dell's plate will look amazing on one of our restored antique tables at the next Snape Maltings Antiques and Fine Art Fair.'

'I thought you were hoping she'd have a load of antique glass bottles hiding in her cellar.'

'Yes, but this plate helps to ease the disappointment. Of course you may have to walk me to the White Hart for a glass of something,' she laughed. 'So, you've heard about my day. How was yours?'

She sat beside him on the two-seater sofa in her living room and rested her head against his shoulder.

'Well, Stickley turned up something interesting today.'

'Stickley, your DS?'

'Yes, we think we may have a lead. One of the local hospices reported a fentanyl nasal spray had gone missing a few weeks ago. The nasal sprays aren't in demand out on the street, so it could be relevant. It might set a trail. You see the timing would be right for it to have been used on Jon Dareham. I'll get Stickley to look into it further in the morning. It'll mean checking out the hospice staff and talking to the Regional Organised Crime Unit again to see if they've heard anything new.'

'You mean the drugs unit?'

'Yes. You can see how it would be easy to overlook one fentanyl nasal spray going missing amongst hundreds of ampules of the stuff being passed on for IV use out there.'

'Right, it's the same in accounting. It's classic to hide the one dodgy transaction amongst hundreds of seemingly innocent ones. Although I wouldn't describe the ampules going missing as innocent, but you know what I mean. Poor Jon Dareham.'

'Yes, and more on the supposed business connection between Toussaint and Jon. Well we now finally have access to all of their accounts.'

'Hallelujah! The wheels of officialdom have turned.'

'And you were right, Chrissie. It doesn't look as if the large irregular payments going into Toussaint's account came out of any of Jon's accounts.'

'Really? Now that's interesting. I told you not to jump to conclusions, didn't I?'

'Hmm, sounds like the pot's calling the kettle black.'

'Now that's not fair, Clive.'

'Oh?'

'I've sometimes wondered if I should have specialised as a forensic accountant, rather than giving the whole thing up.' She stopped mid-track as memories of Bill flooded back. What was she saying? She'd tossed away her accountancy job because he'd died and her heart was broken. Carpentry had been the salve. But of course that was before she'd met Clive, and crime had become part of her life.

'Are you OK Chrissie?'

'Yes, yes. I was just… well I was thinking I would never have been savvy enough with the internet to make it as a forensic accountant. Following the money is almost impossible now people use virtual private networks and the darknet. You've almost got to know where to look next.'

'Now don't beat yourself up. "Ideas" is where you're strong. Lateral thinking. You're… well I wouldn't tell you anything about my cases, except you come up with alternatives – crazy suggestions. I don't often agree with you, but the thing is, you stop my thoughts getting stuck in a groove. You're good for me, Chrissie. Just as long as you keep what I say to yourself.'

'Really? I think that's the nicest thing anyone has ever said to me.'

'Come on, let's go out for that drink.'

'Just a thought before we go. Did Jon Dareham suffer with hay fever?'

'Why do you ask?'

'I don't know, just wondering if he could have used the fentanyl spray thinking he was trying a new hay fever spray. Sorry, just another one of my crazy ideas.'

CHAPTER 32

Matt's ride from Stowmarket had been bolstered by a breezy tailwind. It was Thursday morning and the sunshine flooding through the old sash window into the Balcon & Mora office gave an illusion of summer warmth as he opened the door. He shed his denim jacket and hung it over the back of his chair. He'd chosen his tee-shirt with care. Today was going to be special. He had agreed to take Gayle to Lavenham to collect her Honda PES125A scooter. 'You will ride back with me won't you? It'll be my first time riding since my CBT, and….' He'd had to strain to hear her voice.

'You're looking unusually green today,' Damon said, breaking into Matt's thoughts.

'What? Yeah well the tee only came in green. See it says GREEN and 100% DEGRADABLE.'

He would have preferred to wear his PURPLE HILLS tee but it was, even by his standards, rank and in need of a hot wash. And besides, Maisie had bought him the one with green credentials. He figured sporting the tee-shirt showed his loyalty to Maisie, as well as making him seem cool in having a scootering mate.

'Hey, Damon,' he said, voicing something deeper on his mind, 'What you decided about them payin' ancestry tracin' sites? Are we goin' to try 'em out? An' is Balcon & Mora goin' to offer ancestry searches as well as contact info tracin'?'

'Hmm, I've been checking the costs. If we provide the full ancestry package we'd have to pay the GRO site to retrieve and copy the birth certificate for us before handing it on to the client.'

'Yeah, an' that's after we'd narrowed down the GRO volume, page and name we wanted copied, right?'

'Exactly. And the odds are against us getting it right each time. It'll cost us if we have to request multiple birth certificates before we hit on the right one.'

'So what you sayin'?'

'I'm saying we'd have to quote a package price to the client and at the moment we couldn't be competitive.'

'Yeah, but what you really sayin' Damon?'

'It's a *no*, Matt. I'm saying *no* to ancestry tracing.'

'Right, OK. Now I got it.'

What he *got* was that Damon would notice if he requested any birth certificates from the GRO site through Balcon & Mora. Or to be more specific, he'd *got* that it stopped him asking for Camille Martin's birth certificate unless he was willing to pay for it himself. Secretly he was relieved because without it, he wouldn't be able to discover her exact date of birth or see if it matched Gayle's. The bird he knew would simply remain a scootering mate called Gayle, and her background only shadows.

'Sorry, Matt. I guess you're disappointed, but I'm running a business here.'

'No, no I....' He stopped. They'd been through it before; the line between pushing the Balcon & Mora corporate nose into what turned out to be police business, and the legitimate search for contact details for their clients. He reckoned Gaspard Martin's death in 2007 was a closed police case and fair game, but Camille Martin's new identity was current, on-going and off limits. Yeah, he got it. He certainly *got* that there was no client paying for it.

'Then, I reckon I'll get started on me list of names, Damon. See, I 'ave to get off on time. A mate's buyin' a scooter an' I'm givin' her a lift after work.' He felt doubly cool letting slip that his scootering mate was a bird.

It was close on six o'clock by the time Matt rode into Lavenham with Gayle sitting behind him on the Vespa. The temperature had dropped from its earlier high of 17°C but there was still plenty of daylight left. Her grip tightened on him as they turned into the cul-de-sac off Lower Road, the back route into Lavenham. Ahead, the Honda scooter stood on its parking stand outside the closed garage doors of number 184, just as it had five days earlier. The frisson of Gayle's excitement was infectious as he slowed to a halt and she leapt from his scooter.

It brought back the memory of his first time; the exact moment he'd clapped eyes on the Piaggio Zip he was going to buy; its splendour and size, the colour, the excitement and awe. It was love at first sight, an instant bonding with a brown-coloured scooter back in 2010. Except for him the emotion had been mixed with a tinge of disappointment and angst. There'd been disappointment because he'd longed for a Vespa but could only afford the Zip, and angst because his older brother Tom was lending him the money.

Bloggin' hell, he didn't want to think about Tom and now here he was summoning up his memory. He still felt the churn in his stomach when Tom came into the equation. Chrissie had once told him the scars from bullying and intimidation transcended time and space.

He shifted his gaze from the Honda and focused on Gayle. Had she been bullied, he wondered. Was it the reason he felt a bond with her? He certainly hadn't thought to ask how she was paying for the Honda. And what would he have done if fate hadn't stepped in to save him? Would he have moved away and changed his name if Tom hadn't left? He reckoned he'd have picked a moniker fit to roll off the tongue, something with style, something Italian.

While Gayle spoke to Steve, Matt waited by his Vespa and concocted variations of his Italian handle, *Matteo*. He watched idly while they used the Honda saddle as a make-do table for the paperwork. Nods and smiles and the handshake were easy to follow as a wodge of cash and papers were exchanged. But why Gayle's sudden step back when Steve touched one of her hands with the pen they'd been using? From where Matt was standing it passed for *don't forget to take your pen*, or possibly a *good luck and safe scootering* gesture, before she took the proffered ballpoint.

He held fire with any questions while she fixed her L plate above her rear number plate. 'All done?' he finally asked, struggling to read her face and match emotions like excitement and pleasure to her frown and set jawline.

'Yes, sure. I'm… I hope I'm going to be OK. You will be right behind, won't you?'

'Yeah, just indicate and pull in if you got a problem.' He figured it was bloggin' obvious she must be excited about her first proper ride on her own scooter. 'Hey, how's about we do a circuit: here to Monks Eleigh then Wattisham and back to Woolpit? The last bit'll be followin' the route you'll be takin' when you're ridin' to work an' back.'

'Cool.' Gayle teased the Honda slowly out of the cul-de-sac and down Lower Road. Matt kept a safe distance behind, ready to jam on his brakes. She came to dead stops at each junction before turning onto roads clear of any approaching traffic. He cruised behind, matching her speed as it crept up from 20 to 30mph, then 35mph. They followed the road out of Lavenham, heading towards Monks Eleigh, but instead of turning off to Bildeston she sailed on round the corner and along the road, ignoring all signposts until she swerved off towards Elmsett.

'What the bloggin' scam she doin'?' he hissed as he tooted his horn and indicated to pull in to the side of the road.

He pushed up his visor when she got off her scooter and walked back to him.

'What's wrong?' she asked, her face framed by her new full face helmet and impossible to read.

'Where you goin'? I thought we were headin' to Bildeston and then Wattisham and the Clegg & Jax workshop.'

'Yes, it's this way, isn't it?'

'Nah, we'll end up goin' past the Elmsett airfield and then into Elmsett. Unless…do you fancy a drink in the pub there?'

He pictured the pub. It was opposite the phone box where the anonymous caller had made a call to Damon. Matt remembered turning his scooter in the pub's parking area, but he hadn't given the pub much attention; his eyes had been on the phone box at the time.

'No thanks,' Gayle said and dropped her gaze.

'What's the pub like, then?' he asked, not sure if she meant no to the pub in Elmsett, or no to a drink anywhere.

'I've never been there. I wouldn't know.'

'Right.' But he couldn't make out what it meant when she still avoided looking at him straight in the face. He'd read on the internet about people looking away when they lied. But why bother to fib about visiting a pub in Elmsett? Or was it about not wanting a drink?

'So how do we get back then?'

'What? Well it'll be quickest if we turn round here. Do a u-ey an' then follow me.'

He led the way back to the B1115 and Bildeston, all the while keeping an eye on her in his wing mirror. She looked very upright on her Honda; steady on the straights and leaning stiffly with the scooter into the bends. He waved her on to overtake him and ride in front, once they'd passed the turning to the Clegg & Jax workshop. From there she'd know her way.

When at times she crept up to 40mph, he supposed it reflected growing confidence. At least speed couldn't lie. It was something measurable, a happiness indicator and so much easier to interpret than a smile. If only faces were as easy to read as a speedometer.

Beep-itty-beep! Beep-itty-beep beep! The strident ring-tone sounded from his pocket as they drew into Woolpit. He slowed to a stop and extracted his mobile, happy to leave her to ride the last section of her journey alone.

'Hi, Nick,' he said, speaking into his phone as she rode out of view.

'Watcha mate. How are you lined up for Saturday?'

'Saturday? How'd you mean?'

CHAPTER 33

It was Friday and Nick had stopped mid-morning for a coffee break with the other carpenters in the Willows office-cum-restroom. He scrolled through his mobile phone's log of recent calls. It was as he thought; his last call had been to Matt. They'd spoken at about seven thirty the previous evening when he'd rung to ask for help with the move into his new flat. He might not be the most physical of his friends, but he'd figured Matt should be able to park his scooter easily enough on Saturday morning in Bury, and more to the point, he'd be a whiz at helping set up their home Wi-Fi and computers. Jake had ideas of turning the living room into a makeshift music room. It was going to be awesome.

'Wahoo, we move tomorrow!'

He almost punched the air. Saturday was less than twenty-four hours away, and if he didn't ring Silvia now, while it was still Friday morning, his apothecary bottle gift would get forgotten in the all excitement and upheaval of the move.

So how long ago had he spoken to Silvia? He scrolled back further. Monday? Hell! He'd promised to tell her the size of the bottles for the apothecary box and… well, he hadn't. God, what had got into him? He wasn't usually this scatty.

'Everything all right, Nick?' The foreman's voice cut into his thoughts.

'What?'

'I don't know; you young'un's and your phones.'

'No, it's not like that. I'm using it as a calendar note-book, OK?' He let his eyes drift back to his mobile, the modern scourge of conversation according to Alfred Walsh, the elderly foreman.

'I've just realised I haven't passed on the details for some antique medicine bottles I was after for an old apoth-ecary box,' he added by way of justification. When Alfred didn't say anything he read out Gayle's text message; '*2 bottles, colourless glass - 4cm x 8cm base. Height 16-17cm.*'

'Ha! I remember my nan had an old blue glass bottle we weren't allowed to touch. She kept it in her kitchen,' Tim, a thin wiry carpenter, murmured.

'That'll be cobalt blue giving the colour to the glass,' Alfred said.

'She used to give us kids a spoonful from it; Easter and All Hallows'. Tasted foul. I reckon it were worming liquid.'

'Nah, it can't have been worming liquid; look at you now. You're still as thin as a rake,' Dave laughed.

'It'll have been a warning - the coloured glass. If you woke in the dark, you wouldn't want any mishaps from what's in the bottle, would you? We're going back a bit, but without electricity, your only light would've been an oil lamp or a flickering fire - so the colour, shape and feel of the glass helped tell you what's inside,' Alfred explained.

Nick pulled his attention away from the conversation, and blanking out his fellow carpenters, faced the filing cab-inets set against the wall. He pressed Silvia's number on his recent calls log.

She answered almost immediately. 'Shinton Dredging. Silvia speaking. How can I help?' It was the same efficient voice he remembered. Not exactly warm or friendly, but neither was it cold. Professional; that was the word.

'Hi, I'm Nick. I was going to get back to you about some bottles for an old apothecary box.' The words came out pat. This time he felt in control. 'I'd like two bottles, about sixteen or seventeen centimetres tall and rectangular in shape; their bases - each four by eight centimetres.'

'Yes, of course, Nick. Now let me make a note of that. Four by… eight,' she mumbled, as if writing it down.

'So, do you have any bottles that size? I was hoping I could drop by after work.'

'Today? Yes… that should be all right. I'll take a look through what's here and get out any bottles that size. It's unlikely there'll be two identical ones. We close at five.'

'Great.' He ended the call and slipped his phone back into his pocket.

Where had his week gone? Monday had been taken up assembling Mr Coady's bridge with Dave, and then he'd returned alone on Tuesday to paint it with wood preservative. And for the last couple of days? He'd been helping in the workshop with a rush order making bespoke garden furniture. Time had flown and now he was in the final countdown before his move. The excitement was rising, just as it had when he was a primary school kid waiting to sing solo in an end of term carol concert.

By four o'clock he'd put his work aside. Filled with anticipation, he drove out of the Willows parking area and turned into the road. A breeze wafted through his open car window and massaged his face as his Fiesta tracked across the tarmac. Catkins blanketed the surface. They'd been shed by the silver birch growing near the road in front of the office showroom. He wondered if Silvia's bottles came in the same shades of green and brown as the dropped and crushed catkins.

'Oh no-o, I didn't say Chrissie's are clear glass. I bet Silvia's will be coloured with moulded ridges or patterns,' he moaned. And then another thought struck. God; the labels! Why the hell hadn't Gayle's text mentioned the labels? And why didn't he notice at the time? He could have kicked himself. It was too late to contact Gayle; he'd be at Silvia's in another twenty minutes.

Nick's route took him past the Wattisham Airfield and Great Bricett, following the B1078 before turning off for Naughton. Hedgerows partially obscured his view across acres of yellow rapeseed, patch-worked with fields of green wheat and barley. He threaded his way along ever narrowing lanes to Whatfield, and then headed towards the Elmsett Airfield. The road seemed to follow the old field boundaries as it twisted and turned, making right-angled bends until, almost without warning, a standing stone to one side of a Y-shaped track off to the right, announced the Elmsett Airfield.

'It's got to be somewhere around here,' he murmured.

A corrugated metal barn the size of a disused hangar, stood out amongst the hedgerows. Some of the full-height sliding panels that formed one end hadn't been fully closed, and a gap wide enough for a man to step through had been left open. Nick drew up in front and got out of the Fiesta. He peered through the aperture. There was no sound of people or voices, and the natural light didn't penetrate far inside. It made it gloomy, but he recognised the grubby yellow hydraulic excavator fitted with a dredging bucket. Dozens of heavy-duty road mats, 3 metres wide, were stacked on a trailer. The equipment looked familiar; he'd seen it in use at the moated farmhouse near Eye. This had to be the depot for the dredging firm; but where was the business office? He hurried across the concrete area in front of the giant sliding panels and traced the long side of the barn.

'SS Shinton Dredging,' he breathed, reading the notice on a door set into the corrugated metal. He couldn't see a bell, so he turned the handle and pushed.

'Hello?' His voice was swallowed by the roomy depot.

'Over here! I'm in the office. Can I help you?'

He recognised Silvia's voice. It issued from a generous sized and well-lit box-shaped cabin, set as if dropped into the barn and positioned up against one wall. Large glass window panels made it seem part of the hangar-sized space. The door was widely open and Nick caught a clear view of a woman inside with short curly brown hair.

'Silvia?' She wasn't as he'd imagined, although he wasn't exactly sure what he'd imagined; certainly not someone with the same stocky build as Shaun.

'Hello. I'm guessing you must be Nick.'

'Yeah, hi.'

'Come into the office. The light's better in here. I've got out all the bottles I thought might be the right size for your box. If not, I've got more glass at home and of course, I can ring round my contacts.'

'Thanks, that's brilliant.'

He stepped into the office, his eyes at once drawn past Silvia's solid shoulders and neatly cropped hair, to a table laden with glass bottles. 'Wow!' he breathed.

Cardboard boxes spilled from the far end of the table to the floor, log jamming the space, while scrunched up newspaper threatened to escape the opened boxes and take over the office. Without thinking, he moved nearer and picked up a clear glass bottle with ridges embossed on the glass.

'I call that a green aqua glass,' Silvia said, moving closer to him. 'See it has a kind of green colour if you hold it up to the light. Those marks on the front are from the label, and those,' she leaned forward and pointed, 'are from being in the silt for so long.'

'It's nice, but the top is chipped and it's round, so it wouldn't fit,' Nick murmured.

'How about this one? It's oblong and it's got a wider neck.'

'Yes, but the shape is more of a square than oblong. It wouldn't fit. Hey, but this one looks more like four by eight.'

'And it's got LUNG TONIC embossed on the glass.'

'Neat - but it's kind of blue.'

'I call it medical blue – almost clear but yes, there's definitely a faint blue colour to the glass.'

'Sorry Silvia; I should have said; the other bottles in the box are all colourless... you know, clear glass,' Nick blurted, finally coming clean with what he should have said at the start. His face burned.

She didn't seem to hear him, but reached for another and continued, 'Now this one's unusual. It still has part of its label. If you look closely you can just about make out the letters.' She read them out; 'I P E C A C U A N H A.'

'Awesome. So what's ipi..kac...?' he struggled.

'According to the internet it comes from the root of some kind of South American plant. Apparently it makes you vomit. So if a kid swallowed something poisonous, then a glug of this and back it all comes with the poison.

That's if they've been given it in time. And catarrh – it helped you cough catarrh from your chest.'

'Right, and it's kinda cool with its label. But the bottle has a round base, you know - cylinder-shaped, not oblong. It's not going to match the others in the box.'

They fell into silence as Nick ran his hand over a collection of old brown-black beer bottles. The problem was obvious; they were all cylinder-shaped. There just weren't many flat-sided bottles, and the glass, whether it was coloured, completely clear, or with green or blue tones, was likely cracked or chipped, and marked from years reacting to elements in the silt and water.

'I suppose it's inevitable the label will be lost if a bottle's been submerged in water. And I can see from all those boxes; you must've looked through loads just to find these ones for me. I'm sorry, Silvia, but none of these are going to fit or match. It's hopeless. I guess gold and bronze objects, and bits of pottery are better finds in the dredging world,' he sighed.

'A cylinder-shape bottle is usually stronger than one with flat sides. So it's hardly surprising we've found more of them; they're the ones that survive, like the beer bottles here.' Her tone had developed a hard vein, as if on the defensive but at the same time patronising.

'No. Sorry, Silvia. I didn't mean anything. It's just none of these are right for the apothecary box.'

She faced him with silence. Hell! What had he said to make her take that attitude? Was it because she'd missed out on a sale? He scratched his head.

'Look, I'm sorry if I've wasted your time, Silvia. It's just that Shaun said....' He caught the flash in her eyes. 'Hey, maybe there's something else I could give my friend?

Tell me about the other things you dredge up. Maybe there's something like an old coin, or a lucky horseshoe, or–'

'*Gold and bronze objects, and bits of pottery*, is what I think you said a few moments ago,' she finished for him.

'Well yeah, there was that Dunwich Jewel. I heard about it on the radio. They said it was found in Suffolk – somewhere near Dunwich. I mean things like that get found, right?'

'Not by us. Not by anyone I know.'

'No, well I guess something like that must be pretty rare.'

Nick watched her face as Dave's voice played back in his head. He'd said something about the dredging and metal detecting worlds being the ones to know who was behind the undeclared treasure find. It was a case of ear to the ground, word on the street – that kind of thing. She was bound to know something.

He wondered if she wanted to be coaxed and flattered.

'But I thought Shaun said the firm had been doing a dredging job near Walberswick? And the metal detecting and dredging worlds are small,' he said, slipping into chat-up mode.

'Yes, I suppose you could say that.'

He sensed her tone soften. 'And it must be pretty exciting when something out of the ordinary is found. People boast, maybe exaggerate? You know, like fishermen's tales?' he cajoled, smiling.

'You mean like finding a single coin and then telling everyone it's a hoard? That kind of talk could end up meaning it's classified as treasure and has to be declared, whereas the single coin is between you and the landowner. Exaggerating can land you in trouble, so no fishermen's tales.'

'Oh yeah, that's right: anything from 2 or 9 coins could be counted as treasure, depending on their age and gold or silver content. Yeah, I've heard that.'

'Seems you know more about this than you let on,' she laughed.

'Well, nothing compared to all you know, I'm sure.'

He was rewarded with her first warm smile since she'd invited him into the office.

'So, how about I look out a coin minted around the date of the apothecary box? Would that be something you'd be interested in?'

'Now that would be really cool. I can give it to Chrissie instead of a bottle. I can't go wrong with that. Yes – better than a bottle. She can slip it in the box! Thanks, Silvia.'

'Any specific date or date rage?' A shadow seemed to cross her face as she continued, 'Is she your…?'

'No, no…just a good mate; it's a kinda thank you. She goes mudlarking, so it's… well she's bound to like it.' He guessed he was sharing too much; generally he didn't talk about other girls when he was in smooth-talking mode. And he certainly wasn't going to let slip the reason for the gift - an unspoken thank you for helping dispose of the laughing gas canisters strewn outside his attic lodging. He noticed Silvia was watching him with unusual intensity.

'Right, the date on the coin,' he said firmly. 'I reckon mid- or early Victorian would be OK.'

'So, something around 1840?'

'Cool.'

'OK then. I'll have a look through my coins and get back to you.'

'Thanks, Silvia.' He sensed she would have said more, but he didn't want to waste any further time on the bottle project, at least not while his final packing for the move was still waiting. And anyway, it looked as if the bottle was going to become a coin. 'I'll wait to hear from you then,' he murmured and rattled off his mobile number before quickly smiling his goodbye.

'Goodbye,' she called after him as he headed out of her office and the barn-like depot.

Back in his car, he shot a text to Chrissie: *Won't make Nags Head tonight – packing. Any help moving tomorrow would be great. If you're busy, no worries.*

He started his Fiesta and pulled away slowly, passing Shaun driving in the opposite direction. Shaun, sitting tall in his 4X4, seemed to look surprised. Nick smiled and waved, and drove on.

CHAPTER 34

Clive made a couple of mugs of coffee while Chrissie read Nick's text message. *Won't make Nags Head tonight – packing. Any help moving tomorrow would be great. If you're busy, no worries.*

'Anything important?' Clive asked.

It was Friday and unusual for Clive to already be at home for half past five. They were both in the kitchen and still in the process of shaking off the day, not quite ready to make the transition from work.

'It's from Nick. He's moving to a new flat tomorrow so he won't make it to the Nags Head tonight. He's packing,' she added by way of explanation.

'St Andrews Street South, didn't you say?'

'Yes, that's what he told us last week. His text also says *any help moving would be great*, but he's been staying with Jake and all his stuff is round at Jake's. They're both moving into the flat, so they can help each other. I'll only get in the way. I thought I'd drop round once the worst of it's over.'

'Right. And the Nags Head?'

'I'll give it a miss now you're home. You aren't going out again? I mean you're not still working, are you?'

'Not really. Some paperwork, but I couldn't face it this evening. It can wait until tomorrow.'

She caught his tone and the frown, not the fleeting shadow but the persistent furrow across his forehead.

'What's up?' It was obvious something was troubling him. When he didn't answer, but stood leaning against the butler sink and sipped his coffee, she tried a different tack.

'Talking of Nick and his move, has anything come back on those bin liners full of the laughing gas canisters?'

'Hah! How the hell did you know Forensics are giving me hassle, Chrissie?'

'I didn't. Why? Have Forensics found something?' Cold dread gripped her stomach.

'Good God, they don't work that fast, and it's hardly a priority. No. They're baulking at dusting hundreds of canisters for prints, and they're threatening a massive bill. It's not going to pass unnoticed through the books, and when it's questioned it'll come out that the request wasn't authorised by the chief. I've had an awkward conversation about it this afternoon.'

'Oh no, and it's all my fault. Do you think they might play ball if you asked for less? Only to look at the boxes which the new canisters came in? You know, the pieces of box card saying *144 Cream Chargers*. Remember the black lettering? It might be possible to trace who supplied them... or there might even be some prints on them.'

'Hmm, yes I suppose....' He seemed lost in contemplation of his coffee mug.

'So, did anything good happen today? I mean anything positive to move the case forward?' she asked.

'What?' He seemed to drag his attention back from his coffee mug. 'Well I suppose Stickley is turning up some interesting stuff. He's been following up on the hospice lead. It seems fentanyl isn't the only drug that's gone missing. Some vials of a high strength preparation of midazolam are also unaccounted for.'

'Really?'

'Yes, apparently the high strength midazolam is pretty much only used in hospices. And since Stickley's been sniffing around, the missing midazolam has come to light. Or rather, the hospice has checked through everything and there's some midazolam they can't account for.'

'So what's midazolam?'

'It's a rapid onset, short acting sedative. Not a pain-killer or anaesthetic agent like fentanyl, but it has the ability to stop you remembering things as well as taking away anxiety. At least that's what I've been told.'

'Right, so if it's all gone missing from the same hospice, do they think it's been stolen by the same person?'

'Too early to say. And yes, before you ask; we've checked with Jon Dareham's medical record, and yes, he was on a regular prescription for a nose spray for hay fever.'

'Well there you go. So he could have taken the fentanyl spray thinking it was something new for his hay fever.'

'Possibly... but it's a bit of a long shot. I mean the packaging... and if he'd recognised the name, or the word fentanyl in the contents, it would have been a bit of a give-away. No, I think it's more likely it was forced on him. There was blood in his nose.'

'Oh yes, I remember you saying.' She let her thoughts curve back to Nick, her mind alive with the snippets of information. 'Do you think the anonymous tip off to the police could be linked to someone who'd been watching him, like a stalker? I mean it doesn't have to be the person who dumped the laughing gas canisters.'

'Him? Are we talking about Jon Dareham, still?'

'No, I meant Nick. That's who we'd originally been talking about. Have you got any closer to discovering who the female caller to the police was?'

'No, and it's unlikely we ever will.'

She knew his tone, recognised his irritation. His words might be intended as a full stop to her line of probing, but she couldn't let it rest there; not while she blamed Sarah for over reacting and being too quick to accuse Nick, and then her. It was a betrayal.

'The thing I can't get my head around is the way Sarah behaved in all this. Do you think she could have been the anonymous caller?' Chrissie said, voicing her deepest suspicions.

'What? Now slow down, Chrissie. You can't seriously think Sarah dumped the laughing gas canisters?'

'No I don't, but I bet she'd been watching Nick. She's always secretly fancied him.'

'But I've never had Sarah down as a watcher. She's always struck me as a doer.'

'Yes, I agree but I need to hear it from her. I need to know she wasn't the one who tipped off the police. Otherwise, well - I'll never be able to trust her again.'

'But you can't–'

'Yes I can. Tomorrow you'll be at work writing reports, so I'll go round to see her for a coffee and a chat. Anyway, what type of person would you say was a watcher, then?'

'I'd say the quieter, retiring type. You know, more like Gayle than Sarah. Someone who isn't open enough to say they fancy Nick and can't handle rejection. Or it could be someone who is obsessive, with few or no close friends, but somehow feels empowered by watching.'

'Really? Chrissie frowned as she tried to match the traits with Gayle and Sarah. Gayle was unquestionably quiet and retiring, didn't seem to have any friends, and had never struck Chrissie as being a doer. But a watcher? Weren't good apprentices supposed to be watchers?

Clive must have read her mind. 'I'm not saying it's Gayle. I'm talking personality types, not specific people. There's a big difference between being a good observer and someone who's an obsessive watcher or stalker.'

'But Gayle moved here from the Midlands. And she's learnt to ride a scooter. That has to make her a bit of a doer underneath all her shyness.'

'Yes, and without knowing more about the how and the why behind her move, this is all just pointless speculation, Chrissie.' Clive sighed and briefly shook his head before draining the rest of his coffee in a single gulp. 'So what are we doing for supper?' he asked as he rinsed his mug under the tap.

'Well if you're on duty call now, then let's eat here. It won't take me a moment to cook some pasta and toss it in some green pesto.'

'Hmm, and there's some cooked chicken leftover in the fridge we could have with it.'

'And salad,' she smiled.

Chrissie felt disappointed. The knotty subject of personality types and traits might have been closed, but at least her mind still had plenty to work on with all that he'd said.

•••

The following morning Chrissie was surprised to feel slightly apprehensive as she walked to Sarah's house. It was Saturday and later in the morning than she had intended. The wind had already wiped the sky clean and only a few clouds remained, allowing patchy sunshine to warm her through her light cotton coach jacket. She may have been the one who had initiated the meeting, but Sarah was the one who had suggested the chat over coffee would be more fun if combined with a glass of wine over a lunchtime snack.

Chrissie supposed, as she walked through Woolpit's small triangular marketplace, that the suggestion of wine over lunchtime snacks was what made Sarah fun and why she'd always thought of her as generous, friendly and forgiving. Except with Nick and the cream chargers she'd been anything but forgiving. In fact she'd been quite out of character, even going so far as to make accusations against Chrissie. And that was at the heart of it. In Chrissie's book, trust worked both ways. If Sarah didn't trust her to be upfront about drugs and Nick, then how could she trust Sarah?

A rhododendron peppered with crimson blooms came into view, dwarfing a garden wall as she walked past more houses and turned into a quite lane. White flowering hawthorn filled sections of wild hedgerow as she neared the entrance to Sarah's house, the gate open, as always.

She spotted Sarah's car parked in the driveway and recognised Gayle's scooter, almost out of sight alongside the double garage with the garret lodging above. Before she'd had a chance to reach the kitchen door, Sarah flung it open, her arms outstretched in welcome, her face smiling and her black feather-cut hair shaping her head.

'Hi, Chrissie. Come on in. I haven't seen you in weeks!'

'Hi, we have spoken, though.'

'Oh yes, that... business.' She guided Chrissie into the kitchen, doubled in size by incorporating the old breakfast room. It was mildly untidy, with a pile of washing heaped on an ironing board. The house had been built in the 1930s, but the kitchen breakfast room combo had a more modern feel.

'I thought we'd sit in the conservatory,' Sarah said, opening the fridge and taking out a bottle of Muscadet. 'I've already carried a tray through with some glasses and snacks. And there are olives. I know you like them.'

Sarah led the way out of the kitchen and through the hallway and living room. Large French windows opened onto the conservatory and Sarah's pale kaftan dress swirled around her calves as she walked. Chrissie waited as she put the Muscadet on a glass-topped coffee table.

'So how are you getting on with your new lodger?' Chrissie asked in a conversational tone.

Sarah didn't answer, instead fussing with a couple of glasses and pouring the wine.

'Well?' Chrissie prompted and sank onto a cushioned rattan chair.

'She's... I'm hardly aware Gayle's here. I hate to say it, but I miss Nick - his friends coming round, his old blue Fiesta in the drive. You know he used to play music into all hours of the night?' She waved one arm expansively.

'So why did you ask him to go?'

Sarah handed her an overfull glass of the Muscadet before pulling a *how do I know?* face.

'Come on, Sarah. You must know. He'd been your lodger long enough for you to know he wasn't into drugs.'

Sarah smiled weakly.

Chrissie raised her eyebrows.

'How long have you known me, Chrissie?'

'Since... I'd say January 2008?'

'And in all that time, haven't I always preferred younger blokes? Take the fencing instructor.... It was a bit of a downer when Nick wasn't interested in me, but it was still nice to have him around. And there was always a chance he might change his mind.'

'But why kick him out if you fancied him? And why call the police?'

'Call the police? You think it was me? Why the hell would I do that? The last thing I wanted was the police crawling all over my property and the whole of Woolpit knowing about it.'

'But someone tipped them off. Have you ever stopped to wonder who that person was?'

'No.'

'Well, it's been bothering me, particularly when I discovered from Clive that it was an anonymous female caller.'

Sarah didn't say anything, just stared at Chrissie. 'Well I can assure you it wasn't me. As it happens, I had a dental appointment in Ipswich in my lunch break that day. I always get anxious about the dentist. It's probably why I lost it with Nick in the morning. It freaked me out when I found those cream chargers thrown all over the place.'

Chrissie frowned. 'Is your dentist–'

'Young? No, and I hate going to the dentist.' Sarah set her jaw and gazed through the French windows for a moment. With a sigh she placed her glass down on the coffee table.

'Look, Chrissie – I don't know what came over me. I can't explain it. I don't even know why I overreacted like that with Nick. And now… I wish I could put it right.'

'Yes, we've all got a bit bruised over this, and, well, I suppose in a way Nick has landed on his feet.' Chrissie sipped her wine. 'You do know you upset me, Sarah. It really hurt when you accused me of not having told you Nick was some kind of nitrous oxide addict. Well he's not... and he was set up. He was the one who discovered that bloke who was found dead from laughing gas, near Eye. Don't you understand, someone's trying to incriminate him, land him in trouble with the police?'

'Is that what this is all about? I'm so sorry, Chrissie. I was just lashing out. I had no idea Nick might be in trouble. Hell, why didn't you say?'

Conversation died as they sank into their own thoughts. Chrissie sipped her wine and nibbled on the smorgasbord of crispbreads, cheese, salami, gherkins and olives.

'So if neither of us tipped the police off, who do you think did?' Sarah said slowly.

'I don't know.'

'Have you talked to Gayle about it?'

'And why would I do that?'

'I don't know. It's just that Gayle kind of benefitted from Nick getting kicked out. She might have heard something.'

'But....' Chrissie bit her tongue. She had already said too much about the case. All the details around the anonymous call to the police should have stayed with her. Why hadn't she kept her big mouth shut and Clive's information a secret? If she hadn't been feeling bad about it all before, she certainly felt bad now, and she wasn't going to fall into the same trap again and start talking character profiles.

'What were you about to say?' Sarah asked.

'This Muscadet goes well with the salami and cheese.'

The conversation moved to easier subjects: Sarah's holiday planned in Majorca for later in the summer, and

Chrissie's Limoges plate bought for a song from Mrs Dell in Sudbury. Time passed and Chrissie mellowed. She almost forgot about Clive's cases as Sarah talked about her up-and-coming role as Lady Bracknell in the local am-dram production of The Importance of Being Earnest. Bit by bit, they relaxed and things slipped back to normal between them. Of course the third glass of Muscadet helped.

'Is that the time?' Chrissie said eventually, focusing on her watch, 'It's almost four o'clock.'

CHAPTER 35

Matt sat on the floor in the centre of the largest room in his friends' new flat. It could only be described as cramped: a galley kitchen, bijou bathroom and smallish living room, all stretching over a baker's shop. Above him was the attic, reached by a steep narrow staircase and made up of two small rooms, each barely wide enough to take a double bed and virtually nothing else. He'd maintained his floor-sitting position for the last twenty minutes, while Nick and Jake moved furniture and boxes in around him.

'Your plug sockets are over there on the wall,' he mumbled. 'I s'pose it'll be where you plug in your speakers an' amp.'

'Cool; speakers and amp in the middle of the living room!'

'Nah, Jake – well maybe. But you'll have to plug 'em in on the wall there.'

'Right, so we'll put the double futon opposite. It'll work as a sofa for the moment. Oi, shift your butt, Matt; you're in the way just sitting there,' Nick muttered.

'It looked larger when it was empty. How about you move these boxes into the kitchen, Matt?'

'OK, OK, Jake. You 'ave noticed the kitchen aint too big, aint you? It might be a squeeze for 'em?'

He had hoped, when he'd arrived three hours ago, he'd miss the worst of the lifting and also find a bite to eat. Fortunately, Nick and Jake had already carried the divan beds through the narrow ground floor doorway, up the stairs to their flat, and then up again to the attic bedrooms. The sausage rolls and sticky buns had been eaten, but Matt had been lucky to find a can of lager going begging. So he'd screwed the legs on the divan bases and swigged lager.

When he checked the time on his phone it felt as if he'd been there for ever. 15:58. Saturday afternoon was about to drift into early evening. Fraggin' malware, he was hungry. And when was Chrissie coming?

•••

Chrissie lingered in Sarah's kitchen while she loaded the dishwasher with the dirty plates from their smorgasbord lunch. Chrissie's glass went in, but she noticed Sarah left her own one on the kitchen table. Chrissie guessed she intended to fill it with another glug of wine from the fridge, just as soon as the kitchen door closed behind her.

'Bye, Sarah. And thanks.'

'Yes, we should do this more often. Give my love to Clive. I hope he gets back early enough for you to spend the evening together.'

'I'm sure he'll be home well in time for dinner,' she laughed, and for once she didn't mind that he'd spent far longer than he'd said he'd take to write reports and piece loose ends together. He might have been called to something urgent, but even that thought couldn't shake her relaxed mood. 'Goodbye,' she smiled and stepped into the warm late afternoon.

It had felt good to chill out with Sarah. Somehow it had restored her sense of proportion and humour, straightening her mind, and focusing her on her work and business. It was patently obvious that normal people, if Sarah could be considered normal, didn't spend their time fretting over murder investigations, times of phone calls, and laughing gas. They picked over relationships and people, and with relationships in mind, she noted that Gayle's scooter was still parked exactly as it had been parked when she'd first walked down Sarah's drive earlier that day.

So, was Gayle all right? Was staying in for most of a Saturday normal if you were aged nineteen? Chrissie didn't know. She was beginning to wonder if she could even tell what normal was anymore.

In a flash she knew what she must do. With sudden purpose in her stride, and emboldened by the Muscadet, she headed for the outside steps to Gayle's room above the double garage. Barely pausing to listen for any sound or voices inside, she knocked on the door and waited. There wasn't time to worry if she might be stepping over the line between trainer and uninvited guest. The door catch release clicked and the handle turned.

'Chrissie?' The surprise in Gayle's voice was palpable.

'Hello, Gayle. I was just passing and… is this convenient? I-I can drop by another time. It isn't anything important,' she said, trying to read Gayle's face.

Gayle opened the door more widely. 'No, come in.' Her words failed to exude a welcome and her face expressed something akin to wariness.

'Did you just say Chrissie?' a new voice asked.

'What? Oh, I'm sorry, Gayle; I didn't realise you had a….' The words died on Chrissie's tongue as she stepped inside and met the appraising gaze of a stranger dressed in lightweight jeans, trainers and a cropped hoody sweatshirt. Chrissie's mind might have been Muscadet-fuzzed, but her curiosity wasn't blunted. It spun into action. The clothes were unisex, the body stocky, and yes, there were breasts. The short curly brown hair was styled to an androgynous length.

'Hello. Are you Gayle's…?' Chrissie asked, not sure whether to say mother or friend.

The stranger smiled and glanced at Gayle.

'No, I don't know her. She's someone just come to see Nick,' Gayle explained.

'Well, it was more to bring him something,' the stranger added.

'Right, you said when I opened the door. I'm sorry, but I've forgotten what you said your name was.'

'Silvia.'

'Hi, Silvia,' Chrissie said with lunch-induced amiability.

'Look, I don't mean to intrude, but I thought Nick lived here. I came because he asked me for something from our dredging finds. Something he wanted to give as a thank you. He didn't say why, but the name Chrissie came up. Are you… the Chrissie he mentioned?'

'Ah, now I've got what this is about,' Gayle said in her small voice, her forehead smoothing but the wariness never leaving her eyes.

Chrissie waited, her attention torn from Silvia to Gayle, who quietly closed the door.

'Is it about an apothecary box?' Gayle asked.

'What, Gayle? Are you talking about my, sorry… your apothecary box project?'

'Yeah, Chrissie. Nick said it was his surprise.'

'But it's your project, not his. I don't understand?'

'And I don't get it either, at least not all the fuss about the stuff in the box. I mean, it's only a crappy old chemist's box, right?'

'What? Is that what you really think, Gayle?'

'No, s-sorry, Chrissie. I didn't mean the box, just the stuff inside.' Gayle's cheeks flamed. She dropped her gaze, but she was obviously addressing Silvia when she continued, 'So am I right? Is this about, I mean… are you here with something for the apothecary box?'

'Oh, this is getting awkward. Where's Nick? I just wanted to give him….'

'Give him what? W-What's in your… b-basket?' Gayle's voice came in slow breathy rasps.

'Woah, Gayle? Are you…?' Chrissie's words died as Gayle's knees sagged. 'Gayle!' She grabbed her waist. 'Help me, Silvia. I think she's going to faint!'

Together they guided Gayle's collapsing body.

'Just as well it's cramped in here; otherwise we'd never have reached the bed,' Chrissie puffed, as they let her body slump onto the mattress and raised her legs off the floor.

'There's barely space to swing a cat.'

'Nick called it cosy. Hey, Gayle! Gayle?' Chrissie watched the girl's pale face. She looked peaceful, her breathing gentle, almost silent.

'How do you know she's fainted?'

'Because she's always fainting. She'll pink up and come round in a moment.'

Chrissie looked past Silvia. The furniture was in the same positions as when Nick had lived there. The bed was still pushed against the long wall where the ceiling sloped above it, and the bedside cabinet still stood like a makeshift headboard across the pillow end of the bed. Gayle didn't appear to have stamped her presence on the space at all, apart from the tidiness. Despite being small, it felt empty, haunted by the ghost of a guitar in the corner, dirty mugs in the sink, clothes flung over the only chair, and CDs in chaotic stacks. Nick's absence was almost palpable. Chrissie's foot caught against something.

'Sorry, Chrissie. I shouldn't have put my basket there.'

'Oh, is it yours?'

'Well yes, I had to use something to carry the things here for Nick.'

'Did you have to walk far, then?'

A breathy moan cut in from Gayle.

'Ah good, I think she's coming round,' Chrissie whispered, switching her attention back to Gayle, 'It's all right, Gayle. You just fainted, that's all.'

Thank God her face looked pinker. Chrissie knew she'd sounded sure and experienced talking about faints a few moments ago, but really, seeing the life drain from Gayle for twenty seconds was terrifying. It had to have been the Muscadet talking to make her sound so certain. Oh no! Her breath probably smelled of alcohol. Did they think she was... drunk?

Silvia's voice butted into her thoughts. 'So why a thank you present? Nick's gone to a lot of trouble over this.'

'What? Oh I don't know. It's probably because I helped him dispose of some rubbish.'

'I-I'm... so sorry. My head went all floaty.' Gayle's thready voice held the room.

'Oh Gayle. Poor you. No, don't try and sit up for a moment. What about... would a glass of water help?' Chrissie cooed.

'I've got a bottle of my elderflower cordial in my basket, if you'd like some. I only made it last week. It was... I brought it for Nick, but... well he isn't here so you might as well have it. It'll probably be better for you than just a glass of water.'

'Yes, loads of sugar, and... and plenty of fluid. Good idea. You probably haven't been drinking enough. And probably not eating enough, either,' Chrissie said, maintaining a mixed tone between trainer and mother hen.

She watched Gayle nod in weak agreement while Silvia rummaged in the basket and lifted out a bottle with a metal spring-release stopper. Chrissie heard rather than saw the tumbler being taken from a shelf near the sink, a bottle being opened, liquid being poured and water running from the tap. The sounds were homely and comforting. They softened the stark functionality of the room.

'Have you known Nick long, Chrissie?' Silvia asked in a business-like manner.

•••

Brr brr, brr brr! Nick paused as he decanted plates, cutlery and pans from one of the boxes Matt had shoved into the galley kitchen. The ratty drawers and shelves were simply not large enough for all the stuff. *Brr brr, brr brr!* Great; at least he had an excuse to stop for a moment while he retrieved his phone from the deep pocket in his cargo shorts.

'Yes?' he said and wiped the sweat from his forehead. Jeeze, it was getting hot in the flat.

'Hello? Is that Nick?'

'Yeah, hi.' He recognised Clive's voice immediately. 'I don't suppose you're offering to come and give us a hand, are you? Chrissie said she'd be over sometime.'

'Ah, I was hoping to catch her. Is she with you now?'

'Afraid not. Have you called her?'

'Yes, but she's not answering. I wondered if she'd slung her phone and bag down somewhere in your new flat and hadn't heard it ring.'

'Can't help you, I'm afraid. Do you want me to give her a message if she calls or turns up?'

'No, it's just... well you can say I'd tried to call her. Nothing urgent. OK, then; sorry to trouble you. Oh, I haven't asked. How's the move going?'

'OK, Clive. But it's bloody hot. I reckon we're right over the ovens.'

'Ovens?'

'Yeah, we're over a bakery. They bake early morning, not Saturday afternoon. God knows what it'll be like when they're baking. Bye.'

Nick checked the time on his phone before slipping it back in his pocket. 17:30.

•••

'So you've known Nick for nearly five years, you say?' Silvia rested back in the only chair and looked at Chrissie. It was the same appraising stare she'd given her earlier.

Chrissie sat on the edge of the bed, leaving space behind her for Gayle's feet, while Gayle lay with her head and shoulders propped up on pillows and sipped the elderflower cordial.

It occurred to Chrissie, as she met Sylvia's stare, that they were probably of a similar age. Could Silvia possibly view her as a love rival? Did this woman with curly brown hair have a romantic interest in Nick? Well more fool her. Perhaps it was time to have a bit of fun with the woman. After all, she couldn't imagine Nick actually wanting to be pursued by Silvia. He usually went for someone more Gayle's age. So, still fired with the Muscadet, she cast caution to the wind, and launched into a string of half-truths and misleading statements.

'Yes, Nick's mother was very concerned when he started hanging out with a woman twice his age. And as I said, we've been,' she paused for effect, 'good friends since we first met in 2009.'

'So does he confide in you?'

'Now that's an interesting question. In what way do you mean, confide?'

'Well, our firm was dredging in the same location where that poor man died. Laughing gas, I'm told. We'd always known him as Tuscan Grabb when he worked for us, but it seems his real name was Toussaint, not Tuscan.'

'Why do you want to bring that up?'

'Well, I've always wondered what really happened, and Nick was first on the scene. I'd love to know what he's said about it. He must have told you something.'

Gayle stirred behind her. 'Yeah, Chrissie. P-please tell us.'

'No, nothing. He's said nothing.' Chrissie's words came a little too fast.

'Hmm….' Silvia frowned. 'And what about you, Gayle? Why are you…? How do you fit in here? I thought this was Nick's room?'

'Yeah, well he left. I'm the lodger now.'

The mattress moved a little, and Chrissie felt Gayle tap her arm. 'Please, Chrissie. Please… what did Nick tell you?'

'I've already said. Nothing, Gayle. And anyway, why the interest? It was before your time. Before you came to Stowmarket, unless…?' Chrissie broke off. Why had she always assumed Gayle had transferred straight from Leicester to the Academy? She could have been in the area for weeks before the term started.

Now Silvia was staring at her. No, she was staring at both of them, an odd expression tightening her face.

'It sounds as if Nick has been playing the field with you two. I think he's been devious, really d-e-vious.' Silvia let the word drag before continuing, 'A little bird told me you were interested in mudlarking, Chrissie. Tell me, have you been up to the British Museum recently to look at aestels?'

'The British Museum? Yes, but it was for the Viking Exhibition.' Hell, she was losing control of this game. Where was Silvia leading? She needed to clear the Muscadet from her head.

'Ah! So I was right. You have been up to the British Museum recently. And Nick told me he's interested in metal detecting and dredging finds. So it seems you two are well matched. But I don't need to tell you that, you already know.'

'Bottles! Nick asked you for antique glass – old bottles for the apothecary box.' Chrissie smiled. It was a guessing game, and she'd finally worked it out.

'Yes, well done. But Nick also asked about something else.'

'Aestels? You mentioned aestels.' She was getting the hang of this. She'd be even sharper if she could clear her head. Some water or…, 'Hey Gayle. How was the elderflower cordial?'

'It's nice.'

'Oh good,' Silvia beamed, 'Do you want some more, Gayle? And Chrissie; how about you? Do you want to try some?'

'Well if Gayle liked it, then yes please.'

Chrissie tried to focus her thoughts while Silvia fussed with the basket and tumblers, taking longer this time to pour the cordial. If this woman was from the dredging firm and knew Nick, then…. A shadow of a thought flicked through her mind, but it was too fast to grasp.

'Thanks,' she said, as Silvia handed out the tumblers.

'Have you made it stronger?' Gayle asked, as she sipped her cordial.

'Oh sorry, do you want more water in it?'

'No, no; it's nice. I like sweet drinks.'

'Hmm,' Chrissie murmured. 'So what am I tasting? Elderflower, and sweetness, and… a hint of lemon. And there's something else. Hmm, the elderflower comes through strongly.' She checked the time on her watch. Hell! It was after six o'clock. Where had the afternoon gone? And she had supper to cook. She reached for her bag. She ought to ring Clive and let him know she was running late.

'Aren't you going to finish it?'

She caught Silvia's hurt expression and swigged back more. She really could have done with extra water in the cordial, but asking for it would have slowed things up.

'It's delicious,' she said and glanced at Gayle to check if she thought the same.

Gayle smiled.

It struck Chrissie that it was the first time the girl had smiled since she'd been there.

'You know, I only popped round to check you were OK, Gayle. But with Silvia being here, I've got side tracked. I hope you're settling in all right.' Chrissie made to move but her legs felt tired. Now where was her phone?

She scrabbled in her bag but…. Hell, she must have left it at Sarah's.

CHAPTER 36

Nick and Jake sat, or rather half lay on the futon, their legs stretched out and each holding a bottle of beer. Matt sprawled on the floor, an empty can of lager balanced on his chest, arms straightened as if spread-eagled, and his eyes open and gazing at the ceiling.

'Looks like the can won,' Nick said, and drank beer from his bottle.

'Yup, a knock out,' Jake added.

'I see a song.'

'I hear pain.'

Brr brr, brr brr! Nick grabbed his phone. 'Yeah?'

'Hello, it's Clive. Is Chrissie with you yet?'

'No. We could do with an injection of energy. Has she answered her phone yet?'

'No.'

'Or the house number?'

'No, but I've discovered where she left her mobile. I remembered she was seeing Sarah today so I called her. Sarah said she left at about four o'clock, but without her phone. It's still at Sarah's.'

'Four o'clock? But that was almost three hours ago. You don't think she's had an accident or anything, do you?'

'God, I hope not. Mind you, Sarah sounded like she'd had a skinful. At least Chrissie had the sense to walk to Sarah's, so I guess she knew she'd be having a glass over lunch.'

'Could she have called in to see Gayle? I mean she'd have walked past her room.'

'I asked Sarah to check, but no, Gayle hasn't seen her. Anyway, she hasn't driven to you, right?'

'We've not seen her all day.'

'OK, then I'll go straight home now. She could have… well those stairs are bloody steep.'

'Call me if she's there, Clive. No, call me anyway. You've got me worried now.'

He'd grown used to Clive; he'd heard him irritable and curt before – but rattled like this? What was Chrissie playing at? 'God, I hope she's all right,' he muttered. He checked the time on his mobile again before slipping it back into his cargo shorts. 18:52.

•••

Chrissie came-to with the suddenness of a light bulb. It was as if one moment she had been scrabbling in her bag for her phone; the next she was opening her eyes, one cheek pressing on a worn carpet. But there was a problem. She couldn't summon any memory between the two moments.

A leg and foot in lightweight jeans and clean white trainer stood close to her; so close it almost brushed her forehead. It took Chrissie a moment to process the information: she was lying on a carpet.

She knew the carpet, recognised its threadbare appearance, its tired colour. Woah – she was lying on the carpet in Nick's old room. Gayle's new room. She turned her head a fraction. Was she staring at the underside of a bed? God, she was lying under the bed. What?

She tried to move her arm, but it was trapped under her chest, pinned down and numbed by her own weight. How the…? Had someone rolled her under the bed? She was about to cry out, but an icy thought caught her breath.

Somebody must have wanted her to be under the bed and out of the way. But who? And why?

She blinked, wrinkled her nose and swallowed. Yes; she was awake. Yes; she was alive, and yes; she really was under a bed. She strained to catch the faintest sound. All she caught was silence. But she knew she wasn't alone; there was a person wearing jeans and white trainers in the room.

She focused on the things she remembered before the nothingness, before she thrust her hand into her bag for her phone. Hadn't she held a tumbler? Yes, she remembered the feel of the glass. That's right – elderflower cordial. Of course, Gayle and – Silvia!

Oh, no… the trainer was on the move. It edged towards the head end of the bed, paused and without a sound, stepped away. It made a couple of paces with its partner and then *crash!* Shiny metal ampules, the best part of a box-load of cream chargers, bounced, rolled and cavorted onto the carpet. Chrissie flinched.

A metal release valve for the cream chargers landed heavily on the floor, *clunk!* It sent a shiny metallic ampule spinning. She held her breath and caught the sound of something being shaken. A handful of unused party balloons landed near the release valve. A moment later two large clear plastic bags floated to the carpet. Then silence returned, along with an uneasy stillness.

What the hell? Instinct kept her quiet. Confused and frightened, she centred herself by focusing on what she could remember. Gayle had fainted and Sylvia had helped to lay the pale limp girl on the bed. Yes, and then Chrissie knocked her foot against something. Silvia had said she needed a basket to carry things in. That was it! Silvia's basket must have just been tipped onto the floor.

Chrissie's stomach flipped. The carpet was covered in the kind of things Clive had found with Toussaint, dead in his boat. He'd called it laughing gas paraphernalia. Except why the plastic bags? She didn't recall him mentioning bags.

Something stirred above her on the bed.

'Gayle? Gayle, I need you to stay quiet for me.' Silvia's voice broke the silence.

Chrissie recoiled at the sudden command. It pierced the invisible barrier between the space under the bed and the rest of the room, the words more frightening than the crashes and bangs.

'We don't want your landlady knocking on your door again, now do we, Gayle? We don't want her knowing you've got guests up here. You enjoyed playing the connection game, didn't you? And now you've told me all about how you're connected with Chrissie, Nick, Toussaint and all those lovely artefacts, you've... won the game. That's why you get to go first.' Silvia spoke, as if to a young child; coaxing and cajoling in honeyed tones.

'You get to try it before Chrissie. And you know how much you loved my elderflower cordial. Well this is going to be even better.'

A hand in a white cotton glove reached down for one of the plastic bags, scooped it up and lifted it out of view. There was a snappy rustle as if the bag was being shaken open.

Chrissie waited, a coldness gripping her.

The gloved hand stretched down again, but this time picked up a cream charger along with the release valve. The trainers moved closer to the head end of the bed.

'Now, let me help you lift your head a little and then we can slip this over....'

In a flash, Chrissie understood. This was a replay of Jon's head in a tumble drier filled with nitrous oxide. Except of course, this was going to be a plastic bag over Gayle's head... and then hers.

How long would it take to suffocate? Six minutes? Maybe seven? The clock was running, and Chrissie needed a plan. She was desperate. If she was going to save Gayle, she had to act now. Surprise was her only weapon.

With stupendous effort, she rolled silently off her numbed useless arm. She swung her legs deeper under the bed. Now her feet were in easy contact with the wall. It would be her starting block. She bent her knees and thrust hard with both feet. 'Out!' she shrieked and aimed her floor skimming exit at Silvia's legs.

Thwack! Her shoulder connected with Silvia's shins. She flung her good arm out like a net and encircled Silvia below the knees. Silvia stepped back, freeing one foot from Chrissie's hold. Chrissie hung on to the other leg; her arm sliding down to clutch Silvia's ankle and trainer.

'Get off!' Silvia bellowed, and kicked with her free foot.

Chrissie held on, her face pressed hard against the lightweight denim. Metal ampules scattered across the carpet.

Silvia stamped down onto Chrissie's shoulder.

'Aghh!' Chrissie gasped and clamped her mouth on the lightweight denim and the fleshy calf underneath. She bit with every ounce of grit she had until she tasted warm salty blood.

Silvia screamed, lost balance and toppled backwards. The movement wrenched and twisted Chrissie's neck, her teeth still biting as Silvia fell. *Wham!* Silvia hit the floor like a skittle. Chrissie couldn't hold her any longer and let go. Panting, she scrambled on one elbow and both knees to reach Silvia's inert torso. She steeled herself to grapple her again. But Silvia looked peaceful: her eyes were closed, her curly brown hair almost cherubic, and there was no hint of the evil showing from within.

She must have been knocked out by the fall, Chrissie reasoned, and shoved her elbow hard onto the woman's chest, so as to be sure. Good, there was no reaction, no sudden intake of breath to disrupt her easy breathing, not even a frown. The woman was out cold.

'Gayle! Hey, Gayle!' Was she OK? Was she still alive? In the struggle, she had momentarily forgotten the girl. Chrissie's stomach twisted as she scrambled to her feet, stumbling across the cream chargers to reach the side of the bed.

Gayle lay motionless, her breathing soft and regular. Chrissie focused on the plastic bag. It was a transparent bin liner, the type sold on a roll to line medium-sized waste bins. Gayle's head was well into it, but clearly visible through the plastic. Her colour was pale, but normal for Gayle. There was still space, or rather air, in the bag.

'Come on, Gayle. Let's get you out of this,' Chrissie sobbed as she tore at the plastic. 'Hey, wake up, wake up!' She shook the girl's shoulders and was rewarded with a groan.

She cast around for the release valve with the cream charger attached. Thank God, it wasn't in the bin liner; it lay, gently hissing into the bedding between the pillow and wall. As far as she could tell, it had never been in the bin liner, or if it had, then it had been dislodged when she'd launched her shoulder at Silvia's legs. What the hell had Gayle done to be treated like this?

Gayle needed an ambulance, but where was her phone to call one? Chrissie tried to think, but all she got was nothingness; the memory blank between scrabbling in her bag for her phone and opening her eyes, one cheek pressing on a carpet.

'Help!' Chrissie yelled, 'Somebody help!' She ran, jumping across Silvia, still prostrate on the carpet, and unlocked the door. She staggered onto the wooden platform outside and shrieked, 'Sarah, somebody; help! Ambulance! Police! He-e-lp!'

CHAPTER 37

'I'll never be able to move again,' Matt groaned. He hadn't changed his position since Nick took the call from Clive; the one saying Chrissie wasn't answering her mobile and Clive was going to drive back to Woolpit. That had been five minutes ago.

'Well you can't lie there forever, Matt. Anyone for pizza?' Jake asked and got up from the futon.

Matt raised his head, conscious of the muscles pulling in his neck and shoulders. He winced. 'Are you offerin'?'

'Ha! I thought that'd get you moving. Hey, Nick, are you OK, mate? You've got your moody song-writing face on.'

Nick grunted from where he still sprawled on the futon.

It was an effort, but Matt propped himself on his elbows to view Nick's moody song-writing face. He'd never heard anyone's face described like this before. 'Aint it your tired look? I didn't know you were writin' songs when you were sittin' with your legs out straight.'

'I'm not; well not at the moment. I don't get why Chrissie isn't answering her phone.'

'Have you called her?' Jake asked.

'Yes, I've tried twice just now. All I'm getting is, *number unobtainable*.'

'You mean she's switched it off, or her battery's flat?'

'Maybe, Jake.'

While Matt was propped on his elbows, his brain felt more alive. 'Did you say summut 'bout Gayle?'

'Yes, but Clive said Gayle hasn't seen her either, according to Sarah.'

Something fizzled in Matt's mind. All the stuff he'd found on the ancestry sites, or rather the FreeBMD site, seemed hotter than ever. It flamed in his head alongside the report he'd discovered in the Coventry Tribune. He couldn't contain it any longer.

He'd known for weeks that if Gayle had really been given the birth name Camille Martin, then she was not all she seemed. Not only that, he'd already made the connection; Toussaint Martin and Camille Martin had the same surname. Toussaint was dead. And so was Gayle's father, Gaspard Martin. Coincidences weren't coincidences in the world of people-searching. But up until now he hadn't cared about the Martin connection, not while Gayle was a scootering mate. After all, in his comic-strip books, weren't Harley Davidson motorbikes the gel holding Hells Angels together? He reckoned mates could be bonded by scooters as well as motorbikes. Except if Chrissie was…. Was what? Missing? In trouble? Lost her phone?

'But Gayle's a mate; me scooterin' mate,' he said, half voicing his thoughts. It felt like a betrayal.

'So? What's that got to do with anything?' Nick asked, a frown replacing his tired, moody song-writing look.

'Nothin'.' Matt dragged his mobile from his jeans and automatic dialled Gayle's number. He listened to a long tone, and the words *number unobtainable*. 'Gayle's phone aint answerin' either.'

'I thought Maisie was your girlfriend,' Jake said.

'She is, and I'm meetin' her later. But that don't mean Gayle aint a scooterin' mate.' And that was the point – on her Honda, Gayle was cool. As a mate, he wasn't going to grass on her. But what if it came to a loyalty choice between Chrissie and Gayle?

'Did you say Clive's gone back to Woolpit lookin' for Chrissie?' Matt asked, a plan taking shape in his mind.

'Yeah.'

'So when are we eatin' pizza?'

'Dunno, Matt. Soon? I thought we'd go out for something. Right, Jake?'

'Yeah, I'm done with unpacking for tonight. I need a break. It's time to sample the beer round here. How about you, Matt?'

'Nah, I reckon I'll be gettin' back. Got to meet Maisie and… yeah I'll call in at Woolpit an' see if Chrissie's home.' He didn't want to say he'd drop by Gayle's place.

Outside on the pavement, the air felt warm and breezy. It was barely ten past seven and there were still almost another couple of hours of daylight left. Matt stood for a moment and looked up at the flat over the baker's shop. A first floor window gaped at him, the sash held open from the bottom, propped on a can of lager. 'Frag; so that's where me other can went.'

The old brick facade projected an air of times gone by. The paned bakery windows began at knee height and were far larger than the first floor sashes. Blue shop blinds blocked any view inside.

It was time to get moving. He pulled his helmet on and rode his Vespa fifty yards along St Andrews Street South before joining the Parkway junction. The traffic was light and he was tempted to take the back route to Woolpit, but hunger and anxiety stoked his sense of urgency. He chose the A14 and rode on full throttle. Around ten minutes later he left the dual carriageway and sped into Woolpit. He headed straight for Gayle's room over Sarah's double garage.

As soon as Matt pulled into Sarah's driveway, he saw Clive's black Mondeo. It was parked at an angle, as if in haste. Matt braked hard, parked his scooter close to the waste bins and hurried further into the drive on foot. He pulled off his helmet as he reached the base of the wooden steps outside Gayle's room.

'Matt? What the hell are you doing here?' Clive's voice boomed from high up the steps.

'Clive! And Chrissie!' Thank blog he'd found them. It took a moment to take in the scene.

Clive sat on the platform outside the door, his knees bent and his feet resting on the second step down. Chrissie sat next to him, his arm around her and her head on his shoulder. She looked odd, her blonde hair ruffled and one cheek a little swollen. Sarah stood behind them and held a large broom, her eyes wild as if guarding the open doorway.

'Where's Gayle? Clive, I've got summut I need to say. I should've said it before,' he rushed.

'You better be quick. The police and ambulances will be here in a moment, Matt.'

'And Stickley. I heard you call Stickley,' Sarah added, raising her voice as if the name and broom could ward off who or whatever was in Gayle's room.

'What's happened? Where's Gayle? Are you OK, Chrissie?' Panic rose in Matt's throat.

Sarah stiffened. 'There are two people in here: one on the floor more or less out cold; and… there's Gayle. She's

308

on the bed and making no sense. You tell me what's going on.'

'Chrissie, what's happened?' Matt asked, his voice breaking. He turned his gaze on Clive and searched his face.

'We're not entirely sure what's been going on, Matt. Chrissie has been knocked about, but when I ask her, she's a bit vague about it all. What I do know is that this is a crime scene and I think there's been an attempted murder.'

'What? I better tell Nick.'

'No, Matt. And you, Sarah; this applies to you as well. Nothing either of you see or hear of this is for public consumption. I'll call Nick. I said I'd phone when I'd found Chrissie, and anyway I've got some questions for him.'

'OK, but there's still somethin' you need to know 'bout Gayle.'

'I think I might have an idea what you're going to tell me, Matt.' The distant wail of sirens cut across Clive's words. He waited a moment before continuing, 'And if I'm right, then I think what you've got to say may best be said behind closed doors.'

As if on cue, the wail erupted into ear-splitting intensity as two ambulances and a police car, blue lights flashing, swept into the drive.

•••

Nick took the call from Clive, anxiety churning his stomach. 'Have you found Chrissie? Is she all right?'

'Yes, we've found her now.'

'That's great. But is she all right? Where was she?' Nick asked, relief flooding though him.

He slumped on the futon in the flat's living room. Jake was ferreting through a box in one of the attic bedrooms for a sweatshirt. They still hadn't set out for a pizza and concern about Chrissie, tinged with exhaustion, was even threatening the proposed pub crawl. Nick checked his watch. It was twenty minutes to eight.

'Come on, Clive. Tell me,' he prompted.

'She was in Gayle's room over the double garage. At least that's what I understand.'

'But I thought you said Sarah checked and she wasn't there.'

'Hmm, it seems there was another person there as well.'

'Right, but Chrissie's OK, isn't she?'

'Yes, she'll be fine. She needs a quick check at the Police Investigation Centre; fingerprints for elimination purposes, that kind of thing. The real surprise is it seems this other person was looking for you.'

'What?'

'Yes – so can you do me a favour?'

'Like what?'

'I'll be at the Police Investigation Centre in Bury in about forty minutes. Can you meet me there?'

'But why?'

'Convenience. This isn't about you; it's about this other person. I need to clear up a few queries with you, and as I'll be there anyway, it makes sense to get it out of the way.'

Nick wasn't sure. 'This other person… everything is OK, isn't it Clive?'

'Yes of course. Why shouldn't it be?'

'All right then, I'll see you there at about eight thirty.' He ended the call.

'Come on, Jake. Get a move on. At this rate there won't be time for a pizza,' he shouted up the stairs with newfound energy.

The centre was a brisk, fifteen minutes' walk away. Nick, fuelled on pizza, split from Jake and cut along the footpath from the Rougham Road, crossed River Lane and headed for the reinforced glass entrance door to the modern Police Investigation Centre. He felt as if he'd left Bury St Edmunds behind. Only the sound of traffic on the busy Rougham approach road and A14 exits connected him with the vibe of the town and Saturday night. The fast walk had helped to work off his anxiety, but it didn't alter the fact that police and police stations made him feel uneasy. If Clive was there, then it had to be OK, he told himself.

He gave his name at the entrance desk and was ushered by a uniformed policeman straight to an interview room. 'Dead on eight thirty,' he murmured as he cast a brief eye at the plain walls and skim of sound proofing material. A table was bolted to the floor, and two plastic stacker-style chairs were placed on either side of the table – four in all. Even the chairs had been secured to the carpet-tiled floor by chains. DVD recording equipment was safe in an alcove alongside the table, and wall mounted cameras completed the look. The overall colour was a pale calming aquamarine.

Before Nick's guts had a chance to go into meltdown, Clive strode into the room.

'Hi, Nick. Thanks for dropping by. Don't look so worried, this isn't an interview under caution. Nothing is being recorded. There are just a few questions I have for you. Sit down, make yourself comfortable. Stickley, my DS, may join us when he gets back from Woolpit.' Clive smiled mechanically. Nick thought he looked exhausted.

'What's going on? What d'you want to know?'

'I want to know how you know Silvia Shinton.'

'Silvia? She's Shaun's wife. You know... from the dredging firm. They dredged the moat while Dave and I were on a job at a moated farm house.'

'OK, but how do you know her?'

'I don't. I've only met her once. That was yesterday. I rang her on Monday, the beginning of the week, to ask if she had any old glass bottles. Shaun said they dredge up loads. I wanted to give Chrissie some bottles to replace the ones missing from that apothecary box she's got Gayle repairing. I'd never spoken to her before Monday.'

'So what happened?'

'Nothing happened. She asked for details about the kind of bottles I wanted. I haven't seen the box, so I said I'd get back to her.'

'And then you met her?'

'No. Gayle texted me the sizes. I couldn't ask Chrissie – I wanted it to be a bit of a surprise. I rang Silvia yesterday, gave her the details and she said to drop round to have a look. I went over after work. Probably got there at about four thirty.'

'And where was this, exactly?'

'The Shinton Dredging office. It's in the depot where they keep all the dredging machinery. It's near Elmsett Airfield.'

'And that was the first time you'd met her?'

'Yeah, and the only time, as I said. Look, what's all this about?'

'Do you fancy her? You know, have you been chatting her up?'

'What? You are joking?'

'Did you give her your address?'

'No; but she let on she knew it was in Woolpit. I didn't bother to say I was moving. Why all the questions? Was Silvia the other person with Gayle today? Bloody hell – she was, wasn't she? You think she may have called in to see me?'

'Possibly.'

'Chrissie warned me to watch my back, but I didn't think she meant....'

'That'll have been to watch your back with Shaun. He asked Balcon & Mora to trace your contact details. Money for old rope, I'd call it. Matt was assigned.'

'How come you know? Matt never said. And why would Shaun want my contact details?'

Clive ignored the question and pressed on, 'I suppose Shaun must have told Silvia. So, was she bringing you some bottles? She told Chrissie and Gayle she was bringing you something, and then produced some elderflower cordial she'd made.'

'What? Elderflower cordial? No, the bottles she showed me were no good. She was going to find me a coin instead; the same period as the apothecary box. Something dated around 1840.'

Clive nodded, and Nick sensed a subtle change in his attitude. He seemed to relax a little and the smile reached his eyes when he said, 'I also know why you had to leave your room at Sarah's. No, don't even ask. So tell me, why do you think Shaun and Silvia Shinton might have wanted to harm you?'

'What? That's a serious question, right?'

'Yes, Nick.'

'Well… I suppose Shaun was worried if I'd noticed anything odd about the laughing gas paraphernalia in the boat with Toussaint. And they might have thought I was fishing when I asked about the sort of treasures they dredged up. Silvia got a bit funny with me when I mentioned the Dunwich Jewel; you know, the Anglo-Saxon aestel. So maybe they thought I'd guessed they'd been up to no good.'

'Hmm. And what exactly had you guessed they'd been up to?'

'Nothing specific; I was just talking. They've opportunity to sell things they find. It's got to be a temptation for them. Now come on, Clive. You've got to tell me what's happened to Chrissie? And Gayle?'

'I don't exactly know exactly. That's the truth. Chrissie can't remember what happened after she drank Silvia's elderflower cordial. After that it's hazy; a nothingness. Gayle's the same. The duty police doctor's taken blood for toxicology. They'll find some alcohol on board for Chrissie but I'm guessing there'll be evidence of midazolam in both of them.'

'Midazolam? What the hell's that?'

'According to the duty doc, it's a fast-acting benzodiazepine. It's something that makes you drowsy and relaxed, and I think Silvia may have had access to some. The awkward side for us is that while midazolam is in your system, it stops you being able to laydown new memories. So you see, neither Chrissie nor Gayle can be reliable witnesses, not after the point when they drank the midazolam.'

'You mean they'd been drugged with the stuff?'

'Well they're acting as if they're recovering from being drugged with something. And I figure toxicology will find it in the elderflower cordial. Silvia's defence will have a field day with their statements. Whatever Chrissie or Gayle tells us now about what happened after they drank the cordial is going to be patchy, or quickly forgotten. It won't stand up in court.'

'But there must be more evidence you can get. Forensics must be able to come up with something.'

'Well Chrissie's got a bruise on her face and Silvia's got a human bite mark on her calf. Silvia says she was attacked by Chrissie and had to fight her off; hence the bruise on her face. Silvia was knocked out, so she's recovering from a concussion. I'm not going to be able to formally interview Silvia until tomorrow, and by then she'll have the best legal representation Shaun can buy for her.'

'And I guess Silvia will be the only one of the three not to have midazolam in her blood, but then she's suffered a concussion.'

'Something like that, Nick.'

'Bloody hell.'

CHAPTER 38

Chrissie sat at home with her back propped against the arm of her sofa and her legs resting on its cushions. It was Monday, nine days after the incident in Gayle's room. She had hoped to be back at work, but her shoulder was still sore and she had been advised to rest. Her initially swollen cheek had yet to complete its journey through the rainbow colours of a resorbing bruise. The blood had tracked downwards to her lower jaw so that now the last trace of it was a yellowy-green stain under her skin near her jawline.

She had been told she was lucky Silvia was wearing trainers designed for aerobics; the soles were cushioned and flexible. The doctor figured if they could absorb some of the shock of impact to the wearer's feet, then it followed the soles might have also reduced the impact to Chrissie's flesh. She wasn't convinced.

But this was small fry compared with what really freaked her out. Silvia had accused her of assault. The outrage of it! As if she would ever simply attack someone.

'But the bite mark on Silvia's calf is compatible with your dentition,' Clive had said, 'and more to the point, it's your DNA in the saliva on the leg of her jeans.'

'But it was self-defence. She kicked and stamped on me. I've the bruises and a sore shoulder to prove it. She was going to kill me next.'

'But can you remember her kicking and stamping?'

And that was the problem. Chrissie had little snapshots of memory. She could recall opening her eyes and being instantly awake. She knew she'd been under the bed because forensics had found her hair fibres caught against the underside of the bed frame. She must have torn open the plastic bag covering Gayle's head because her fingerprints bore it out.

Silvia had been found wearing cotton gloves, the kind used for handling artefacts. Why would she do that unless she didn't want to leave her prints on the evidence? It was all circumstantial but in Chrissie's mind, it pointed to Silvia's guilt.

But there were hard facts as well. Most damning were the empty vials of midazolam in Silvia's handbag. Traces of midazolam had been found in the tumblers Chrissie and Gayle had used to drink the elderflower cordial, and the blood and urine toxicology now confirmed Chrissie and Gayle had ingested midazolam. And as for Sarah – well she could describe and identify the voice she'd heard through the door saying Chrissie wasn't there and to go away. Sarah was even prepared to swear in any court that it wasn't Chrissie's voice. In Chrissie's opinion, Sarah, her blood alcohol level not having been checked at the time, would have to be viewed as both a formidable and reliable witness.

And so Chrissie had gone over and over the events, anxiously biting her fingernails, unable to eat or sleep properly, and hoping to recall something to prove Silvia was a murderer.

When Clive arrived home early that evening, Chrissie guessed something had changed. He hurried through the front door and down the hall; the lightness in his step was new. Even the exhaustion in his face was replaced with a smile as he bent to kiss her.

'Something's happened today, hasn't it? Is that Silvia woman dropping her claim of assault? Come on, Clive; tell me.'

'I'd say taking on an apprentice was a smart move, Chrissie.'

'No, please don't start talking in riddles. Just tell me.' She swung her legs off the sofa to make space for him to sit down.

'Everything hinges on Gayle. We all knew when she came here she had a past; some trouble with her previous apprenticeship.'

'Yes, but how does that help the case?'

Clive sat down slowly. 'The longer she's been with you and the more you've told me about her... well, I figured she was in witness protection or had a new identity, but I didn't know the details. You'd think as a police force we'd have access to all information – but there's no central register, nothing that someone at my level can directly access, and certainly not when the enquiry hasn't anything to do with a case I'm working on. Add to that a probation service so overstretched and chaotic that whatever may have been set up in Leicester doesn't percolate down to here. Different providers don't communicate. People get lost to the service. Clients and offenders can just disappear.'

'Yes, yes, yes... but I don't follow. What are you trying to say?'

'I suppose I'm trying to say that I was curious about Gayle, but met blanks on my initial search and drew my own conclusions. I hadn't reckoned on Matt. He met the same blanks and found out more.'

'He never said anything to me.'

'Because it was sensitive and he had no proof.'

'More likely it's because she rides a Honda scooter.'

'Possibly. But he's subsequently come to me with what he's discovered. It's meant that at this stage I've been able to ask Gayle more probing questions and, well I've persuaded her to co-operate. We know she had a connection with Toussaint. He was her cousin. The probation service couldn't have realised the significance, partly because he chose to use an alter ego, Tuscan Grabb, and anyway, I doubt they had the staff or resources. Gayle and Toussaint mainly communicated using WhatsApp and his Tuscan Grabb moniker. I think she found him through a link to his bottle-selling website.'

'But… are you saying she killed Toussaint?'

'No, quite the opposite. He was the last person she would have wanted dead. She came to this area because she wanted to be closer to him. And because, and this is key – he'd told her about the Dunwich Jewel as an example of how lucrative it was to sell dredging finds.'

'What?'

'Exactly. And not only that - he indicated that even if it wasn't his own find, there was money in keeping quiet about what he knew. He wrote to her on WhatsApp, *even my own boss is paying me to keep my mouth shut.*'

'So why didn't you find that on his mobile?'

'We couldn't get access to his WhatsApp account. But Gayle will let us have the relevant messages still on her mobile, as long as we keep her past identity secret.'

'But why didn't she come forward with this before? Didn't she want justice for Toussaint?'

'Yes, but remember she's come through the system and her concept of justice is warped. It's only since Silvia tried to kill her that she's prepared to come forward. I'm guessing Silvia found most of this out while she was drowsy and compliant under the effect of the midazolam.'

'But–'

'But you on the other hand had alcohol on board, went out like a light and had to be rolled under the bed in case Sarah came in when she knocked on the door. I think that if Silvia hadn't been asking Gayle all those questions, she'd have got straight on with killing her, then pulled you still unconscious from under the bed, and killed you.'

'Oh my G–'

'Exactly, but now we have motive. And do you know what? We can ask for access to the SS Shinton Dredging business accounts, as well as Silvia and Shaun's personal accounts.'

'Right – so this time the forensic accountants will know exactly what they're looking for. So you think Shaun was in on the murders as well?'

'I don't know. She's the brains. I think he knew, or suspected his wife was behind the killings, even if he wasn't the prime perpetrator. No, Silvia's the one; she was a hospice volunteer, and we've linked her to the theft of the fentanyl nasal spray and the midazolam from the local hospice. Same batch numbers on the drugs – that kind of thing. We know she had access to the 4x4 Defender Toussaint was driving because the firm's depot and office are under the same roof. And, we know she uses a nasal spray for hay fever because while she was detained at the Investigation Centre after being arrested following her discharge from hospital, her regular meds include a nasal spray for hay fever.'

'And the cream chargers?'

'I'm hoping a search of the depot and office will find something. Otherwise it'll be down to her internet buying and PayPal records. And of course now that we have a main suspect, forensics may be able to find evidence placing Silvia in Jon Dareham's home.'

'It's funny how you can only really search for evidence if you've arrested or charged someone.'

'Yes, it's a double-edged sword protecting the accused. But we've enough to charge her with now, and the evidence will trickle through. I don't think we've got it wrong.'

They sat without talking for a moment, Chrissie deep in thought.

'What do you think would have happened if Nick hadn't moved out?'

'Come on, Chrissie. You know what we'd have found. Nick full of midazolam and his head in a plastic bag filled with nitrous oxide. And the coroner's verdict would have been: death – unexpected; unnatural cause; hypoxia.'

Chrissie shivered. 'And don't forget the cream chargers she'd have strewn around to set the scene. You do realise she must have been planning his death from the moment she first chucked that first batch around. Do you think you'll ever be able to prove it was Silvia?'

'It'll be circumstantial, but if we find evidence in the Shinton depot, then maybe. Do you fancy a glass of wine? I feel we have something to celebrate.'

'You bet! And as wine saved my life last Saturday by making me need less midazolam to knock me out, I reckon I'll have a full glass and toast Bacchus, the God of wine.'

CHAPTER 39

It was Sunday the 22nd of June 2014, five weeks after the fateful incident in Gayle's room in Woolpit.

Matt, as always was following his nose. This time it was the smell of crèpes that drew him, as he walked through Sudbury's town centre with Maisie holding his hand. She flapped and waved her *Taste of Sudbury Food & Drink Festival* programme with her other hand as she spoke.

'There's goin' to be cookin' demos,' she said as they elbowed a path through the crush in the marketplace close to St Peter's Church.

'I s'pose them demos'll be on the stage, over there, Mais. If we're near the front, we'll get the best of the free tasters.'

'Oi, why you headin' back there then?'

'I just spotted the Suffolk Cheese stall, an' guess who's there feedin' their faces?' He waved to Chrissie and Clive, huddled over a plate of sample tasters.

'Is Chrissie OK now? I mean she were off with her shoulder, weren't she?'

'Yeah, she don't mention it anymore.'

'Hiya!' Nick tapped him on the shoulder and grinned. 'I've just bought some Mauldons Real Ale. You ought to go and get a taster, mate. So what's that you're wearing?'

'Yeah, it's kinda cool, aint it?' Maisie squealed.

Matt glowed with pride and freeing his arm from Maisie's grasp, smoothed his tee-shirt over his chest and belly.

'Bloody hell, is it Italian?'

'Nah, well yeah,' Maisie said, 'I used one of them free English to Italian translator apps when I ordered it online.'

She sounded out the words printed in bold across the white cotton: '*AGENTE DI TRACCIAMENTO* - you know, a tracin' agent. And then coz I knew he were into food and we were comin' here, I had the *LASAGNE to VERMICELLI - no job too small* printed on it as well. I mean it's all Italian, aint it?'

'Awesome.'

'Thanks mate.' Matt basked in it.

'How's Gayle doing? Anyone know?' Nick asked.

'Yeah, she's off on her scooter today. She said somethin' 'bout ridin' the coast road out Dunwich way, dint she Mais?'

'Yeah.'

'Oh hiya, you've found us,' Nick said as Chrissie and Clive joined them. 'I've got something for you Chrissie. Or rather I've got a substitute for what I was going to give you.'

'Really?'

Nick glanced at Clive before continuing, 'It's to go in your apothecary box - a kind of thank you from me, except the first one, which I never got, can't go in the box because... well it's evidence and the police have it. It's taken me ages to find this one.'

'Ah, that's really sweet of you, Nick. It sounds like just my kind of gift. What is it?'

'I expect it'll be a Victorian coin,' Clive murmured, 'We found one on the carpet near the bed in Gayle's room.'

'Really?'

Nick pulled a coin from his tee pocket and handed it to her; 'It's a farthing. It's dated 1840. Look. It's got Queen

323

Victoria's head on it. It's around the same sort of age as the box.'

'You realise that'll be her young head. Her older head was minted in the later years of her reign, to celebrate her longevity,' Clive said.

'But it's wonderful, thank you.' Chrissie turned the coin over to look at both sides. 'So you didn't think a later one would be right for me, Nick?'

'You mean a coin with an older head on it? Like in *great, you're a survivor...* or old head, as in wise?' He grinned.

Clive looked heavenwards.

'So what older date you talkin' 'bout?' Maisie asked.

'Well,' Clive smiled at Chrissie, 'on coins, Victoria's head is usually referred to as *young, bun* or *old veiled*; and that alludes to her aging face and hairstyle as her reign proceeds. So right towards the end of her reign, a farthing dated 1900 has her *old veiled* head on the coin.'

'But I still don't get it, coz if Chrissie's 1840 farthin's got a young head, it's still an older coin, right?' Maisie looked genuinely puzzled.

'Yeah, but that's why it's right for the box, Mais.'

The End.